Those Memories of Love

Robert John Goddard

Copyright © 2024 Robert John Goddard

All rights reserved.

ISBN: 9798866856275

DEDICATION

To all my Italian friends from the past and in the present and future.

1

March 2020

The letter

All stories that I know start and end at some place and at some time. As Italians might say: *Ogni cosa vuol principio,* everything must have a beginning. Initially, I wanted to say that the story I am on the point of writing begins and ends on the terrace of this house in the hills outside Treviso. However, second and third thoughts suggested that, even though the story might begin on the terrace, the story does not end there at all. However, I would say that the terrace has the finishing line well within its sights so that a more accurate description of the story might be this. The story I am about to write starts and has the beginning of its ending on the terrace of this house in the hills outside Treviso.

The reader might well be wondering at this point who this fussy storyteller is, and how he or she knows when, where and how the story begins and when, where, and how it ends. To borrow from the world of magic, may I say that all shall be later revealed? At this moment, it is sufficient to say that Tony Meldrum, one of the book's characters, is well known to me. Actually, Tony Meldrum is probably more than just one of the book's characters. He might better be described as the main character because he drives the plot. I would not go so far as to call him a hero, but I'll leave that for the reader to decide.

It was Tony who told me that the beginning of this story's ending was signalled by the arrival of a letter. Immediately after reading it, he felt the irresistible onset of sleep. This drowsy sensation was not new. It was very similar, Tony said, to the onset of tiredness that had always come over him in the back of his father's car on interminable trips to some summer resort when he was a child. But this drowsy feeling was not a reaction to the movement of a car but a response to shock or a disturbance of some kind. In this case, the disturbance was caused by the letter's contents and he had fallen into an uneasy slumber from which he was now surfacing.

This slow return to wakefulness was marked by spasms, random words and partly-formed sentences that emerged from his dreams while he snoozed and snorted on a deckchair on the terrace of his house in these hills outside this town in the northeast of Italy.

"That place," he muttered, "I know it."

Tony's eyes flickered behind lids now closed to the perfumed delights of evening, and his hands, lightly clenched and resting on his knees, jerked into life along with more coherent whispers.

"Yes, I know that place and those people. At least, I knew them once."

And then, of a sudden, Tony was aware of a sound, the touch of paper skimming over the tabletop in the breeze. He opened his eyes, lifted his mind from the dream and put it where it belonged, and it belonged here on an unusually warm and light-breezy evening in March. The sun had shone from dawn to dusk and its warmth was still radiating from the bricks of the garden walls, the paving stones and the tabletop; and on the tabletop, the ball of paper was wandering hither and thither on whims of the breeze. The ball of paper had entered his life some two hours previously as a neatly folded letter, and what was written on it seemed so absurd and so ridiculous that, in an uncharacteristic burst of irritation, Tony had screwed it up and tossed it to one side. Tony now blinked, blinked again, and put out his hand to smother the paper before it rolled off the table and flew out of sight.

No, the letter belongs in the waking world, and I am not ready for it. I can't believe what I read. I don't want to believe it. God, let the dream go on.

Closing his eyes, he rested his chin in the palm of his hand and he licked his lips. Nobody would have noticed anything untoward in Tony's behaviour, and the presence of the letter had barely seen a single hair turn on his head, but had anybody asked him he would have told them a different story. Tony told me, because I later asked him, that the letter had been as intrusive as a pistol shot fired in the middle of a concert performance; a slow movement from a Mahler symphony, perhaps, or a renaissance Italian madrigal. He needed, he told me, several minutes to find a way back into the contentment of the dream.

And the happy feeling, the place I knew, a happy place created by happy people.

And one of these happy people was his father, Captain Meldrum. A very able and capable man, his father had not only founded a language school in the nearby town, he had also snapped up this piece of land in 1960 when Tony was born and had built a villa on it. Designed in the typical Veneto style, the villa was situated in the hills a few kilometres north of the town of Treviso and, at an altitude of 300 metres, Captain Meldrum and his family and friends had an excellent view of the Dolomites in general and Monte Grappa and Cima Palon in particular. For

Tony, these winter-snow-clad peaks dominated his childhood, and he saw them as signposts that pointed back to memories of the pure and memorable kind; his father, for example, working in the garden shed, a typical English structure, for hours at a time and emerging with a piece of Italianate furniture for the house or garden. Then, there were the parties on the terrace in which his mother would get local help to make local cakes, the coffee-flavoured *tiramisu,* for example, or the crumbly *fregolotta,* and she also got advice on choosing the right white wine to embellish her own English fish-paste rolls, cucumber sandwiches and blended, black tea.

For Tony, the house was full of sunshine and light, but his favourite place, both as a child and as an adult, was the terrace and garden around the house. The garden boasted oak trees, possibly to remind his father of England, linden trees, cypresses standing sentinel and a terrace full of Mediterranean plants. Within sight of the terrace, and on a clear day, Tony was able to see Cima Palon and the not-so-far Monte Grappa massif where so many soldiers had lost their lives in WW1 and where so many partisans had lost theirs in WW2. I swear there were tears in his eyes when Tony told me that if he gave himself over to the past and looked at these mountains long enough, he heard the wind, and felt the memory of death on his face.

The breeze in these hills, on this evening outside this provincial town of Treviso, carried the same warmth as that of the day, and Tony felt it brush the skin of his cheeks, his forearms, his lower legs, but now the moon was shining in a shade of blue, and Venus was posing in her sky, inviting her admirers to enjoy her presence along with the conjured-up memories of moments from other warm evenings in this place, of times past and past friends rambling on about this and that, and this and that were interrupted by a dream or two of futures emerging in a haze of night perfume. Such a notable evening had occurred 35 years before when they had all been together for the first and last time, his brother and his girlfriend, he and her and she and him and his mother and father and on this very terrace in the sun, and the day had been as warm then as it was warm now and the evening air full of the scent of flowers and faraway rumbles of thunder.

And what had happened to this version of me, that young, handsome and happy man?

It was something other than an interrogative that came to him with this thought, perhaps an exclamation mark, because, in his dream, Tony was young again, 25 years old and on the brink of life, and he now knew that something had happened in the flicker of an eye, and that something was called ageing. Ageing had happened and left him used up and twitching and dreaming and dozing in the evening of his life and in the evening light and wondering why he was uncomfortable and whether this discomfort was down to the coronavirus circling the house or this hazy dream, but one or the other was making him feverish and exaggerating this dream and this memory of his parents and two women and two men gesticulating and mouthing off while they related their stories and dreamed their dreams and hoped the hopes of their youth and, in his mind, he watched and listened to these youngsters and sometimes muttered along with his inner voices. He surfaced, shook his head at these old dreams that had come to visit him while realising that they had been invited no doubt by the same warmth, the same sultriness and the same air perfumed with jasmine.

And this sameness of air and this sameness of perfume bring a sameness of feeling and a sameness of longings; yes, I know them well. The same perfume gives me that same sense of her presence, a presence I still experience from time to time with a power that is quite extraordinary. Yes, I know that sense of her. It has visited many times.

Yes, many times before had he seen and smelled these night trees, relived the power of love, the power of her, the promise of more, the promise of a gleaming future, a future of promise and yes, he had relived that evening many times before.

That evening was the evening in 1985.

Indeed, it had happened here, and what happened here and the feelings that accompanied it remained in the stones, the trees, the buds of spring and in the light of the stars. This might have surprised him, the passing of so many years, but it did not. Tony was only too aware that the sense of time had speeded up and then accelerated so fast that he was unable to keep up with it. She arrived in his life with the sound of USA for Africa urging the world to help the victims of an African famine but she went away when there were other young people, and few of these others had heard of that historic musical event or the famine which gave birth to it. It had all happened in the blink of an eye. But its speed no longer concerned him. Time was punctuated and measured by memorable events, and when he was young there had been a flow of new things to interest him and leave a lasting impression: the first time he rode a bicycle, his first kiss, his first job, his first child and this constant flow of newness made time appear to pass slowly. But at some point, fewer new and notable events occurred in his life and fewer new ideas were received so that time speeded up.

No, this no longer surprised him. What surprised him, or so he told me on several wine-fuelled occasions, was that, with a movement of mind and feeling that was quite extraordinary, she had transferred her allegiance to somebody else, and its shockwaves still rocked him and reminded him of her faithlessness and his stupidity. What he meant, of course, was that the event was as fresh in his memory as it was still fresh in mine but from a different perspective.

I prefer the scent of the blossom and its reminders of the youth I was, memories of a person I once was but am no more. Yes, I have changed, but some feelings remain, hidden perhaps, but they remain, and occasionally they reveal themselves when you least expect them.

Tony opened his eyes and shook away the lingering dreams but a residue of feelings, with a life of their own, had mixed with his blood, and these feelings would likely stay in place for the rest of the evening and into the night, if past experiences were anything to go by, and might even spark off a music-from-his-youth binge and all those sad songs from a yesteryear that contained hope for a future that had already become past. He had never lost touch with those feelings, he told me. They might disappear for long periods but they were ever present in the songs, their words and their melodies and they infused his dreams.

Tony reflected, as most of us later do, that first love was a love that did not grow on trees and affairs of the heart were not things that often happened when a man was in retirement, and trust and feelings of betrayal didn't get better when you were older even after you had done the building-a-home-and-raising-children thing. And those raised children were now autonomous individuals. Mario, now 33, and Julia, now 31, were doing their own thing in London and succeeding miraculously well given that he still saw them as his babies. Mario was a restless individual and working in the field of fine art while Julia, who took after her mother, had enormous ambition and was in Telecommunications.

And they say that first love never quite dies and all that. And they, whoever they are, put their finger on it. How can love die when your very own children are not only that love's product but also a reminder of the hopes and living proof of the dream?

And Tony still believed, as many of us want to believe,

and even more of us do believe, that those first moments with her had been special, really special, and, along with other significant moments, he often relived those early times from long ago. One such memory had him walking down that street again and he felt her presence and knew she was there somewhere, and from this somewhere she was looking at him and when he looked up and through the crowds of people, their eyes had met over a distance of at least 100 metres. And there were times, silent times, hand-in-hand and dreamy times, when they had broken the silence at exactly the same time, each tripping over the words of the other and breaking into gales of laughter, and there were those extraordinary moments their thoughts had met, had revealed themselves in a simultaneous exchange of telephone calls, electronic pulses colliding in space.

Some people might say that these are lovely memories. But some people don't have a clue. She was hot and cold, near and far, and ambition was in her DNA, and ambition destroyed us.

But how will I tell it, this story of betrayal? Tony was 60 years old now and it had all happened such a long time ago, and I wonder if the story had all been the way Tony's mind had recorded it and, subsequently, how accurate it was. Was it all fiction? Was it partly fiction? And if it was partly fiction, could I put a number to it, a number like 1% or 99%? What I am getting at is this. Was Tony the unreliable narrator intent on reconstructing events in order to give them a different focus, a focus which sat more comfortably with his own ideas about what or who was right or wrong?

And now that story was coming to an end, and the end was signalled by the letter now wandering willy-nilly in the light breeze and tossing from side to side in a manner that suggested it had not a care in the world; but this letter was not getting anything rolling. It seemed as though it was bringing the whole and sorry story to a dead and crushing end, a story that had started, at least he saw in retrospect, that night in 1985 because "that night" marked a point of change. Tony was happy for a while, but the events of that evening returned to haunt him and later turned his life into a cold-north-wind-infested night.

He and his brother were celebrating the end of the academic year and their father's retirement and their ascension to legal ownership of their father's legacy. And on that evening, there had been no indication that it was going to end in March 2020 with a letter arriving like a pistol shot. He had screwed it up into a ball, thrown it onto the table top, and it was now blowing around to the whim of the wind. The blue official envelope, the one stamped and ablaze with the words: *"Polizia dello Stato, Verona,"* looked like a traffic fine or a reminder of some kind and anything other than what it actually was, something that required a trip to Verona, a claim of death to validate and accept, a total reshuffling of the cards, so to speak, and ideas to rearrange.

After Tony had scanned the letter, he was in the sort of state a person might experience on discovering that his father was not his father. There was a nonsense going on, a sort of April fool's joke of the worst possible taste. Certainly, the Italian police must have made an error. His brother Ricky, so selfless, so caring and mindful of others could never have done what they said. Tony had seen him the previous week. They had met in Venice and spent the afternoon chatting about this and that, drinking this and drinking that in their favourite café while the band played and the waiters hovered and, amongst all that movement, all that sound and chatter, Ricky had given no intimation of any bad feeling or malicious intent. He even said he understood why Lucy was thinking first and foremost about the health of her parents and she was right to do so. Both were in their mid-eighties, a high-risk group at this time of Covid-19.

But Tony had to think of himself and act quickly because he had been ordered to Verona immediately, and immediately did not mean when he could find the time, it meant now; except "now" was not an ordinary now. "Now" was now in the time of the coronavirus, and that meant the meaning of the word "now" was now up for interpretation. There was a new normal and a new normal meant a new way of understanding the world and its time, a new now, a new then, and a new future. Several friends had commented that the coming of the virus had ushered in their generation's World War 2, and suggested that it might be the event that changed their understanding of adverbs and adverbial phrases like now, instantly, immediately, without delay or any other words or phrases that they might later utilise to place everything they did in time's perspective. If that turned out to be the case, their lives might soon be divided into that time before the virus and this time after the virus lockdown. Nonetheless, in the final analysis, the lockdown and its fear, its isolation and anxiety, its role in the increase in alcohol and drug usage and insomnia, at least that was what the newspapers claimed, would all be forgotten and buried in the grave with the dead and the truth got covered up or reinterpreted.

And the end was starting now, on this evening during this pandemic in 2020 and it was beginning where it had all begun some 35 years earlier on this terrace, with those youthful dreams, with those views of the mountains, and with that warm and early-spring night and its haunting legacy of love, betrayal, ambition and death.

2

May 1985

Ponytail 1

Hovering between house and terrace, Tony allowed his thoughts to idle from his father, to his father's retirement and to his own future. Feeling the transition bar through the soles of his shoes, he rocked between inside light and outside starlight and eyed a corner of the terrace, where a group of employees was waiting for the dancing to kick off. He was not surprised to see brother Ricky, now clad in linen, and darkly unshaven for the summer, slumped in a chair to one side of them. With the ankle of one leg resting on the knee of the other, and one arm across the chair back, Ricky was flaunting vast amounts of skin and body hair and was just close enough to be part of the crowd but far enough away to act alone and strike should a young and pretty female candidate break away from the group and appear alone and vulnerable and open to Ricky's undoubted good manners and charm.

In contrast to Ricky, the group was jumpy, tense and waiting; they were bright and baggy, dripping with bangles and other accessories, and all of these hooped and hanging, big and bright, and tension moved amongst these people with their hello-or-hi greetings and my-name-is-this or my-name-is-that intros, firm or floppy handshakes, one-after-the-other apologies and smiles amid jokes unfolding with gales of laughter and glasses of *vino rosso, vino bianco* or *grappa*, and everybody convinced they were having such a blast.

"*Una serata meravigliosa*," someone said.

"*Adesso, vogliamo ballare*," said someone's friend.

Tony nodded. It was indeed a wonderful evening and the group of colleagues was restless, ready to dance the night away. Tony leaned forward and tottered on the tips of his toes, balanced for a second between being on the terrace and not being on the terrace and, in order to test his memory, he decided to play the game he sometimes played with himself in the classroom, and pick out the people he recognised and put names to their faces. There were people he had seen at interview; people he had placed in the right school and people whose teaching skills and personal presence he had observed in the classroom. He was troubled by the one person he had, apparently, never seen before and assumed she was either a visitor or one of the very few standby-staff he had not chosen. He stared at her and glimpsed Ricky walking behind and away from her. It was only a fleeting glimpse, seen from the corner of Tony's eye, and Ricky was gone in an instant and disappeared in the crowd.

Tony settled his eyes on the girl again. He would have remembered meeting her, but not because of her clothes. Like the other guests, she was all colourful rings and padded shoulders. It was her ponytail that marked her out, at least initially, and once seen he could not take his eyes off it, so short, so blond and so out of place in the fashionable and voluminous curls and waves of the others; and how it showed off her fine facial features and those oh-so-bright and perfectly-blue eyes. He assumed it was the wine that was responsible for his pleasant and not-quite-in-this-world feeling, and it seemed to him that she of the pretty ponytail was an apparition created by the swirling, sweet and herbal-smelling smoke as if one gust of wind might blow her away.

"I'm going to find a job here," she said.

He was wondering if he was drowning in the fragrance of jasmine plants when he heard himself say: "Language is the key," and assumed he had floated across the terrace with the herbal smoke and was now facing her in a shapeless and shadowless world.

"Of course, it is. Learning Italian is vital," she said. "You're not going anywhere without it."

"I'm Tony Meldrum."

"Yes, I know who you are," she said and looked up at him with those large blue eyes, smiled and cocked her head towards the group of waiting dancers. "They told me…"

"Told you?"

"Who you are."

"Why did you ask them?"

She shrugged.

"I didn't, but they seemed to think I might be interested to know."

"Why did they think that?"

"Don't ask me. Why don't you ask them?" she said, indicating the teachers with her head.

His desire to deal with these gaps in his knowledge and ask his colleagues was crowded out by an odd need, very odd, he later reflected, to rush out over the local hills so that the skin of his arms would be touched by the breeze and it would be a thoughtful touch, a caring touch, an affirming touch, an attentive touch, and he longed to put out his hand and touch her, a brief touch like a quick handshake, a quick pat on the arm or a stroke on the shoulder. She said:

"I am Lucy. I've escaped from Thatcher's Britain and I'm looking at my options."

Knee-jerk questions concerning Thatcher's Britain and Lucy's choice of the word "escape," remained unasked. His suspicion that this introduction had been carefully prepared was forgotten in an instant because her outstretched hand had dislodged a strand of her hair from the ponytail, and it now framed her face and skimmed her throat. Tony stared at it, alarmed at the need to stroke the hair away and feel the skin by the jugular vein. He was also touched by her clothes. Soft and airy, billowing and cool, they fell over her body with a suggestion of promise.

"And I'm staying near here with friends for the summer. One of them works for you. She invited me along this evening. I hope you don't mind."

"I'm glad you came," Tony said.

"That's what your brother claimed," Lucy said.

"My brother?"

Tony was about to say more when there was a riot of movement, colour and bagginess. At long last, a blast of music from the house had aroused and invited the waiting dancers and they now pushed through the sliding doors and crowded into the house. In a blink of an eye, Lucy had blown away and joined them, and he chased after her, stumbling over the transition bar, tripping into the house but losing sight of her, her hair and her throat, and there was nothing but the music, its thumping and shaking, and the dancers now throwing themselves around in a frenzy of sound and vibration, and Lucy, if he recalled her name correctly, seemed to have disappeared in a dizziness of big hair, faces and scarves, jackets and bangles flying. Then, there was the almost silence, a ringing echo in his ears, so that he did not register that the music had stopped, nor was he distracted by his brother, hand in hand with a girl, and both were jostling past him and making their way to the relative cool of the terrace. There was an English voice at his elbow.

"Don't you like to dance, Tony?"

He stammered to reply but her neck, evenly developed, soft and white, was now so close, he felt an almost irresistible desire to sink his teeth into it.

"Tony?"

"Yes?"

The music returned with a crash, he sensed movement from behind, heard voices and stumbled into the room behind her. She seemed delighted to see him there.

"Wicked," she said.

Snatching for her outstretched hand, he tripped after her. Ignoring the gasps and protests of the others, he was determined not to lose her and pushed and jostled forward. Lifting and positioning his right leg, he bent his arms and copied her movements; leg down, slide the foot backwards, and not once did he look away from her and nor did he think of others while he danced his way through an undergrowth of legs and flaying elbows, but he glimpsed other boys pushing and other girls sliding, and faster and faster they danced, louder and louder got the sweetest music he had ever heard, and there in front of his eyes was this apparition, and with her head half turned she seemed to be mouthing: "Come, Tony, and follow me, follow me," and Tony followed, mesmerised by the ponytail sparkling in the flashing light and faster and faster they danced, and his world and her world became a jumble of wriggles and a medley of cries and laughter hanging in the air.

And then, in a moment, the music seemed to lose its steam, the dancers their wind and the singing stopped and Tony bent over to catch his breath before looking up at the dream standing and smiling over him and he became aware of a feeling of satisfaction or even happiness. He took a deep breath and said:

"Well, it's nice to meet you, Lucy."

"Likewise," she said. "But I must tell you something."

"What?"

"Actually, I needed to know who you were and so I asked."

Their eyes met, and both allowed their gaze to rest there for a moment, and it seemed to Tony that so much had been revealed in their two comments and that this "so much" was creating images in his head with she in his arms, giving in to his advances.

"Shame my dancing partner was here all the time and I didn't recognise him," she said. "And to think I nearly stayed at home today. I don't like crowds. They diminish me. I'm staying in Montebelluna, so I don't often come to Treviso."

Tony pictured Montebelluna, a one-horse town with a bus-stop on the way to the hills.

"I can assure you that you're undiminished," he said.

"Had I known how much potential there is here, I would've come sooner," she said with a smile. "There are some things I wanted to ask you about the school and whether there were any openings for people with a master's degree."

"You have a master's degree?"

She nodded.

"A master's in linguistics."

Tony did not turn his eyes from hers and did not comment on Linguistics. Instead, he found himself thinking of the lost potential of all the spring days that had already passed by. Those days now seemed drab without her perfect presence. He turned his head towards the sliding doors and caught sight of his brother. He was sitting at a table in a corner of the terrace, the ankle of one leg resting on the knee of the other and one arm across the chairback next to him and on this chair sat the object of Ricky's desire.

"That's my brother Ricky," he said with a twist of the face that could have been a grimace or a smile.

Lucy glanced at Ricky and smiled.

"He's very good looking," she said. "He asked me to dance. Didn't you know?"

"No," Tony said. "A good job you refused him."

And later that evening, Tony told Lucy that his brother's desire was driven by the need for someone to love, someone to care for, someone to help in an hour of need. Ricky's desire was, so Tony said, focused on everywoman, and a very specific kind of everywoman. She was the woman who made Ricky feel adequate for a while, masculine for a while, strong for a while, loving and caring for a while until the novelty wore off and he let her go. And the novelty had worn off many a girl so that nobody took his loves seriously any more. But it never crossed his mind that, by telling her this, he was actually saying that he was not like Ricky, that he was trustworthy and true, and capable of something much deeper and real. It certainly never entered his head, not even for a split second, that his description of his brother might also apply to him.

"He's just a womaniser," Tony said.

"I see."

"So," Tony said. "Why don't you come by and bring your CV with you."

"And there's so much I would like to ask you," she said in a tone that suggested his comment had created vivid pictures in her head.

"I look forward to seeing you," he said. "Tomorrow?"

Tony later said how disappointed he was at not getting a reply or a warm smile or a kiss on the cheek. Instead, she turned her head, stared towards the hills, and disconnected.

"And who did you say you were staying with in Montebelluna?" Tony said.

But she appeared not to have heard his question. She was nodding and smiling as if at some inner voices congratulating her on the achievement of a deep and personal need, a need from which Tony felt firmly excluded. She turned her head towards him and, almost as an afterthought, she said:

"Yes, tomorrow would be fine."

And the music restarted.

3

June 1985

Almost

Immersed as he was in Lucy's ideal presence, his ideal love, this ideal evening on a warm terrace, Tony almost missed the puff of air on his cheek. It came from a plosive P, the watery parting of lips and the word, carried on two heavy outbreaths, in his ear.

"Powwow."

And the word was accompanied by a boom-booming echo from a roll of distant thunder. The storm had announced itself as flashes of lightning soon after sunset and had sparked off comments of the let's-hope-it-stays-away variety, but Tony liked the sound and drama of thunder because it seemed to connect them all. It was, he thought, like a heartbeat and brought a regular balance to the evening that all could feel and hear and, in the main, he was proud of Lucy and her knack of doing and saying the right thing, most of the time, to the right people. However, this comment was different. Never before had she used the word "powwow" to describe these family gatherings.

Nonetheless, he succeeded in side-lining her less-than-respectful comment and told himself that her choice of word was an unfortunate aberration. Tony took a deep breath, shuffled on his chair, and glanced at the people around him until a voice from the hammock, his father's master-of-ceremonies voice, barked out:

"For all those who haven't met her yet, can I introduce Lucy. She…"

Her hand was on Tony's arm, and she squeezed it before saying:

"…hasn't been in Italy long. Left university and came to visit a friend."

She punctuated her utterance with a nervous laugh, but her words of introduction were met with silence, his father withholding comments because he was polite, his mother in order not to upset, Ricky, who was staring into his current girlfriend's eyes and Tony, who was trying to stay positive.

How forthright she is. And such a breath of fresh air.

"I've just completed an MEd," she said, "and I'm now considering my future."

She smiled her winning smile at Tony's mother and father who, as the family elders, dominated the centre of the terrace, and then she winked at Ricky and his current interest, Mary, or was her name Mariah or Mara? Tony could not quite remember. To him, this everywoman was disposable and required to do nothing more than sit there, smile at everybody, and look young and pretty.

"The world's appearing to be my oyster," Lucy said.

"Interesting use of the progressive 'ing' form," said Tony's mother.

A clap of thunder rumbled away and left space for a single high note vibrating from cicadas, and the note filled the terrace, the garden around the house and the valley below, while the house and garden had also surrendered to the scents of the valley, the fragrance of flowers and the stars twinkling in the night sky.

"And where in England are you coming from, dear?"

"Dorset," Lucy said. her eyes darting from one person to another, in ascending order of the hierarchy, from Ricky's girl, to Ricky, to Tony, to Tony's mother and then to the hammock and Tony's father.

"Thomas Hardy country," his mother said. "I'm loving it."

"I call it Jane Austen country," Lucy said with a smile, "and I love it, too."

"Indeed," said his mother, puckering her lips and clenching her jaw as if wishing to show that she did not bite.

"Indeed, indeed," said Lucy. "We must not forget that Jane Austen often visited Lyme Regis. Her novel *Persuasion* is partly set there."

To Tony's surprise, his mother did not reply, but she offered the smile that he had last seen when she had been pulled over by a traffic policeman and she had tried to charm him into letting her off with a warning. From the direction of the hammock came his father's voice.

"And I suppose your father was too young to have…"

"Been in World War 2? Indeed, yes. He was born in 1935."

"Just a child then."

"And an orphan at the age of 5. He lost his parents in a bombing raid."

The arms and legs unfolded from the hammock, and a head and shoulders swung up and round to reveal a balding man in late middle age.

"Sorry to hear that," he said in a tone and with a look in the eye which suggested both an understanding of death and sensitivity to the fact that when someone is killed, someone else survives and feels a sense of loss.

"He was brought up in an orphanage in Devon."

Tony's mother struggled to control the I-told-you-so

tightness of her mouth and, fighting a losing battle, she said:

"And right at the beginning of the war. With five years to go."

"We only know that now," Lucy said. "Dad thought he'd stay there forever."

"Right," Tony's father said. "Hindsight is a wonderful thing. Looking back on historical events is not the same as living through them."

"Frederick, dear, what has that to do with this young lady's father?"

"Everything, dearest. It's hard to see the plus side of some things, war for example, or growing up in an orphanage, when you're living through these experiences."

"Does war have a plus side?" Tony's mother said.

Captain Meldrum hesitated, thrust his chin forward and looked over the wall of the terrace in the direction of Venice and the sea.

"Perhaps yes and perhaps no," he said.

The old soldier rarely spoke extensively about his wartime service but, over the years, both Tony and Ricky learned that their father had served with the Surrey Fusiliers from their part in the invasion of Sicily in July 1943, through the landings on mainland Italy, where he had added a slice of his nose to the litter of body parts on the beaches, fought his way up to the Sangro river where regimental spirit and blood had turned the river waters red, and he had left half his mind with the corpses littering the slopes of Monte Cassino.

"Yes, I suppose war could have positives if you were prepared to look for them," Tony's father said.

Captain Frederick John Meldrum would never have admitted that the war had shaped him but, 40 years after the war's end, it was as clear as daylight, at least to Tony, that his father had indeed looked and found and made the best out of the war and things out of his control. At the time, his father said, nobody could guess when or how the war would end. In effect, he did not know who would survive and who might die. Captain Meldrum said he was aware that the after-the-war world would be very different from the pre-war world but he had no idea what these differences might look like.

"Too many good people died," his father often said. "We just got on with the job at hand. We were not heroes. We were all just doing what was expected of us in a time of crisis."

Being the positive man he was, Captain Meldrum had tried to learn from his wartime experience by focusing on the plus side and doing what he could to create a post-war society that was built on sympathy and understanding, and sympathy and understanding grew from better communication, and better communication grew from one common language and, to that end, Captain Meldrum stayed in Italy after the war working first for the Military School of Languages in Treviso and later setting up his own English language school, The Speak English School, as a civilian in the 1950s.

"Yes, you have to look for the positives," Lucy said. "But people who live through events have no idea what's going to happen. For my father, the orphanage was always in the here and now, a constantly shifting reality without an end and without the context that retrospect can bring. That was all dad ever said about his stay in the orphanage. He always referred to it as 'that institution'."

Mrs Meldrum raised her eyebrows.

"A constantly shifting reality? Interesting," she said.

"Must have been tough," said the old soldier. "Not for the faint of heart."

"And how," said his mother, "do you think the 'constantly shifting reality' of 'that institution' affected him? Losing one's birth family and being placed in an orphanage, regardless of the age it occurs, is traumatic. It must have influenced his life and yours, too."

"As your husband pointed out," Lucy said with a sweet smile, "everything has a plus side, if you look for it."

"Does it really? For example?"

"He learned to survive," Lucy said, "to depend on himself, and he knew the value of having goals."

"Well," said his father. "That's grand."

The word "grand" was one the old soldier often chose, an adjective open to interpretation, designed to please as many people as possible with a flexibility of meaning that ranged from "not bad" to "outstanding." On several occasions, Tony had heard his father use the word "grand" to describe Treviso's suitability for his language school. But, on other occasions, the captain said his decision to choose Treviso as the town in which to establish his school was entirely accidental, the result of a random request made in 1944 and based on a spontaneous decision by person or persons unknown to send the British army one way and the US army another way and Captain Meldrum had been ordered to accompany units of the US military as liaison officer, and he found himself, one day in March 1945, marching into the city he later came to call home.

"Your father was ambitious then," Tony's mother said in a tone that suggested she did not approve of ambition.

"For himself and for me," Lucy said. "He always wanted me to go to university."

"So, what does he do?"

Lucy shuffled on her chair.

"He used to be a teacher."

"Used to be?"

"He retired early, due to ill health, or so I was led to believe."

His mother winced as if a stone had passed to close to her head.

"I see," she said.

Tony was almost sure what his mother saw. It was highly likely she saw ill-health as a weakness. Perhaps, she saw a man without grit and determination. Probably, she saw a man with no backbone, a man who had just given up.

"So where did he teach, my dear?"

"A school in Manchester."

"Manchester? Manchester Grammar?"

"No, a primary school in Oldham."

"Coal town," his mother said in a triumphal tone that suggested she had, at last, found the answer to a crossword puzzle clue that had been eluding her.

"Correct," said Lucy. "Dad saw himself as a reformer and believed in educational change, the ideas of Steiner, Montessori and A S Neill."

"So, playing around all day."

"No, not exactly. He saw activity as a guide to education and didn't believe in repressing it. Unfortunately, he found himself in a more backward-looking school which…"

"…which focussed on learning? The problem today is…"

"Just let her finish, dear," Tony's father said.

He smiled at his wife and nodded to Lucy.

"Carry on, dear," he said.

"When he started, class sizes in the middle 1960s were large, often over 30 children to a class. Dad was horrified by the discipline he was expected to administer, by corporal punishment, the chalk-and-talk style of education and children sitting in ranks and facing the board. Times tables were learnt by chanting aloud and poetry would be learned by heart for homework."

"And is there anything wrong with repetition?" Tony's mother said. "We use this technique in our schools, don't we Frederick? It seems to work, you know? The Italians love it."

"Times are changing, dear," Captain Meldrum said. "The situation today is not the same as it was in our day. Remember, dear?"

He squinted into the night shadows of middle distance as if his memories were hovering in the darkness and he said:

"I can still see myself drifting through the streets of this town in 1945, and I see and feel the huge impact the war had on those who lived through it."

And then he fell silent while scanning the palms of his hands.

"You know," he said, "before the war, the town of Treviso boasted around 115,000 inhabitants. By the end of the war, that number had fallen to 51,000 people and most of these were living in cellars. On top of that, with no cinemas, no restaurants or bars, public life had come to a standstill."

He turned his hands over to reveal his knuckles before inter-twining the fingers of both hands as if in prayer.

"So," he said, "have you ever wondered how a city like this got back on its feet? Have you never wondered who led the reconstruction of life in the city?"

Tony's father remained silent, gave his audience space to imagine, sparing himself the trial of explaining everything he had been witness to when what he really wanted to do was forget.

"It should be no surprise to you that so many of the officials and local politicians here in 1945 were ex-members of the defeated Fascist party. It's easy to condemn this, but who else was going to lead the reconstruction?"

And then he went off again searching his memory for those images of the past that haunted him until, in a matter-of-fact tone, he added:

"And make no bones about it, the tasks these people in Treviso faced were daunting. Most of the city had been destroyed. Most houses were uninhabitable and the rest were badly damaged. The streets were full of rubble, there was nothing to eat and disease was rife. I felt a need to do something that would help in preventing such a thing happening again, something new and innovative that was open to everybody and not just the rich and educated. And so, we set up the school and developed our method."

The captain's generosity of spirit was always present in his use of the words "our" and "we" when the reality was that, in the beginning, he had acted alone. Captain Meldrum's "method" was, at the time, a novel approach to language learning that focused on spoken communication rather than on grammatical accuracy and was a huge success. Within a few years, the Speak English School, commonly known as S.E.S., had become the most successful language school in the Veneto with branches in most towns and cities in the region.

"My dad also thought it might be better to ask if there was something better," Lucy said.

"A troublemaker who upset the status quo?" said Tony's mother.

"An innovator who reacted to circumstances?" said Tony's father.

"Perhaps an agitator who helped bring about needed reforms?" said Lucy.

"Well," said Tony's mother, "it'll always depend on your perspective."

"And change takes time," Lucy said. "Most movements for change are full of hidden heroes."

"Well," said the old soldier, "there's no doubt that times have changed again. But that is something I've left my sons to deal with."

On reaching his sixty-fifth birthday earlier that year, Frederick had announced his retirement from active school duties. It was the most natural thing in the world for Tony and Ricky to step into their father's shoes and continue his work. The sons had divided this scholastic empire into two halves: the western half, based in Verona, would be run by Ricky while the eastern half, based in Treviso, would be run by Tony.

"And what about you, Mary?" Tony's father said, turning to Ricky's friend.

"Marion," said Marion with a smile.

"What do you have to say about your schooldays, Mara?"

"Don't know," Mara, or Marion or Mary said.

"Well, that's grand," said Tony's father. "So, how did you meet young Ricky here?"

"It's all above my head," she said before announcing that she had been travelling and was on a train to Venice, and when she woke up, she found her passport and money had been stolen.

"And I bumped into Ricky in the centre of Treviso."

"So lucky to have met such a caring individual," his mother said. "He's always been so thoughtful and somebody to trust. And how do you see your future?"

She giggled and glanced at Ricky.

"Don't know," she said. "Future's a long way off."

"Well, you're so right," said Tony's mother and while she said it, she smiled a conspiratorial smile at Tony before continuing with: "Plenty of time to enjoy your youth without looking at silly things like futures and commitments. When did you say you were going back to England?"

Tony was no more impressed by his brother's latest offering than his mother was. What bothered him, in the manner of a sudden pain, was the realisation that he had no opinion of his own. Just like his mother, he thought that Mary, Marion, or Mara seemed packaged instead of dressed. Just like his mother, he thought she seemed like something edible and, perhaps, artificial and, just like his mother, he was sure Mary, Mara or Marion would be sent packing, broken-hearted, back to wherever it was she had come from. Until now, it had never occurred to him to wonder what he really thought. Until now, it had never crossed his mind that thinking like his parents was the easy option, the line of least resistance that caused no friction.

"And no doubt we'll be seeing you again," his mother said to Lucy. "Tony was always such a conservative child. He's Mr Perfect with such high standards, dear. Do you think you can match them?"

"I'm far from perfect, Mrs Meldrum, but instead of looking for imperfections, we might choose to look for the perfect in each other."

Why can't mother see that Lucy and I somehow connect at the level of our souls?

Tony was only too aware that his mother was not quite the dominant force she had once been; and what she had been was slowly disappearing with the daily pills she took at breakfast. She was still fun-loving enough to lay the pills out like soldiers on parade but they seemed to make her sad and tired and sometimes argumentative. Tony knew that Lucy was different from most Italian women but that did not make her odd. Lucy was independent, forthright, and assertive but these attributes did not make her rude and, even if she was a follower of her own star, that did not make her ruthless or ambitious. Yes, it was true that she was imperfect but that just made her wonderful and wonderfully human.

"Wonderful words," Tony's mother said. "But we mustn't forget that perfection's rather like beauty."

"In what way, Mrs Meldrum?" Lucy said.

"They say that beauty lies in the eye of the beholder," Mrs Meldrum said. "And I suggest that the same may be said for perfection and many other concepts."

"For example?"

"Truth, for example, reality, good and bad, to mention but a few."

Tony might have agreed. He later told me that, on that evening and on that terrace, he had glimpsed a change in himself and that change involved an understanding of the nature of things. Retrospect is such a fine thing, I told him, but Tony was adamant. That evening, he said, his mother's words marked the beginning of change in his outlook and opinions, and this change was brought about by questions concerning the existence of absolute truths of any kind. Was there an unchanging and everlasting reality, he wondered, fixed and permanent, or were all opinions and reactions simply points of view? Perhaps, he said, all things were in a state of flux, a never-ending process of movement and hard-to-pin-down change.

The thunder had now rumbled away but, every now and then, the spaces between the trees and the bushes were filled with flashes of lightning and the trees wandered to and fro in a wind which had been rising since sundown and it brought with it the perfume of the flowers and the grass. Ricky drifted past him and he stopped behind Lucy and while his eyes wandered to the walls, the trees, and the house, he put his hand on Lucy's shoulder and stage-whispered in Lucy's ear:

"I like your ponytail," he said. "Let it grow. It really suits you and looks really attractive."

But Tony did not hear his exact words, immersed as he was in Lucy's almost ideal presence, his almost ideal love, this almost ideal evening on a warm terrace now stamped forever on an almost perfect memory.

4

1988

Perfect

"It's a dog she needs," Lucy said, "not a daughter-in-law."

Stretched out and dozing on the lounger, half in and half out of the house, Tony was barely visible in the shadows of the room but his presence was signalled by the skin of his legs glistening in the terrace sunlight. There was a fumbling for the armrests of his lounger, and his head and torso shot into view. He swung his legs sideways and shifted himself into the shade.

"Sometimes you confuse me, dear," he said while scratching his head. "Why does my mother need a dog?"

Lucy was on her hands and knees, in the centre of the sitting-room. The morning was hot and windless, and Lucy was surrounded by piles of washing: a small pile for her, a bigger pile for him and a variety of piles for baby Mario.

"A dog doesn't answer back; that's why."

Tony cocked his ear to a distant sound, perhaps an accelerating car reminding him that there was a world beyond these aromas, the garden walls, and this ongoing and disagreeable tension between the two women in his life.

"Well, she was born in another era. She's a product of a different time"

Lucy raised herself on her haunches, arms akimbo.

"And what does that mean, Tony?"

"It means…"

"It means that, I too, was born in another era," Lucy said. "It means that, I too, am a product of a different time. Perhaps, I need a dog."

"And what sort of dog would you need?"

"A dog that barks at disagreeable women, and a dog that keeps them away until they're invited."

Tony let his head fall forward and he scanned the floor between house and terrace while muttering as if he were irritated at losing something.

"I can't hear you," Lucy said. "What did you say?"

"I asked you if a dog would make you happy."

Lucy lifted her shoulders while rotating her forearms outwards and extending her fingers, the palms now parallel to the sky.

"Bah," she said while putting her lips together and raising her eyebrows. This gesture, designed and made in Italy to express powerlessness or disengagement, was carried out by Lucy in such a controlled way, so slow and deliberate that it lacked Italian spontaneity, Italian flair, and lightness of touch but, Tony thought, it had power, plenty of power. Lucy cast an angry eye over the piles of washing that surrounded her.

"There are such things as disposable nappies nowadays, but what does she expect?"

"What does she expect?"

"She still expects our son to experience the terror of washable nappies and safety pins."

"Oh, come on. You…"

"Just look at all this stuff."

"What's wrong with it?"

"None of it is mine."

"You mean you don't wear it?"

"I didn't choose it."

"Some of it must be your choice."

"No. It's all blue."

"What's wrong with blue?"

"Whoever said that blue is for boys and pink is for girls?"

"Isn't that the norm?"

"Since when has blue been the norm? Why not green or yellow, or even pink?"

"Do you really expect my mother to say 'to hell with the norm'?"

"Why not? To hell with the norm. See? It's easy."

She put her hand into the wash basket and pulled out a pink cardigan.

"I got this for Mario. I got it because I will not, repeat not, be a replica of your mother."

"Nobody's asking you to be anything other than who and what you are, dear."

"She's a control freak."

"She's just trying to help."

"No, Tony. She wants to control me like she controls you," Lucy said while searching for another nappy to fold. "Whose side are you on anyway?"

"I'm not on anyone's…

"Shit," Lucy said, letting a safety pin fall to the floor, inserting a finger into her mouth, and sucking at it while she grimaced in pain.

"Perhaps, we should've moved into the flat," Tony said. "She still thinks this house is hers."

Lucy pulled her finger from her mouth and held it in the air.

"It is hers. We're just renting. Remember?"

The flat to which Tony referred was in the centre of town. Many years previously, his parents had bought it for their retirement because it was the fashion amongst the well-to-do and retired Treviso elderly to move into accommodation in town centres. An added, but minor consideration, was the proximity of these places to the facilities that the elderly might need.

"It's the perfect solution for my perfect son," his mother had announced with a smile.

Tony turned his face away from this memory as though he had been slapped. He rested his elbows on his knees, his chin in his cupped hands and rocked to the rhythm of his thoughts. Perhaps there was no perfect solution. What was "perfect" anyway? After all, his perfect meat was clearly Lucy's poison.

The word "perfect" had entered his life and Ricky's life during their early childhood and it had never gone away. It had brought a series of perfect expectations and problems with it and these had never been identified, addressed, and dealt with. So, he reflected, and in a way, what was happening was not his fault. Both he and Ricky had been brought up, passively, and raised, actively, like most people, and they had been perfectly trained, by perfect parents and accompanying adults, to act and react in perfect ways, to judge and to condemn in perfect ways, to think and believe in perfect ways, forever and ever, until death did take them away. But Tony now realised that it did not need to be like that, and he was now ready to deal with it. After all, it was neither his fault nor his brother Ricky's fault because they did not bring themselves up and fill their heads with all that perfect nonsense. But only they could change it.

It was porridge that had set the perfect tone of Tony's

life. Even now, he recalled the steam on his face when his legs were still short and his feet would not touch the floor, and he drew the spoon through the porridge to separate the cereal into half-moons. The trick; no, the necessity, was to put the spoon in the mouth and repeat the action before the half-moons met again. If this happened, Tony knew it would cause a calamity, the world would end or he would die. One morning, runny porridge appeared at his nose. Believing himself unable to carry out his task, Tony was struck with terror. He refused to touch his breakfast.

"It's too runny," he said.

"Mr Perfect, are we?" his mother said. "Is there no room for something different in your life?"

And the name, "Mr Perfect," like a virus, spread through friends and family until its point of origin was forgotten.

"Oh, perfect Mr Perfect. What a perfect boy he is. Why can't you be like the rest of us ordinary, adaptable and imperfect people?"

And then, their views spread to infect other aspects of his character and personality. Not only did he need perfectly cooked porridge, so they said, but he also needed the world around him to be perfect, too, perfect relationships, for example, or the perfect holiday, the perfect hotel and so on. It also meant, so they argued, a dislike of change because a changing world was a disorderly world and far from the perfection required, so they said, by Tony.

Something similar happened to the caring Ricky. Long ago, and so long that neither Ricky nor Tony remembered it, they were out in town and carrying their mother's shopping, at least that was how the family story went, and they said that Ricky noticed an old lady hovering on the edge of the pavement and he ran over to help her, so went the story.

"Bless him, just look at that," said their mother. "How he loves to help and please people."

And somebody else, although Tony could never remember who, said:

"Such a caring and kind individual."

From that day on, Ricky was condemned to carry this burden, and he became the caring Ricky, the thoughtful Ricky, the kind and sympathetic Ricky whose generosity of spirit would take him so far in life that he would become a "somebody," perhaps a caring doctor, a caring teacher or even a caring social worker. Some people, more thoughtful people, perhaps, said that he had better be less caring and more careful and remember to look after himself otherwise, so these thoughtful people suggested, he might leave himself open to the machinations of others who might not, they opined, have his well-being at heart.

"Too universal to give it all to one person," they said, and although they, whoever "they" were, were now vanished and gone, their ghosts always returned to haunt and taunt him. And Tony thought, as if struck by a revelation, that there had always been something of the priest about Ricky. Tony fidgeted at the arrival of this idea. Something of the priest? Maybe a little bit, but not enough to become a real mediator between God and humanity. Tony knew that his younger brother had problems enough of his own without having to deal with the confessions of others, advise on their marital problems, their lack of spiritual direction, attend marriages and perform funerals and burials. Nonetheless, having a priest-like figure as a brother meant that whatever Tony did, he was not quite good enough. He was not completely bad, but bad in comparison with the priest-like goodness of his sibling. And so, when Ricky opened his mouth to speak, Tony always expected to be lectured loftily while an accusing finger wagged between Ricky's arched eyebrows.

What utter nonsense it all was. They got it all wrong. Neither of us was like when we were younger and we are not like that now.

Then there was a click, the sound of a key turning in a lock. and a voice was raised, its expectant words gathering in the sitting-room:

"Darling, I'm here."

"Talk of the devil," Lucy said.

"She's not the devil," Ricky said. "She's just my mother. Please, do try and keep the peace."

5

1988

Pink

To Lucy, the slamming of the front door was a personal affront, a deliberate challenge, an expression of displeasure at best and rudeness at worst, unless it was an accident and the perpetrator apologised. Lucy waited for the apology that never came. Instead, there was a rustle of clothes, an intake of breath, the wipe and rub of shoes on doormat, the crackle of cloth against cloth, cloth against skin, a fumbling for the clothes hanger, the metallic crash of keys thrown on the door-side tabletop. There was a voice, a loud and confident voice, from the doorway.

"I'm home, dear."

Lucy stiffened, her mouth dropped open and her eyes stared in disbelief.

"The key, did you really give her a key?" she said. "Without asking me?"

Tony pushed himself away from the lounger and stood up, the right leg-opening of his shorts stuck at the hip and making him look ridiculous.

"I didn't know she had one," he half-whispered. "But she and Dad are the owners of the house."

"Did you or did you not give your mother a key?"

Tony held out his arms in a gesture of helplessness.

"So, you did give her free entry into our house and you didn't tell me."

"It is her house," Tony said.

Lucy shook her head.

"No, it's our house," she said and nodding at his shorts, she added: "And for heaven's sake, make yourself respectable for your mummy."

Tony was about to respond but Lucy's face told its own story, and that story was going to get told, come what may. She was staring into his eyes, shoulders hunched and her hands clenched into fists.

"Not while I'm here," she said between her teeth. "No, not while I'm here and paying the rent. I don't give two hoots who the landlord is."

Tony opened his mouth to respond but a voice from the entrance hallway cut him off before he could utter more than a grunt.

"The garden will need weeding again," Mrs Meldrum said. "And soon, by the look of things."

Lucy was still glaring into Tony's eyes when her mother-in-law clip-clopped out of the vestibule towards them. This pillar of the community, this famed hostess, at least in the town of Treviso, this happily-married-for-decades woman, known for her pastries and hybrid cooking as far away as the boundaries of the province, carried her status and her right to treat Italians like colonial subjects into the room beside her.

"Shall I ring the gardener for you? I just popped in to check up and… You look tired dear," she addressed Lucy directly

"Oh, it's teething problems," Lucy said.

Mrs Meldrum tossed her head and appeared to ignore Lucy's response. She was waltzing through the piles of clothing on the floor when she stopped and looked down.

"What a lovely colour pink," she said, eyeing the pink cardigan that lay on the floor before turning to her son and saying: "Is there something that you're not telling me, dear, something more important than teeth?"

"No, I'm not pregnant," Lucy said with an imitation smile.

"We would love a sister for Mario, wouldn't we?" Mrs Meldrum said to her son.

"We've no plans for more children," Lucy said.

"The best laid plans of mice and men can always go wrong," Mrs Meldrum said over her shoulder while striding towards the kitchen.

"I'm not a mouse," Lucy said.

"That's not what Mum meant," Tony said with a frown.

"Exactly, dear," Mrs Meldrum said from the kitchen. "The fact is that humans are animals too, and it doesn't matter if you're a mouse, a farmer or a king."

"What is that supposed to mean?" Lucy said.

"It's not supposed to mean anything," Mrs Meldrum said, isolating the word *supposed* and emphasising it with a shake of her head. "However, it does mean that life's full of negatives and that we have to learn to live with them, dear, don't we? Even Mr Perfect must see the value in that."

"The value of what?" Tony said

"Tolerance, dear."

"I've got no idea what you are…" Tony began.

"So," Mrs Meldrum said. "Have you decided?"

"On what," Tony said.

"The date for the ceremony."

When this statement was met with silence, Mrs Meldrum looked hurt.

"The date for the baptism?"

"I don't recall…" Tony said.

"And have you decided on the Godparents? And please don't forget that boys wear a blue ribbon on the robe as a symbol of their gender."

"We will wait," Lucy said, "until Mario's old enough to make up his mind about these things."

Mrs Meldrum visibly paled but Lucy had not yet finished.

"We will not impose our religion or anybody else's religion on him. We're going to let him decide what he wants, or doesn't want, to believe."

"My dear, the country in which you've decided to live is a very Catholic society. Entry into the church is expected. There are no good reasons for parents to avoid baptising children. Who are you to make this decision? There are things in the bible, things implicit and explicit. We can discuss this again later. I didn't come to argue about your child's future."

"There's nothing more to discuss," Lucy said. "We'll inform you of our decision when we're ready."

She managed a soft tone, a tone which was not charged with a stack of resentment-making memories: the wedding invitation extended to one of Tony's oldest girlfriends, for example, or Mrs Meldrum's meddling in the affairs of the school. To Tony, it all seemed so natural he scarcely noticed until Lucy brought it to his attention.

"By the way, dear," Mrs Meldrum said to her son. "I've been darning your socks and I wanted to ask you for Mario's trouser size. They do grow so quickly, don't they?" And I came to invite you…"

Lucy swivelled and marched into the kitchen and announced her disaffection by clearing the kitchen with as much banging and crashing as she could muster. When there were no more plates and cutlery to throw into the sink, Mrs Meldrum continued with:

"…to our party."

"We'd love to come, wouldn't we, Tony?"

"Bit late for lunch, isn't it?" Mrs Meldrum said.

There was a sudden crash that stopped them all in their tracks. Mario had managed to climb half-way out of his chair, had lost his footing and fallen to the floor.

"Look what happens when you're not paying attention. Neglect can kill," Mrs Meldrum said.

Lucy was checking for bruises and bumps or any other injury when she said:

"Please leave us alone."

"You'll need to be vigilant for the next 12 to 24 hours."

"Please…"

"We'll be fine," Tony said making a sign to his mother that she had better leave.

"Very well," she said. "I'll leave you in peace."

When Mrs Meldrum had left, Lucy nodded towards the closing door.

"I want you to make a solemn promise," Lucy said.

"Always be polite to my mother?" Tony said.

Lucy shook her head and nodded towards the front door.

"She will never come uninvited again. Promise?"

Tony glanced towards the floor and took a deep breath.

"I'll do my best." he said.

6

1990

Still

On that particular day, the return-home-at-noon-for-something-to-eat-with-the-family-time turned out to be much more than the usual click of the doorlatch, a push at the door, a rough rubbing of wood on carpet, a quick hello, a snack, a peck on the cheek and a speedy goodbye. Something else was going on, and it was entirely unexpected, unless one looked at it in retrospect, in which case, it was visible as part of a thread in their lives, but that moment, the moment when he knew his emotions were back in their usual place, he had not seen coming.

The realisation hit him before he had even entered the house, and he was watching her through the glass side-panels of the door, and he knew immediately, or at least recognition came immediately, that the special "she" and the special "he" or, in other words, those two special people he once thought to be connected at the level of the soul, were victims of nature and were now spinning further and further away from each other.

I would like to jump in at this point, a moment's digression, and say that I am not passing judgement here, but suffice it to say that the course of true love invariably, but not always, runs downhill with the arrival of children. And it is ironic because so many couples, Tony and Lucy among them, believe the myth that the birth of children will be the final act that fills some gap or fulfils some need that brings couples closer together. Despite all the evidence to the contrary, this myth is tenacious, a pulling of wool over the eyes of those who are young and in love. It is almost a miracle that this belief persists despite the fact that social scientists have found consistent evidence, or so I have been led to believe, that there is almost no association between having children and happiness.

The front door opened into a magic cloud, and Tony knew it was the smell of roasting pork and an image of his mother cooking it, that transported him to this place he had mislaid and which marriage had not even begun to replace. This lost-but-not-forgotten place was childhood along with all its defining characteristics, its sense of security, belonging and connectedness, its sense of love, warmth and appreciation. There were no images to go with this time and nor could he call it a memory. It was just a sensation of such intensity that it prompted Lucy to look at him, and then to stare at him and say:

"You look as though you've seen a ghost."

"Oh, I think I have," he said.

"Whose ghost?"

"No, seriously, it's just the damned fog."

"What about it?"

"It's keeping the students away," he said while studying his face in the mirror by the entrance door. When he was satisfied that his facial features were the same as they had been the day before, he added: "The pork smells lovely, by the way."

He closed the door on this throw-away comment, on

the silence and on the fog and on the cold, swirling and curling around the house, but there was a darker silence in the lamplight over the meal table while the kitchen clock ticked and tocked, and an equilateral triangle of eyes was waiting in silence. Lucy faced him and, for a moment, she reminded him of Christ the redeemer with arms receptive and open and over the heads of three-year-old Mario and his sister Julia, who was learning to feed herself.

"Students?" Lucy said. "Isn't it time to call them what they actually are?"

Tony took in a calming breath, held it for several seconds before slowly exhaling. She was having a bad day, finding fault with everyone, he thought, and looking for someone to hang her mood on. Tony hung up his coat and scarf, tried to keep his tone neutral.

"What are they actually?"

It had been below freezing down in the town, down in the fog, but up here, up in the hills, the sun was coming and going and flickering through the glass panels of the front door, lighting up a side of Tony's face and fading again in the manner of a searching beam.

"Actually," Lucy said, "they're clients, and we should call them as such."

He closed his eyes and imagined the Prosecco Bar beckoning him with its warmth, the camaraderie of teachers, who had invited him to lunch, but who had been turned down by the must-get-back-to-my-wife-she-is-expecting-me kind of excuse he often made. Tony knew what his colleagues would say and do if he suggested they use the word "client" to describe the people they taught. Their gales of laughter would be a welcome addition to other sounds of Prosecco-Bar merriment, shouts for more wine, more sandwiches, more pork rolls, shouts that rose above the polished wood, the engraved window glass, above other customers and their green and uniform-like loden coats. He wished he was there now and feeling at home, feeling the warmth of being with others like himself, sneering and splitting their sides with laughter at those people who referred to their students as "customers" or "clients."

"I think the teachers would have something to say about calling their students 'clients'," Tony said but, even as he spoke, he was conscious again of that sinking sensation in his stomach, that downward glance at his clenched fists and that reluctance to predict in which directions he and Lucy might take the conversation from here and what they would do with these directions and conversations, and what could happen when and if they came to that place called no-man's-land, a churned up place where the past lived and where love was dumped.

"It doesn't matter what the teachers think," Lucy said. "Students are paying for language learning services, so they are customers and we are the service providers."

Tony shook his head. He still believed in his father's ideal of creating a better society through communication and understanding. This meant that, for him, S.E.S. was something akin to a social service. What was more, whole families had learned English there and they, in turn, recommended the school to younger family members so that S.E.S. became the school of choice for many Veneto families.

"So, customer satisfaction is our goal?"

There was a cough from little Mario as he extracted three fingers from his mouth. Lucy bent forward and removed the food from between his fingers and thumbs.

"Exactly," she said.

"And are you saying that the success of the school is to be judged by the evaluation of the students?"

Lucy allowed Julia to win a power struggle over the plastic spoon, and Julia waved it like a windscreen wiper in front of her face while her mother adjusted the little girl's bib.

"Correct," she said into Julia's ear.

Just for a moment he was back again in the Prosecco Bar and chatting with his colleagues, laughing at their jokes, applauding their wit. He could so easily have telephoned Lucy and told her the fog was too thick to drive home, but he did not like lies and deception. These black words were usually a signal that something, somewhere, was not as it should be and, perhaps, worse than it seemed.

"It's just not practical," he said. "Learners have responsibilities, and the school has a responsibility to maintain standards, not to mention a reputation to maintain."

But Lucy had turned her mind to Julia and her back on him, and Tony had seen the bottles of local red wine, wandered into the kitchen and poured himself a cup of "Clinton." And while he poured, he winced at Julia scooping up food from the table-cloth with her hand and he winced at the direction his conversation with Lucy had taken, just like the direction many of their conversations took, and he knew it would finish up with salt on already-cracked skin and already-open wounds. The idea of it produced an involuntary movement of his arm that ended with his hand clasping at his stomach. He picked at similar thoughts that had preoccupied him on the drive home, thoughts that came as questions of a most fundamental kind.

Is love still alive? Does love still have a place in our relationship? Do I still love her? Does she still love me? Do we still love one another?

The word *still* stopped his thoughts in their tracks. It suggested something negative, something that was in decline, on the way out, not for much longer, or dying. Still, he still loved her or was their love a fantasy or a memory of love perhaps, something akin to the memory of town that very morning, with the freezing fog and the dead leaves. He still felt the fog on his skin, still heard the leaves dancing around his feet.

"So," Tony said and he knew that he was going to ask her what he had asked before and he heard her response before he had finished. "You believe that the subjective gratification as reported by students is the marker which we should judge the quality of our teachers by?"

"Indeed, I do."

"And this same subjective gratification is the marker which should be used to evaluate our institution, our ethos and the people tasked with running it all?"

"Yes, that's exactly what I think."

A field of repulsion and negativity closed round him, and he looked down into the sink wondering whether this negativity was the result of differences of opinion regarding the way the school was managed or merely a battlefield on which other conflicts were fought: differences of opinion over the role of women in bringing up children, the use of babysitters, the application of authority, how much freedom to give, to take or allow and how much leeway to give to Lucy. She was certainly different from other mothers he knew, Italian mothers with Italian husbands and Italian children.

"Shouldn't you be focusing on the kids?" Tony said.

Lucy reached forward, slid a notebook towards her and picked it up, held it in front of her face.

"Look," she said. "I've written out the way forward for the school, as I see it."

"Are you saying that Dad's ideas were wrong?"

"No, not wrong, but what might've been right in 1950 is not necessarily right in 1990."

"Can't you leave that to my judgement?"

Lucy did not immediately reply and the long silence was enough for Tony to feel both uncomfortable and inadequate. She had started this silence with a suggestion of a smile and a series of glances at him but as the silence grew, the smile disappeared from her face and she scanned the area around her and finally lowered her eyes to stare at the floor. Eventually, she said on a breath:

"Just read it, please."

"Just leave it on the table," he said. "Please."

"By the way, the pork is for supper tonight."

Tony nodded. Lucy said:

"Be sure to read this," she said. "I'll ask you about it later."

He held his tongue and these, her last words, rang in his ears and roused those other rumblings of discontent that suggested he was wanting as a father, a business man and as an individual with an independent wife who was persuading him to make her, when the time was right, a manager of their limited liability company. She wanted powers to run the company on behalf of the partners and these powers included operating the school on a daily basis and hiring staff. This would give her a role in the company with much more independence than he now felt comfortable with but, believing himself unable to make a decision, Tony's response was one of procrastination Perhaps, the problem lay squarely with him and, every now and then, he wondered if he had loved her too much.

Is it wise to love too much? If you love too much, there is only one place to go and that is not to love them enough.

"Please believe me when I say that I have our business interests next to my heart," she said.

And he looked at her and thought he saw who she was and, while he put his coat back on, he recalled how he thought she had been, the strands of the ponytail brushing his skin, her breath on his cheek, the salty taste, the clasped hands, the skin and the eyelashes and the silence of content, the quiet breathing, the sleep. He at least knew the reason for the absence of the ponytail. It had been an interim measure, a practical and provisional solution when she had decided to let her hair grow longer.

Have I lost sight of myself? Do I still have an identity in my own right?

He closed the door on his questions, walked out into the fog and looked forward to finding himself again with those colleagues who might still be in downtown Treviso in the Prosecco Bar. When the car engine sparked into life, he reflected that his very existence was in a state of flux, of change and under threat, perhaps an early mid-life crisis. What he needed was the familiar and the feeling he was still in control. And if I, the narrator, might add my point of view, I would add that Tony was still in love with the idea of a perfect woman, a kind of never-changing fantasy or fairy story, if you like. But the main problem, in my opinion, was that if you criticised him for being in love with an ideal, he might look at you, shake his head and say, "What is wrong with that?"

7

1992

Ashes to ashes

"She wasn't a real mountaineer."

"So, tell me. What's a real mountaineer?"

"Mountaineers are adventurers, bro. Mum was a keep-the-status-quo type of person. She wasn't a mountaineer."

"But this mountain was always her mountain," Tony said.

"Just as long as she could confine it to imagination," Ricky said.

Tony scanned the summit of Cima Palon, watched another cloud come down and quickly obscure both he and his brother, the rocks, the view and, just as quickly, rise again.

"You remember the stories she used to tell us when we were kids?" Tony said.

"Cima Palon was the only place in the whole wide world where giants lived," Ricky said.

"Giants that could lift and kill elephants, you mean?"

"But were afraid of the eagle," Ricky said.

"Eagles that befriended lost children," Tony said.

"And took care of the climbers who dared to venture onto the summit."

"Talking of which…," Tony said.

He strode to the mountain edge, placed the palm of one hand on his hip and, resting the palm of the other hand on the summit cross, he leaned over the precipice to get a better view of the three roped-up climbers grappling up the spine of a ridge about 500 jagged metres below him. Everything seemed to be in order.

"You alright, bro?"

Tony's world was tilting sideways. His head was spinning. Sickness set in. He grabbed at the upright beam of the cross with both hands and lowered himself to his knees.

"I asked you if you were alright, bro?"

Tony felt his heart racing and thumping against his ribs, heard his breathing both quick and shallow and Ricky's voice both alarmed and caring.

"Bro, what's up?"

Tony was now in survival mode. He fixed his eyes on the rocks at his knees, felt them cutting at his skin while a bead of sweat rolled off his nose.

"Bro. What's going on, bro?"

Tony gave no indication that he had heard Ricky's words, did not react to their tone. His eyes were focused on the base of the beam where it plunged into the rocks and, between shivering breaths, he managed to whisper:

"It's all good, all good."

"All good? Bro, what's got into you?"

Tony threw out his right arm, the palm of his hand facing behind him.

"Stay back."

Tony noted his growling tone, closed his eyes, took deep and calming breaths, and remained still until the mist came down again, and the world dissolved into it.

Gingerly was Ricky's choice of word to describe what Tony did next. He pushed himself back from the rock at the mountain edge, toppled backwards and away from the precipice. Ricky strode towards him.

"Whoa, bro, what's going on? You're as white as a sheet."

"It's nothing," Tony said. "A touch of vertigo."

"Just a touch?" Ricky said. "Bro, you…"

"I'm fine," Tony said.

"But…"

"It's OK. I'm fine."

He pushed himself upright and staggered in a gust of wind.

"I was brooding a bit," Tony said. "Those memories… It's tough."

"It looked like…" Ricky said.

"I don't care what it looked like," Tony snapped. "I told you; I'm fine."

"But you…"

Tony placed his hands on his hips and straightened up.

"I said I was fine," Tony said. "Now, leave it be."

Ricky sucked at his bottom lip while looking around at the rocks, the cross, the sky.

"OK, bro," he said. "Have it your way. We're not here to argue."

Indeed, they had not come to argue. Nor had they come to dominate, claim, win or conquer peaks. They had come to say goodbye and *arrivederci* to their mother, to obey her wishes and scatter her ashes on this mountain. Ricky took a deep breath and, exhaling slowly, he searched for a safer topic.

"You got the ashes?"

"In my sack," Tony said.

Ricky nodded.

"You know," he said, "Mum claimed this mountain as hers. It's visible from the terrace of the Treviso house."

"Indeed, it is," Tony said in a monotone. "But only on clear days."

"She'd stare at it for hours."

"She'd make comments about it," Tony said.

"She would?"

"Yes, she would," Tony said. "She said it was her very own mountain."

"I see," Ricky said with a nod of his head that suggested this information was news to him.

"It's the absence of ski slopes she found attractive," Tony said.

"And the absence of vulgar tourists, I suppose," Ricky said.

"With all the crap they can leave behind, I'm not surprised," Tony said.

"That certainly made her mountain unique," Ricky said.

"Unique? It was her own El Dorado."

"Right," Ricky said. "She never came here, did she? It was all in her head."

"Exactly. That meant she was always in control."

"In what sense?" Ricky said.

"Under her control?" Tony said. "It meant that it could be anything and everything her imagination wanted it to be. Giants, eagles, lost children, and all."

Ricky nodded.

"Yes, I get it. Keep a distance. Don't let reality get a look in."

"Whereas," Tony said, "we are here and staring real life in the eyes."

"Real life? A rough place with the occasional nice view?"

"Something like that, but you must admit the views are impressive," Tony said.

Ricky opened his mouth to reply but managed only a syllable or two before shaking his head at a huge gust of wind that carried his hat and his half-words away. Another stronger blast of air forced the boys to crouch down while the wind tore at the mountain summit, whipped past the cross and thrashed at their cagoules before whistling away.

"Did you say oppressive," Ricky said.

"No, I said they were impressive," Tony said. "When you can…when you can see them."

Tony thought his brother's hand on his was a sign that Ricky had understood or the result of Ricky stumbling on the rocks and losing his balance in the last blast of air. Then, Tony felt his sibling's fingertips searching, finding, and grabbing his hand, holding it tight in his. Tony waited for the wind to ease, for the right time to ask what the matter was, but it was Ricky who broke the silence.

"Is it now? I mean, is this the right time to do what we came for?"

He sounded like a child asking a parent whether it was time to go to bed, time to go to school, time to have breakfast, time to act, time to play.

"Yes, it's time," Tony said. "While there's a lull in the wind."

"And the clouds are lifting. It is a magical moment."

The clouds had risen, and their shadows now cast themselves over the world below, roamed over the ridges and valleys and merged into the horizon. Sunlight was blinking on village churches, bathing their spires in its light and Tony grabbed his brother's arm.

"A magical moment, indeed, and not the magic of giants and lost children. This is magic of a different and natural kind."

The leaves, a perfect mixture of green and orange and burning red, swept down the lower slopes of the mountain, over the crests of hills and into the valleys and left the boys almost speechless. The wind died, and the summit basked in peace and tranquillity and, for a short while, the mountain showed them its calm side. Now was their moment.

"It's Mum's kind of day," Tony said.

"On Mum's kind of mountain."

In one swift movement, Tony swung the rucksack from his back to the ground. He tugged at the zip, plunged his hands into the sack and pulled out the urn. Taking a cloth cover from the top of the urn, he nestled it in his hand. It was a plain earthenware pot but it was by no means plain to him what he was expected to do with it. The two boys stood shoulder to shoulder and checked the direction of the wind.

"Hold out your hands," Tony said. And…"

Ricky did as he was told and Tony poured some of the ashes into them.

"…and remember the last time you saw her," Tony said, "before the illness when she was still in good health."

In the silence that followed, Tony tried to remember his mother at home, his mother in the kitchen, his mother making cakes, his mother working in the garden but, for some reason, he was unable to see her in motion and this reduced her to the eternal stillness of photographs. But pre-war snaps were confined to pictures of his father as were the early-wartime pics in black and white because there was no Mrs Meldrum until the war was almost over and the uniforms were mostly gone. Captain Meldrum often looked uncomfortable in "civvies" and his poses were rather stiff and typical of their time and he did not seem to care about colour because there was no colour. When pictures of his wife finally appeared, they were in shades of black and white; the wedding photos, staged and formal, or the parties on the terrace and the group shots suggesting how integrated both she and Captain Meldrum were and how much fun they were having with their Italian friends. There were images of flared dresses, tight waistlines, cocktail dresses, images of people with cups of tea, soda bottles or whisky decanters, images of perching hats, combs and pins and fox skin or mink.

"Ready," said Tony.

He took a deep breath and tossed some of the urn's contents into the air.

"We love you Mum," Tony said. "And we know you loved us, too."

The dense, sand-like matter fell to the ground but some of the ashes were of powder and became airborne. The white cloud spread out in front of them and disappeared in a second.

"Will her memory disappear so quickly?" Ricky said.

"She'll return in other ways," Tony said.

"Like?"

"A gentle memory; an unexpected presence, or perhaps in a shadow that appears at your feet."

Tony was not sure how long they both stood reflecting on the afterlife in this way, but he sensed a light movement, no more than a twitch of the arm, and Ricky took several deliberate steps forward and flung his arms upwards in the manner of a winter sportsman tossing the caber.

"Fly away, Mum," he said.

While he watched his mum's ashes flying above him, Ricky held his arms above his head with fingers outstretched as if he would catch her should she fall. And Tony looked into his brother's eyes, saw him bearing this cold moment alone, understood that grief was better shared, and he tossed his remaining ashes into the air. Some dropped to the ground, some became airborne and spread out in front of them. At this point, there was a sudden and sharp gust of wind that blew the ashes back towards the boys. This ash seemed anxious to show that it was not the feathery and powdery stuff of his imagination but a gravelly substance that stung the skin and eyes and stuck to hair and faces.

"She might be trying to tell us something," Ricky said.

Tony wiped at his face with the palms of his hands.

"Whatever she is trying to tell us, she's not going without a struggle," Tony said.

"And we'll always have photos to help us remember her," Ricky said.

"What we remember will depend on how we interpret them," Tony said. "I've often wondered about those party pics."

"What about them?"

"It occurred to me that they might indicate an inner emptiness or loneliness."

"Perhaps, they do," Ricky said. "On the other hand, belonging to a group might have flattered her. After all, the terrace was her realm, so perhaps she saw the guests as her subjects. These pictures told Mum that she was integrated, that Dad was integrated, that they were a part of local society. It must've been very satisfying."

"And what about those holiday pictures?" Tony said. "The holidays abroad. Have you seen them?"

"You mean the photos taken in places like *Cannes* and *Juan les Pins*?" Ricky said.

Tony nodded.

"What about them?" Ricky said.

"Do they simply tell the world where she and Dad could afford to relax."

"Well, maybe, but there are also lots of landscape photos taken in our local hills," Ricky said. "I'm not sure what they tell us but they seem to indicate satisfaction with life, don't you think?"

"To me," Tony said, "they show that life was a success, that now Mum could admire nature, escape from a frenetic daily pace, and enjoy the contemplation of natural beauty. But yes, we do have pics to help us remember her."

"True," Ricky said, "but photos don't give you advice you didn't ask for."

Tony smiled.

"Yes," he said. "She was opinionated at times, wasn't she?"

"But let's be thankful," Ricky said. "We still have Dad."

"Yes, we still have Dad," Tony said.

"And you still have Lucy," Ricky said. "And the children still live with you."

There was that word again - *still* – and its suggestion of not-for-much-longer impermanence, and the wind returned with the sound of a howling dog, and Tony looked into his brother's eyes and, while he looked, dislocated memories and whispers came to him. It might have been his mother who once said that a single person might always be envious of those who were married. Was it his mother who also said that the envy of those closest to you might cause the most harm?

"Just dreams," Ricky was saying. "Impossible...that can...be..."

Tony glanced at his brother quizzically.

"What's impossible?" he said into a fading wind. "You've lost me, old chap."

"Finding the right woman is impossible. Look at me, bro," Ricky said.

He opened his arms and held them outwards as though wishing to give the world a big hug.

"I'm no longer a young man, and I'm alone."

Tony shook his head.

"I guess it's hard not to feel alone when everybody else seems to be paired off," Tony said.

Ricky smiled.

"Then," he said, "I might need to be ruthless."

Tony nodded, stepped away from his brother, his smile, his threats, and leaned forward, picked up the empty urn and slid it into his rucksack.

"But first, I have to know exactly what I want," Ricky said.

"So," said Tony with practised disinterest, "what do you want?"

"I need a woman who's supportive of my needs," Ricky said. "I need a woman who'll share responsibility with me but who is also adventurous, experimental, independent and articulate about her own requirements."

Tony raised his eyebrows.

"So, not too much," Tony said. "The right woman is out there somewhere. Mark my words. Just don't make the mistake of thinking she'll turn up…"

"It's alright for you," Ricky said. "You've got a wonderful wife and children. Lucy's amazing. Even Mum came to like her in the end."

Tony frowned at this reference to their mother. He frowned because he was unsure as to whether his mother had ever really liked Lucy or whether she was being unusually pragmatic, because of the children, because it was her son or because it was easier that way. Most of all, he frowned at his brother's choice of the word "amazing" to describe his wife. Perhaps, Ricky should mind his own business.

"And Lucy's a great mother and a great asset to us in the school," Ricky said. "And you've got two wonderful children. Are you going to have more? Does Lucy want more children?"

"We haven't discussed it," Tony said. "To be honest, bro, it's not your business."

Tony grabbed at the drawstring at the neck of his rucksack and pulled it tight.

"You're a lucky man to have such a woman," Ricky said.

Tony raised his eyes, met Ricky's gaze full on and took a deep breath.

"Are you saying I don't deserve her?"

"No," Ricky said. "I mean you were lucky you got to her that evening before anybody else. Don't you remember?"

Tony balanced his rucksack, fumbled for the front compartment zipper and pulled it shut.

"Of course, I remember," he said. "She was standing alone. She was beautiful, enigmatic, one of a kind. How could I forget?"

Tony pulled the side-pocket zippers tight.

"Shall we go," he said.

"Oh, it's easy to forget those things that don't quite fit the stories we tell ourselves," Ricky said.

Still on his haunches, Tony said:

"Are you telling me my memory is just fantasy?"

"I'm saying that our personal memories are trimmed to fit the stories that become our own folklore."

"Folklore?" Tony said. "So, you are implying that it didn't happen in the way I recall?"

Ricky shook his head.

"Who am I to say such a thing?"

"So, what are you saying?"

"I am saying that the past can stick to us like labels. Mum always said I was the caring one," Ricky said. "Why did she say this? Because she once saw me behave in a caring way, it seems, but it's something I no longer recall. What do you think oh-brother-of-mine? Am I really the caring one?"

"Lucy seems to think you are."

Ricky looked up and into his brother's eyes.

"Lucy told you that? Really?"

"You ready to go?"

Ricky was tense, animated, and joyful.

"Lucy told you that I am the caring one?"

"I didn't say that."

Ricky stepped forward, avoiding Tony's eyes, and

threw his arms around him.

"Sorry, bro," he said.

"For what?"

Ricky shook his head and grabbed for his brother's hand.

"I can't stop myself," he said, wiping a tear from his eye. "And you, Mr Perfect, you messed up the throwing of the ashes."

"Perhaps the only positive to take from Mum's passing is that we can now be who we really are," Tony said. "The brakes have gone."

"Perhaps," said Ricky. "Perhaps, we are released. Is that a good thing?"

"Don't ask me," Tony said.

The clouds seemed to be queueing up and waiting their turn to swoop down and cover everything and, in the blink of an eye, the mist had shrouded the summit entirely. Sunshine was blocked out and the view was gone. While they shouldered their rucksacks, tightened their belts and boot laces, Tony felt confused. The future was a shining light beckoning with a range of possibilities and probabilities. But the future was also dark, menacing and threatening the unthinkable.

"Ready? Tony said.

"Let's go down," Ricky said. "Are you feeling…?"

"I said I'm OK," Tony said. "Forget it. It's all good."

But Tony would not forget. How could he possibly forget? The adjectives that Ricky used to describe his perfect woman: supportive, responsible, adventurous, experimental, independent, and articulate were adjectives that Tony often used when describing Lucy to himself.

8

1995

Power

"Thank you so very much for coming," Lucy said. "I'm sure you're busy enough with all your duties and all these changes going on at the moment, but the management team didn't forget your request."

While the teacher delegation shrank before Lucy's elaborate politeness, Tony blinked. He blinked at her attitude, he blinked at her arrogance, he blinked and blinked again at the changes he was seeing in Lucy and he blinked at what his father might say concerning this disregard for his own ideals of human sympathy and understanding. And he shook his head at the cavalier way with which Lucy was handling the situation. He shook his head at the way she was sitting in the high-backed swivel chair behind his desk in his office and in his father's first school and he shook his head when he heard her use the word "team" when the reality was that she had acted, and was acting, alone.

"In fact, we've considered your request from a variety

of angles," she said, "and we soon realised that each angle pointed to only one reasonable conclusion."

And then came the muted tuts, shakes of the head, and catches of the breath. Tony tutted at her bright red outfit. He tutted at the give-away-nothing expression on her face. He caught his breath at the words "management" and "team" and he shook his head at her fake politeness, and he caught his breath and tutted at himself. It was he, in a moment of weakness and after considerable resistance, who had agreed to Lucy's demands to give her the small but significant role in the running of the school she had always asked for. He had resisted until Ricky pointed out that the business was expanding at an almost impossible rate. There was even talk about opening a summer school in London, and Ricky suggested that they needed her more than she needed them. Tony shook his head in memory of her absent words of gratitude, the absent smile, the absent hand on his arm and he stifled groans of disgust in memory of that familiar disconnection, her nod and smile as if she were listening to some inner voices congratulating her on the achievement of a fundamental need.

"And now," Lucy said, "we'd like to inform you of the team's feelings and decisions."

Ricky was standing at her shoulder, clutching a sheaf of papers, sometimes whispering in her ear, occasionally lowering his head or looking sideways at Tony, sometimes with an expression of concern and sometimes as if he were lost in space.

Something is up with Ricky. Has he changed, or have I?

Perhaps, Ricky the caring and Ricky the kind turned out to be just Ricky the gullible, taken in by acts of cunning by those who would take advantage of his caring nature. Was it false memory, Tony wondered, or had he actually seen them both, on one occasion, conversing in a close huddle in the corridor? He had been looking into her eyes and nodding while she had been speaking. Neither of them seemed to have noticed Tony. So focused had they been on each other, they had not even looked in his direction. Perhaps these images were false, a product of reality and imagination. He could not say.

He shook his head and realised that 10 years had passed since those magical moments of first love on the terrace of the Treviso house, but now, with the ponytail long gone, streaks of grey in her hair and the results of two pregnancies evident in stomach-expanding and approaching middle age, Lucy had evolved into someone he hardly recognised. He had avoided the topic of feeling, those do-I-still-love-her questions, by barring the subject of love from his head, refusing it entry on the grounds of inappropriateness and irrelevance. Of course, he still loved her. He took love for granted. He had no choice but to still love her. It was just that their love seemed different from the perfect and everlasting love he knew from books and films. Whatever happened to that flirtatious behaviour, those over-the-shoulder glances, those come-and-get-me eyes, and those dances in the moonlight? The elegant slow waltz had deteriorated into the drooping slovenly gait of family strolls in the park while the slow foxtrot had lost its rhythm to become a stumble with no suggestion of intimacy. Perhaps, their love was just an oath, for better or for worse, for richer, for poorer, in sickness and health. Their love was a memory to cherish, till death. Or so he thought, until the arrival of children changed everything.

"There's no question that your request to improve conditions and wages is a reasonable one in many ways," Lucy said, looking at her hands and adjusting the position of a chunky gold bracelet on her wrist. "And we've looked at the question carefully and from differing points of view. After careful deliberation, these are our findings."

His love was now shared with a hard-nosed individual whose humanity appeared to have been sucked out of her, with somebody who seemed to think that emotions in general and human connection in particular to be weaknesses. Worse than this, she seemed to believe that the wedding vows were words with no meaning. And he believed that if his love was shared with someone who thought that words with no meaning were dead things, perhaps their love was a rotting carcass.

But it never occurred to him to ask her what she thought. There was never a right time to broach the topic and to find out what was going on in her head. And if he had asked her, maybe she would have told him something he did not want to hear, that his own perfectionism was partly to blame for his discomfort and unhappiness.

Recently, Tony found himself returning and returning again to one particular afternoon, a rainy afternoon when a periodic house clearance was going on, and he and Lucy had been looking through Tony's record collection and Lucy commented that his musical development seemed to have been static since the middle of the 1970s.

"It looks like music reached a stage of perfectionism at that time and has never been surpassed," Lucy said.

Tony was unable to recall his reply but he did remember wondering whether he saw people and relationships in the same way and he was still reflecting on it. There was no question, in his mind at least, that he was conscientious, dependable, systematic and had a dislike of change for its own sake, but he wondered whether this last point was his contribution to his own discomfort. Perhaps he had failed to appreciate that the only constant in life and relationships was change and readjustment. Nothing and nobody stood still. Perhaps, he thought, this was the way to be, otherwise, human beings and their relationships would stagnate, atrophy and die.

"And, I can assure you, that our decision was not an

easy one to make," Lucy was saying.

Tony watched her and Ricky, and then he studied the faces of the teachers' delegation and he tried to convince himself that all of the people in the room, management and teachers alike, were none other than himself but shaped by different circumstances and separated from others by conflicting interests.

Nobody in the room is either good or bad, are they? Just different from one another and with diverse interests and concerns.

"But, after careful deliberation," Lucy said, "we are, regrettably, unable to offer you the contractual changes you're seeking. Your request is, for the moment, denied."

A collective sigh of disappointment and a hunching of shoulders from the delegation behind the desk and they shuffled as though did not know whether they should leave or wait until they were given permission to do so. Lucy eyed them, seemed to reflect for several moments, or perhaps, Tony thought, she was relishing the power she had before delivering a knock-out blow.

"But I've decided on some changes in the school and, since you are here, I thought it best to tell you first."

All of a sudden, Tony felt transparent. The words "I have decided" were ominous. She had never before made decisions without consulting him. She was becoming somebody he hardly recognised, somebody moulded, perhaps, by her father, her grandfather and her great grandfather with all the accompanying family characteristics and values he had never known or experienced. And one such never-experienced example was an end-justifies-the-means pragmatism, a pragmatism to which he and his father, and no doubt his grandfather and great grandfather before him, would have attached another word and that word might have been "deceitful," "dishonest," "unscrupulous" or "unprincipled."

And then came those revelations. For 10 years, Tony had kept his head down and played the business by the rules of his father. He was certain that his hard work and natural talents would be rewarded but sleepless nights had begun to disturb him about 6 months previously when she had told him about her "tactical behaviour" when she had met his parents. His feelings for her would, and could, never be the same again.

Six months had gone by since her admissions and here she was, shifting her bottom in her large leather chair, leaning forward, and planting her elbows on the table. To the teacher delegation, she said:

"The decision I'm referring to concerns requirements of my own."

She proceeded to lecture the delegation about the strength of the increasing competition and that this required a response from S.E.S., a response that unless implemented might result in a drop of student numbers and a corresponding cut in teaching hours and, perhaps, jobs.

"I am, therefore, unable to offer the annual increase in salaries this year," she said.

Shifting her bottom in her large leather armchair, she leaned forward and planted her elbows on the table.

"However, given the nature of the competition, we require maximum availability, maximum flexibility and maximum professionalism from all teachers."

She waited for the message to sink in before slamming the palms of her hands on the desk.

"Any questions?" she asked. "No?"

She glanced at her watch.

"No?"

"No questions," somebody mumbled.

"Then, thank you for coming."

When the door shut behind the teacher delegation, Lucy turned to Tony.

"There's no need to look at me as if you've had an epiphany or seen a ghost," she said. "You and Ricky gave me responsibilities, and I intend to carry them out to the best of my abilities. Times are tough and competition's increasing all the time. We'll continue to use babysitters to look after the children, as and when needed unless you, Tony, are prepared to do it yourself? No? Then let's all get back to work, shall we?"

9

1995

Revelations

Later that day, when he was alone, Tony was still wondering to which category Lucy's revelations concerning her family belonged. Was it tactical behaviour, fantasy or a barefaced lie designed to impress? As her husband and business partner, he felt he ought to know, but now that he was putting it all on the table, as it were, he was having doubts. Could he reject her as a liar and an opportunist and somebody never to be trusted or should he simply see her as a new version of someone important to him and an individual corrupted by a variety of social conditions and a product of the world she had grown up in?

Perhaps, he reflected, Lucy herself would answer his question in a different way. Perhaps, she would say her fabrications revealed a desire or a need that she was unable to fulfil in reality, a need like being in control or a need for power. Did her fantasies protect her view of how she wanted the world to be or did she merely desire to please Tony's parents and, by doing so, further her own ambition?

Why did Lucy lie? What would she tell us?

"I had to be creative, for our sake," Lucy said. "I needed them to approve of me so that they'd approve of us."

Tony shook his head.

"You've lost me," he said.

And in one sense, she had lost him. He was lost at sea with a malfunctioning compass and with no idea as to what was coming from over the horizon. But, in another sense, she had not lost him at all. From the beginning of his relationship with Lucy, he had been trapped between the expectations of his mother and the demands of his wife. His mother was unable to see past the values, traditions and prejudices that had shaped her and never saw Lucy as he saw her. His mother's complaints centred on Lucy's need to work all day and deprive her children of a mother's love and attention. For her part, Lucy could not understand why Tony's mother was unable to offer help on her visits especially regarding the children. Tension between the two women ceased in 1992 when Tony's mother had suddenly died.

"I wanted their blessing. So, I needed to tell your mum and dad what they wanted to hear."

"About your parents?"

"About me and my parents. It was all a fabrication," she said.

"Your father was never a teacher?"

"Are you joking?"

"No. I'm not."

"But I told you," Lucy said, "I needed your mum and dad to approve of me and to achieve that, I needed to reinvent myself and my personal history."

"And you think that that was a good thing to do?"

Her mouth dropped open and her eyes widened in disbelief, and she turned her head away from his and giggled; but giggles became guffaws and guffaws turned to gales of laughter that appeared not only to exclude him but also left him obscure in the audience, blind in the jungle, lost in the wilderness and wishing she would stop and re-enter his space. She did stop; suddenly. And she stared into the empty place above his head and lowered her gaze until it found his.

"Well, the end justifies the means, you know?" she said.

"Does it?"

"Of course. If you want to be a success, you have to do whatever it takes. Pa was ambitious and I'm proud to be like him. It's called pragmatism."

"Pragmatism? Sounds like dishonesty to me; like lies, in fact."

"Oh, really? Grow up, dearest. That's the way the world is."

"Come on, Lucy, whose world are you describing? Mine or yours?"

"And is your life so very different? Are the lives of your parents any different? In their oh-so-cosy-middle-class world isn't it more important to do and say the right thing and put a brave face to everything?"

"They're simply adapting to the circumstances," Tony said.

"And I was simply adapting my own history to suit my circumstances."

Tony did not respond but his attitudes were already shifting in the silence. He almost heard the creaking of change within, and whatever was being changed was complaining and forcing him to blink. He saw and knew at last what it was that had been eating away at him, the how and why of all that negativity, in the past and present and forever more.

"Pa's retired now," Lucy said. "But he ran his own business."

"Retired? You led me, and Mum and Dad, to believe your parents were dead."

"Then, you misunderstood," said Lucy. "Both ma and pa are very much alive."

"How interesting. And what sort of business did your pa run?"

"He started life as the general manager of a Soho strip club in the 1960s, but he had ambitions to open his own club catering for a London that was recovering fast from the doldrums of the post-war years."

"And you mother?"

"She was born in Romania but came to London in 1955 where she found work as a dancer and cigarette-girl at a cabaret club, Vincent's, in Black Road. Its general manager was Dad. They began a relationship and married in 1960."

"I see."

"What do you see, Tony? Two lives and two people your privileged parents would never have approved of? What I see is two people, a working-class boy, and an immigrant, very much in love and who wanted to make a life for themselves against all the odds."

"What was privileged about living through a depression and a world war?" Tony said.

"It's not about what they lived through."

"No?"

"No. It was about expectations and the chance of making a better life for themselves," Lucy said.

"Go on," he said.

"Mum and Dad found premises in Soho and opened a new club on Valentine's night in 1963. They called it The Adam and Eve club. The illuminated floor was the first of its kind in the city and the club offered fine dining in the European tradition. It also offered sex and glamour. It was the place to be seen and was frequented by politicians, sports stars, and pop music celebrities. What is it, Tony?"

Tony was feeling a little sick. All those values he had inherited from his parents, values of common decency, accepted and unquestioned, were churning in his stomach. He heard himself say:

"So, I suppose it was an upmarket brothel."

"It's all a question of perspective," she said. "Of course, there was sex, but never on the premises."

"Oh, that's alright then. If you don't see it, it isn't happening, is that right?"

"You are sounding like your mother," Lucy said. "Don't you have opinions of your own?"

Tony sucked in a deep breath, held it and, while he counted to five, Lucy stared at him in a manner that suggested she had seen something in him she had never before noticed. It was not a new clarity. It was not even a new perception or a new attitude. It was an illumination.

"Well, go on," Tony said.

Lucy blinked, and blinked again, her lips parted but she seemed to be in a dream until she shook her head and said:

"By the beginning of the 1990s, the world had moved on. The new strip clubs of Soho made The Adam and Eve Club look tame."

"So, what did your parents do? Oh, don't tell me, they did something pragmatic, drug dealing; perhaps, people smuggling?"

The words were out and hanging in the air, poisoning the space between them, and they had emerged by themselves, a kind of automated response, while Tony watched in despair and wondered whether this tendency to moral righteousness was really his or, as Lucy said, it had been inherited from his parents and had a life of its own.

"There's no need to be so moralistic," she said. "Just a few years ago, he sold the business, and Mum and Dad moved to France, at least for a while."

"Where they died, apparently."

"Oh, I never said they died."

"You never said they were alive either."

"You wouldn't get on with them."

"You never gave us a chance. Don't you want them to visit us, to see their only daughter and grandchildren?"

"I suppose they would if they wanted to," Lucy said. "The last I heard they'd gone to live in Thailand. We no longer have much contact. In fact, contact is restricted to the odd letter."

"Are you saying they just abandoned you?"

"Not at all. Dad supported me during my studies. Without his help I'd never have been able to finish my M.Ed. I'll be forever in his debt."

How, Tony wondered, had Lucy managed to fool him? Perhaps, he thought, a better question might be to ask how he had allowed her to fool him. She seemed to love him, at least at the beginning of it all, and they both seemed to have so much in common. It was almost uncanny. When he wrote a diary, she said she did, too. When he said he went climbing, she said she did, too. He wanted kids. She did, too. He liked seafood. She did, too. But when he realised that they rarely went skiing together, never went climbing together, rarely ate seafood together, that he never saw her writing in a diary, he assumed it was the presence of their children that stole her time.

And now, here she was, 10 years after their first meeting, and giving him a new account of her parents' lives, a rags-to-riches story that could not have been more diffcrent from that of a teacher in Oldham. But why, Tony asked himself, had he taken her at face value? Why had he never checked up on her story? There were no answers to these questions, but there were assumptions. He assumed that he loved her. And because he loved her, he assumed she was telling the truth. Because he assumed she was telling the truth, he had put her on a pedestal.

But while she was on that pedestal, she had lied to him.

Did it matter? Trust, Tony thought, was a quality that belonged to him. It was his quality and he was not going to lose it because she did not deserve it. But it was not easy and, if he was honest with himself, doubts haunted him from that day on, especially at night.

10

1999

Hands

Tony smiled at Lucy.

The memorial service had been in good hands.

The graveside service and burial had been in good hands.

His father's memory was now in old and safe hands.

"Thank you so much for coming," Tony said. "I can't even begin to thank you."

Grit your teeth. Hold back the tears. Just put out your hand. Let him grab it.

"So glad you've come."

There were always more hands. Hands with rings, hands without rings, hands with folds and furrows, hands with cracked and broken fingernails, hands with creases carved and puckered, and hands that shook and hands that trembled towards him, scarred hands, thumbless hands, gloved hands, prosthetic hands.

"So pleased you're here."

And he smiled at Lucy.

She was beside him, chatting, supporting, comforting, lending her hand and being there for him amongst all those hands: this one bruised, that one wrinkled, this one cold and that one scarred. Information about the future could be gleaned from hands, Tony knew, but he was drawn to them as witnesses to the past. Every palm, every knuckle, every scar and every missing finger or thumb was a story worth telling, a story connected to his own father, and that part of him that his dad had shared with these old soldiers.

"Thank you for coming."
"So nice to have met you."
"Dad would be happy you came."
And he smiled at Lucy.

Hold them back. Whatever you do, hold them back.

Some of them, but just a few of them, he knew from past parties on the terrace but there were always fewer of these men, gathering in a huddle as though for protection, they were the old guard, upright and upstanding with chins lifted, facing their own Waterloo and daring the grim reaper to claim them.

"So happy you made it."
"When did you last see Dad?"
"Have you travelled far today?"
"What do you remember about Dad?"
And he smiled at Lucy.

Keep it cool, don't show your feelings, be stoic, like Dad was stoic, like these old soldiers are stoic.

His father had been like these men, these phlegmatic men, these unflappable and detached men come to celebrate the passing of one of their own. The handshakes of these veterans were sometimes weak, sometimes strong, sometimes soft, and sometimes rough, but Tony knew he was touching what his father had touched and, that blue and blustery afternoon, he felt these hands connected to comradeship and love. Captain Meldrum was nearly 80 when he died but Tony was unable to recall a time when his father tried to hide his hands away from the eyes of others. He rarely even mentioned those wrinkles, never seemed to think of them as unsightly. Tony had never imagined that his father, like his men, had simply grown into them and accepted them as his own.

"Thank you so much for coming," he said to a blue blazer and a regimental tie.

Hold it together, like they are holding it together for Dad's sake.

"Thank you for being here today," he said to a man in a wheelchair.

And he smiled at Lucy.

Tony recognised neither the badge nor blazer. But he thought he had seen this man on previous occasions, perhaps reunions on the terrace of private people in military blazers, berets and ties designed for the young and worn by the old, and indicating their belonging to an ever-smaller band of ever-older men. Gathered by the graveside and bolt upright they sang in harmony a soldier's song to the tune of "Lilli Marlene."

"When you look around the mountains, through the mud and rain
You'll find the crosses, some which bear no name.
Heartbreak, and toil and suffering gone.
The boys beneath them slumber on.
They were the D-Day Dodgers, who'll stay in Italy."

"That was wonderful."

Hold them back.

"I'm so pleased you sang that. Dad would've loved it."

Keep smiling.

"So pleased you came."

And he smiled at Lucy.

"We fought our way across Africa," said one old hand. "We were part of the invasion of Sicily and were at Monte Cassino and we took part in the liberation of Rome. We were in the final push up to the Po River and watched the Germans burning all their equipment before trying to swim across the river to escape to Germany."

Things he had never known. Stories he had never heard.

"The war never left him," one old comrade said. "Did the Captain talk much about it?"

Hold them back. For God's sake hold them back.

"He rarely talked about the war but the war was always in the home," Tony said. "When I asked him about his wartime experiences, the only thing he said was, 'We were always cold. always wet, always hungry and nobody cared'."

He laughed. The old soldier laughed.

"I remember the flies," said another old soldier. "They were big and gorging themselves on the decomposing bodies. The stink of death was everywhere. And there, down below was that beautiful valley full of red poppies. At times it was hard to appreciate the contrast: here an atmosphere of death and destruction and, down there, there was beauty, peace and quiet. I thought: how can these two worlds coexist sided by side? But that's how it was."

The old soldier laughed. Tony laughed.

And he smiled at Lucy.

Laugh again, take a deep breath, and hold them back. Hold back the tears. If they can do it then so must you.

"Did he tell you about his unit at Caserta? No? Did he tell you how his commanding officer shot himself because he knew he was responsible for all those deaths? Did your father tell you about his best pal? No? I've often wondered how on earth he managed to make funny stories from horror, but he did."

"Funny?"

"Yes, his best friend was standing next to him and he was holding a cigarette between his fingers. Captain

Meldrum said the colonel drove up in a jeep and asked him what he was doing. Your dad said he was sharing a smoke with his friend. The colonel just pointed at his friend and said, 'He's dead. Return to your unit' and drove off. And your dad turned to his friend and said, 'Hey,' the colonel said you're dead' and then your dad saw the bullet hole. His friend had been shot in the heart. Stone dead, he was, stone dead. How his friend was still on his feet he didn't know. Funny, isn't it?"

Hold them back. Keep your tears for another day.

"No, I never heard that story. So happy you could come today."

Banish that childish sense of jealousy that comes from stories by people I have never met and the man I thought I knew.

And he smiled at Lucy.

But he asked himself if he had ever known his father and, if the answer was no, why had he not known him? He had known him as a father but not as a soldier, not as a husband. He did not know the man who was forced to kill and a man who had gone through hell but at least he now understood why Captain Meldrum constantly scratched at the scar on his nose. What was he supposed to say to those old hands who knew his father better than him?

"Thank you for coming. Dad would've appreciated it."

Then, there was a hand on Tony's forearm.

"Only, your father told us terrible stories," an old soldier said. "And he told them as if they were part of a comedy routine in order to make us laugh."

"He never really talked about the war," Tony said. "But it was often the elephant in the living room."

"You don't truly know the horrors of war," the old soldier said. "Until, one day, you feel your knife cut through flesh and watch a human being die horribly, gurgling in front of you, teenage eyes pleading for a life that you can't return. You just don't know."

"Thank you for coming," Tony said grabbing at the old soldier's hand. "Dad would've appreciated it."

And he smiled at Lucy.

A gentle breeze was blowing through the trees which sheltered the cemetery on three sides. Looking out over the flatlands south of Treviso it was hard to imagine that the green expanses had been bloody killing fields. The evidence was there in the rows of headstones. Tony had come here with his father one day when he was around 6 years old and he had walked and stumbled over the graves and his mother had told him to stay on the paths but his father had said:

"Let him be. These men won't mind a young English boy walking over their graves."

This old soldier still had Tony's hand in his. He was pulling it and drawing Tony closer.

"Killing is a horrible thing," he whispered into Tony's ear, "and the human mind's wired to consider it a horrible thing. We take a human and break him down and rebuild him to overcome this aversion to killing another human, but the mind never accepts that killing another human is normal. Soldiers have to live with memories until they die. Why would you want to tell a story about something that hurts and that your brain has tried to forget? Nobody wants to relive the event. It wasn't glorious. You killed a human being with family, a family that'll never know the love of their son again."

I can confirm that Captain Meldrum had dreams about the war until he died, but he never talked about them. Nor did he have screaming nightmares when he fell asleep, whether it was in bed or on the couch after watching a war film. But we, the family, all knew when the war came back to haunt his dreams because after these dreams he retreated to his shed. When Mr Meldrum was very ill a few years ago, and again just after he died, I took snaps of my own of the inside of his garden shed. I was only around 12 at the time but there was something about its informality that I found exciting and creative and I wonder if it was the improvised nature of the hut that fascinated me, the make-do-ness of it, its unfancy naturalness and a place where he could close the door and disappear for hours at a time, an escape without having to travel. There were photographs there, of his unit, his men, both together as one entity and separately as individuals. But to me, these pictures somehow felt like a portrait of him, portraits of the inside of his head and all the images and stuff he had collected there. For me, these photographs helped me discover his character in a way that all the posed photographs failed to do, and it was all to do with time and mortality and memory, all the moments which the photographer can catch and, in a click, are captured forever. Now, I am older, and every time I think of Mr Meldrum, I see an image of his shed with its door closed and him sitting inside, alone, remembering.

Tony wondered if he, too, had known his father as nothing more than a black-and-white photograph. On the day of his funeral, Tony saw the guests, their uniforms but the regimental song gave a richness and colour he had never considered, let alone seen. Tony now saw his father in all his technicolour glory, in all his real self.

And he smiled at Lucy.

But there were always more hands. Hands that shook, hands with folds and furrows, hands with creases carved and puckered and hands that trembled towards him like the hands of death.

"So pleased you're here."

"Thank you so much for coming."

"It was so nice to meet you."

"Dad would've appreciated it; I can tell you."

And he meant what he said.

And he smiled at Lucy.
She wasn't there.
"Thank you."
"Thank you."
"Goodbye."
"Goodbye."
But Tony was to learn that grief was unpredictable.
Now, now you can let it go. Now, cry your heart out.
He was unable to shed a tear.

Lucy was hugging Ricky, and he was crying on her shoulder.

11

2000

Occasionally

Now and then, he opened his eyes from the torments of dreams only to find them again in the half-darkness of his bedroom and, in this half-darkness, he half-wondered whether it was the dreams that tormented him or his inability to make decisions and act on them. Sometimes, he managed to convince himself that it was the indecision and that, if he was to be free from it, to remain in the game, to pass "Go" collect his salary and his rent, to stand a chance of winning, he had to take matters into his own hands and act. Then, he reminded himself that he had no dice to shake, no pieces to move, and he was the imprisoned participant with no dues to collect. Emasculated, he had failed in marriage and fallen from grace and, in the witching hour and with nothing to hold on to, he was vulnerable and often felt like pounding the pillow.

There were times when he tried to fall asleep again, but the bad dreams were waiting and ready to pounce on him and so he lay on his back, stared in the direction of the ceiling, and allowed his thoughts to drift to this and to that and the other and, more often, to the significance of being an adult orphan. With both his parents now dead, he and Ricky were next on the list. Each day was a gift and could not be taken for granted. And if life could be taken away at any moment, both he and Ricky were obliged to make the most of their lives and not to squander something so precious, something that could be gone in an instant. Obstacles to happiness should be identified and clinically removed so that life would be clean and perfect. Of course, in moments of desperation, it had occurred to Tony that he could remove Ricky and he could divorce Lucy but the very thought of all the nastiness and the subterfuge this might entail brought him out in a cold sweat. He did not need to be reminded that nastiness and subterfuge were a long way from the ideals of the perfect life led by his father and the perfect life he wanted for himself.

So, he told himself to keep a perspective. He reminded himself that he had no evidence of treachery, infidelity, or any other form of wrongdoing other than lying, or worse still, the suspicion of lying. But what was wrong with suspicion? There was good suspicion and bad suspicion and good or healthy suspicion needed that fine touch, a reminder that many behaviours should be taken with a pinch of salt.

Nonetheless, it was something more than suspicion that led him to disbelieve every word she told him about her parents. She had lied once so she could be lying again but he knew that if he kept thinking these thoughts, they might take on a reality of their own. So, he told himself to regain a balance, but regaining a balance would require a holiday but not a stay-on-the-beach-and-roast kind of holiday but a holiday that obliged him to be always on the move. Even if he did not travel far, movement and the sights and sounds of different people and places made him feel awake, alive, and open to the world. And such a holiday might include trains. Tony loved looking through train windows and catching glimpses of crimson leaves whizzing past, of white-capped mountains and of medieval towns and villages. Being in motion helped him evaluate, accept, or discard and to do it at speed. Being in motion helped him put his life and experiences into perspective, but he needed to be careful. Being in motion might also mean avoiding responsibility. Being in motion might mean running away.

Tony needed a pee. He had been putting it off since he woke up. He knew it was the dark night that was competing with the pressure of his bladder, this dark and starless night with the sense of Autumn creeping across the terrace, pulling a few leaves from the trees and bushes, building moss, fading the flowers and berries, and giving the breeze a cold edge.

One foot hit the floor.

When his father had died the previous year, Tony found himself with no role model to please, nobody to go to when times were bad, nobody to go to for advice, nobody to lend him an ear. With his role model gone, Tony was in a very bad place for several months, and he had succumbed to pressure from brother Ricky and wife Lucy to take a step back from his professional duties and to continue a process that had already started several years earlier. Lucy was allowed more responsibility in the running of the company. Tony had always followed his father's advice concerning credit where credit was due and so he told her that she was a great learner and a fine administrator and he encouraged her in her vision of where she wanted the school to go. But he did not tell her that she seemed oblivious to the feelings of others, took the credit when it was due elsewhere, controlled everything, trusted nobody, gave orders without a clear purpose, never expected, or asked for feedback, was aloof from the other employees, mostly teachers, but there were also cleaning staff, admin, and a librarian. He never told her that everybody was frightened of her and he never realised that not telling her these things was also a form of lying and that he was as guilty as she was.

The other foot hit the floor.

He sat hunched and still, heard low-pitched sniffling noises, rattly breathing, and high-pitched inhalations of both his children, now aged eleven and thirteen, suffering from Autumn's common ailments. He did not bother looking for the light-switch but made a daring and falling motion in the switch's direction and set off down the hallway, refusing to catch his reflection in the glass of the framed pictures because he had convinced himself that if saw nothing, it would be a sign that he would soon die in his sleep. When he had emptied his bladder, he rinsed his hands, stumbled back to his room, and fell into bed, pulling feet and hands back where they were safe and warm. He did not bother to tap the clock and allow it to threaten him with its florescent green teeth. He knew it was about 3.00 a.m. because that was the time he drifted from a deep sleep and into a lighter REM sleep, and because brains were more active in REM sleep, it meant that dark thoughts might keep him awake. Lucy had told him this and Lucy was upstairs in the spare room because that was the only place where, she said, she could escape from his disturbed sleep and rest in peace.

Occasionally, he was able to convince himself that he had chosen a good woman and that they were just going through a bad patch, but he was clutching at straws, chasing rainbows, and chancing his arm for no reason. Occasionally, he caught a glimpse of an ambitious woman whose ambition was limitless and whose perception of happiness was, therefore, in perpetual motion, unobtainable and forever out of reach. Occasionally, he realised that all she wanted from him was an official husband, marriage to whom gave her social respectability. It even occurred to him, occasionally, that she had really married the school, and it was in the business of running it that she intended to flourish. When he was honest with himself, he regretted giving her the managerial role and he regretted marrying her and he clearly saw that they were like two bubbles in the air and gradually floating apart.

It was at around this time, on a sleepless night after many other sleepless nights and while he lay in bed with the sounds of autumn crackling around him, that Tony made a decision. The decision was made shortly after Lucy's revelations concerning her reconstructed personal history, as she called it, and this reconstruction marked the beginning of a revulsion and an isolation that prompted Tony to get some kind of revenge and construct his own personal life and history. And he would accomplish this by doing the unthinkable and breaking his own code of conduct. He would do this by committing adultery.

And like everything else he did, he tried his best to do it perfectly, and perfectly meant with no strings attached, no jealousy, no emotional blackmail, and the opportunities were endless. Once he had started, the advantages became so obvious, he wondered why he had not done it before. When he paid for sex, he was the boss. The customer was always right and this gave him the opportunity to explore his deepest sexual fantasies. There was also a wide range of options regarding people types. His partners did not judge him or his performance. Tony even believed that his actions would save his marriage. Essentially, it was good value. It was neat and tidy. He walked out of the door and he was free, physically, emotionally, in every way.

Only now and then, and usually during the process of enjoying sex when he felt the movement of her body with his fingertips, did he realise that the act itself might be an attempt to get back at Lucy and live a life reconstructed, a life that mirrored the way he wanted it to be and, in a sense, he was creating memories for himself and these memories would tell him how good his life had been, a life with sex, with a heartbeat and a soul. Only occasionally, did he look at himself in the mirror and tell himself his life was, at best, a fabrication and, at worst, an out-and-out lie.

And what about me, the narrator? How do you, the readers, feel about me discussing Tony's private acts, sex life and his innermost desires? Lives are meant to be private, aren't they? But let me tell you now that I don't care what you think. I have a story to write, a record to put straight and, I had a right to know the truth. Given what happened to Lucy, and given what Tony did, I could not care less what you think. Occasionally, just occasionally, I think Tony had it coming to him.

12

2003

M.A.R.I.O. and J.U.L.I.A.

It is time to come out of the shadows and reveal my identity. Who am I, the God-like and all-knowing storyteller, and what am I hoping to achieve by writing this story? Perhaps you have already guessed. I am Mario, of course, Tony and Lucy's son, and I am writing this story because I have to. Writing might help me understand how it all started. Writing might help me understand why it all ended in the way it did. Writing might help me figure out whether or not I share some responsibility for that ending and, if I do, how much responsibility I might share. Writing might bring some clarity regarding whether or not I could have done something more to prevent the way it all ended. Perhaps, there was nothing that could be done. Once the wheels were in motion and, given the flaws of character in the people involved, there was only going to be one ending. In other words, the story I am writing is a tragedy, a life unto itself, and beyond the control of its actors and its writer.

By the year 2003, I was 15 going on 16, and I was old enough to see that despite my hopes and dreams, my parents' relationship was past its expiry date. I chose this expression only after a great deal of thought. "Problematic" was another word I considered along with "unstable" and "oppressive." I almost opted for "amiss" because of its suggestion that their relationship was not quite in tune with what I considered "normal." However, in the end, I chose the expression, "past its expiry date," because this did not suggest that the relationship in question had gone bad, but that its peak had been reached and that, thereafter, its quality would decline.

At this point, some readers might ask what a 16-year-old knows about normal relationships. So let me be straight and unapologetically answer that question right now. Anybody who underestimates young people does so at their peril. Come to think about it, how many people, of any age, know what to look for when judging if a relationship is good or bad or if a relationship is or is not in tune with normality? Well, let me tell you something. A 15-year-old can feel that his or her parents' relationship is in trouble even if he cannot easily put those feelings into words. A 15-year-old knows how it is to be with parents who no longer trust one another. A 15-year-old knows what absence of affection looks and feels like. A 15-year-old knows what poor communication is. A 15-year-old knows what presentiments are, what a hunch is, what an inkling is. A 15-year-old knows what feelings of anger are and what feelings of confusion are. A 15-year-old knows what feelings of sorrow are and what feelings of helplessness are. A 15-year-old knows when things are not right and, above all, a 15-year-old knows what desperation is and what feelings of guilt are. Seventeen years have passed but I still remember almost all the details of what I witnessed. I finally understood the situation in all its dreadful glory one day in 2003 when I saw them, and they did not see me, in Treviso town centre.

I was enjoying morning coffee when I spotted them. Before I continue, let me add that although I have used the word "enjoying" morning coffee, I would say, in retrospect, that I was not really enjoying the coffee at all. What I was actually enjoying was doing something adult in the adult environment of a downtown bar. Anyway, I was taking morning coffee in Bar Sporting when I saw two people, a man, and a woman, walking down the main street. I did not recognise them as my parents at first, perhaps because the context was unusual and most people who passed by looked vaguely similar and, anyway, until that moment, my attention was focused on me, my immediate world and whether or not I looked as if I was doing something habitual rather that doing something for the first time. And my world was the smell of fresh and baking bread, the tinkling of cups, the hissing of steam from the coffee machine, the clatter of pouring fresh beans, the chattering of *Trevisan* dialect, and coffee "corrected" with *grappa* for the street workers.

Seen through the cafeteria's vast glass frontage, the world in the street was one of intense movement that came to me as a silent film: a woman and her two children on a moped, an elegant couple with a poodle and a group of men strutting past the bar as if down a fashion runway. And then, imagine my surprise at seeing my very own adoring parents wandering over the cobbled stones and stopping occasionally to look into shop windows. When they were not directing their eyes at the shop fronts, they were treading carefully on the cobbled and ankle-twisting streets, directing their gazes and appreciation at the morning sun striking the yellow-ochre of the walls. There was no eye contact between them. They could have been strangers to each other and each taking a stroll through town alone.

The *barista* opened the bar door, shoved a stopper

under it to prevent it closing, and hot air and assorted sounds rushed in: the toll and clang of church bells, the buzz of scooters and the distant cry of stall-holders from the nearby market. My parents stopped outside the bar and with their backs to the open door. Dad had his hands in his pockets and was looking at his feet while Mum, who wore a shady hat, started to speak and, between cars accelerating and stallholders hollering, their words clipped into the bar.

"I shall be in Verona all next week," Mum said.

"Uh-huh, and why must you be there all week?"

"Exciting possibilities," she said. "Your brother has been putting out feelers. He needs my opinion and expertise."

"Putting out feelers? There are such things as phones you know."

"There is nothing like face-to-face communication," Mum said.

"What will we tell the children this time?"

"Isn't that a bit dramatic?"

"They will want to know where you are," Dad said.

"You can tell them I'm needed in Verona. I'll be back at the weekend."

"Don't you think they might be worried?"

"Why should they be worried?" Mum said.

"It's not the first time you've stayed away the whole week. Why don't you tell them yourself?"

"For heaven's sake, Tony. If I've told you once…"

And their ghastly exchange, made even ghastlier by the complete lack of eye contact, droned on only to be drowned out by the funereal tolling of the church bells and the high-pitched buzzing of the accelerating scooters. For a while, I could have been watching a form of silent art, in which the actors communicated with movements, gestures and facial expressions.

The increasing use of such movements from my mum

and dad revealed emotional distance and a need to protect personal space, and this need was signalled by crossed arms or legs, for example, or by hands in pockets or increased distance between the two of them. This personal disconnection was emphasised by an absence of touch and an absence of mirroring and both of these suggested that although Mum and Dad were together, the togetherness was fake, a product of habit but slowly snuffing out and entering a period of darkness before burial.

At last, the sound of bells and scooters faded and I heard Dad's voice.

"If it helps us, then you should go. We can't let the business down."

He made a movement of the lips that suggested a smile but the eyes were disconnected and exhibited something else, something like disgruntlement or abhorrence.

"My thoughts entirely," Mum said while rubbing her hands and yawning.

I could not understand. At nearly 16 years of age, I was still of the opinion that Treviso was the best city in the world. Why would anybody voluntarily go to the tourist towns of nearby Venice or the slightly-more-distant Vicenza or Verona when there were the attractions of an unspoiled traditional city like Treviso with its fresco-painted medieval buildings, its waterways and with the mountains within easy reach? Nearby *Piazza dei Signori* was the most beautiful square in Italy, the city's heartbeat, and it was surrounded by the *Palazzo* with its card players and the legendary pizzerias and restaurants at its edges. Nothing could be better than Treviso.

The most disturbing memory of that morning, so many years ago in the bar, was not the mime but my mother's words although the word "words" is actually incorrect. She said:

"So, what will we tell M-A-R-I-O? What will we say to J-U-L-I-A? If they ask, what will we tell them?"

This embittering and destructive utterance was spelled out to the accompaniment of more tolling bells, more accelerating cars, and scooters and all to the background hissing of the coffee machine. To me, the spelling out of the names of her children suggested emotional distance or a disconnect of some kind. At the time, hearing my name spoken as a series of letters was shattering: a withdrawal of love, a rejection of me, and I still feel this rejection today.

"Tell them what we always tell them," Dad said. "It's an important business trip."

In retrospect, given what we now know, I have to say that I should not have been surprised by this disconnect between my mother and her children. It seems she was able to withdraw into herself almost at will. Take the photographs of Mum and Dad in their album, for example. Do these photos show a happy couple? No, not exactly. To be honest, I would say that there was no "couple" at all. But there was Lucy, always first, always Lucy, Lucy at home, Lucy in the mountains, Lucy on the beach, Lucy in London, Lucy in Paris, Lucy in charge, Lucy with her hands on top of other hands, Lucy with a hand on Tony's lower back, Lucy with an arm around his waist. Yes, it was Lucy, Lucy the controlling force that told and tells the world who is who and what is what, and who is in charge and who is not, who the dominant force is and who is the star.

"Is that really what we always tell them?" Mum said.

When I see a photograph of my mother as a young woman, I barely recognise her. There is nothing about the photographs that suggests what will happen when she is older and what saddens me most of all is that although I have a number of family albums and boxes stuffed with pictures, there are no family pictures of her own. It is almost as if she came down to earth one day as a fully-formed adult and announced her arrival in her usual confident way but without a past, without a history. She just appeared. She said hello. She went away. And yet, the few photographs have taken on a cruel disconnect. She seems so vital, so alive and caught in a moment and yet, she is no longer here.

"Yes, and it seems to work, don't you think?" Dad said.

Memories of my mother's personal photo collection, and not to be confused with her rare guest appearances in the photographs of others, tell me that the collection was relatively small and, for the most part, they showed Lucy at her desk, Lucy in the office and other formal settings suggesting what was important to her. My feeling now is that she orchestrated her photographic legacy so that it showed any viewer, past or present, that she was not only a professional holding a position of status, but also a woman to be reckoned with.

"Fine," Mum said. "An important business trip it is."

My own interpretation goes a little further. The photographic evidence that we do have reveals Lucy as an open book, a person with no guidance from without and who knew no boundaries from within. Such a person was dangerous, capable of change in any direction and at any time, and a person ready to break ranks, to cross swords, even to break the law if she could get away with it. When Lucy spoke, she expected the world to listen. When Lucy acted, there might be hell to pay. Having said that, I am unable to say with any degree of certainty whether my interpretation has been influenced by subsequent events rather than by the pictures themselves. The same doubts arise when considering the photos that show Mum and Dad together. These, perhaps, tell their own story.

"Then," Mum said, "you know what to say to the children, don't you?"

Lucy's eyes reveal that she did not give a jot about my father. His adoring eyes were met with indifference,

Tony's strengths revealed as weaknesses, caring met with impatience, and he, always ready to forgive, and she, wishing he wouldn't. Their photos say: one day I will rid myself of this lackey. When I am tired of him, I'll walk away. But what do I know? I may be reading things into these images that were simply never there.

My point is that while writing the story, I have only memories, both my memories and those of others, and photos to help me, and both memory and photograph are flawed. Don't get me wrong, sixteen was old enough to know that all relationships have their bad patches. Nonetheless, now that I am older, 33 to be exact, readers might not trust me to write an unbiased story. For that matter, can I trust myself to write an unbiased story? How would I know if my view was objective, partly objective or not at all objective? And what are my credentials? Why am I in a position to know things that others, perhaps, do not? Let's face it, memories of myself at 16 and old photos of the protagonists are hardly reliable, and we all know that memory can play tricks on the "rememberer" by editing events in order to fit into his/her current view of the world. Photos, those records of a particular moment in time, the party on the terrace, for example or the trip to the mountains, often suffer from the over-imaginative stories that go with them.

Perhaps, the only real truth is not the memory or the photograph but the narrative truth, the stories we tell each other and ourselves, the stories we continually reinterpret, re-categorise, and refine, the story I am writing for you. But the narrative truth is now becoming problematic. This story could be a product of my own design, an imaginary product, made up of chosen experiences mixed with scenes from favourite novels or films and daydreams and, hey presto, I have created a coherent narrative about who the main characters are, where they come from and where they are going. And it does not stop there. This narrative tells the reader whom she or he should love, whom to hate and what to do with these emotions. To be honest, when all is said and done, I can look back on the past but I can no longer say, for certain, what is fact and what is fiction.

It seems that Dad had nothing more to say about M-A-R-I-O and J-U-L-I-A. Perhaps he could find no words while Mum wandered away muttering something about her hair-do. I recall watching her scanning the large houses that lined the streets outside the café, the streets with their arched openings, interesting chimneys, cobbled pathways, arcaded walkways, wood or stone balconies, and the tiled roofs covered with lichen and I recall wondering whether she had ever really loved Julia and me or whether she was simply able to file us away as and when it suited her. Dad tagged along behind her, looking troubled, and pretending to be interested in window displays while Mum looked for a hairdresser. And the last I saw of them, they were heading for the cheaper side of town, the post-war side with its architectural copies and fake medieval and renaissance frescos and other revealing consequences of wartime destruction.

I was only 16 when this happened, so what do I know? I now have the finished article to deal with, the end of the story and my book to write. I can see the important memories that stand out because they are a part of the story I am writing.

"Yes, but…," I hear you say, and you, whoever you are, might go on to tell me that I am looking for evidence from the past that supports what I think I know in the here and now. And perhaps you are right. Needless to say, I think you are wrong. I have no axe to grind, no scores to settle and no hidden agenda but you will have to take my word for that.

13

September 2005

Arrivederci

"And you've got to look after yourself, Dad," Mario said, "until we get back so that we can take care of you."

I remember my words exactly because I meant them from the bottom of my heart. I was already feeling some responsible for my father's state of mind and physical well-being. I so desperately wanted my parents to love each other and to be together forever and ever but for some reason they spent more and more time apart. Why was Mum in Verona? Why was she not there on that day of all days when the lives of her children would change forever? What was so important in her life that it kept her away? She belonged here in Treviso with us and not in Verona with him. Was uncle Ricky the reason for Mum not being here?

Please God, do not let it be uncle Ricky. Please keep my family together.

Yes, I remember my thoughts and prayers exactly but, more than this, I can recall exactly how I felt. I felt distraught enough to call on the almighty for his help. I felt worried. I felt anxious and I felt helpless, but I did not show any of this. Nonetheless, I want to record it now for posterity and, most importantly, for me.

"And don't work so hard," Mario added.

Tony thought he had had time to prepare for this day. He believed himself to be ready but here it was in front of him and he was taken aback, knocked sideways, astounded, and surprised. Why now? Why not tomorrow, next week or next year? He needed the time to prepare himself, to prepare for a time when you surrounded yourself with people who knew what you were going through, a time when you accepted that the days of parent-teacher meetings, of football practice, and piano lessons were over. This time was a time to embrace new chapters for you, new chapters for them, new hobbies, and a new trust, new skills, and abilities.

"So, when are you coming to see us, Dad?" Mario said.

"And when you do come, you can visit your *alma mater*," said Julia.

"And keep us informed about *Juve*," Mario said.

As if they couldn't get the information in England.

"Look after Mum," Julia said.

Does she know our marriage is falling apart?

Chatter softened the moment, words eased the awkwardness of this station-platform goodbye, eye contact deterred the teardrops, and everybody was wondering why they had wasted so much time, so much potential to discuss, to understand, to sympathise, so much time to love, so much time to cherish, to get to know, so much time to make memories to ease the moment of parting. And that moment was now, carefully put out of eyeshot, of earshot, of mouth-shot for years but the moment had arrived out of the blue and it was hanging in their faces and hanging in their hearts.

"We'll both be fine," Tony said.

But what will all this mean for me?

Re-ordering his life and settling into newness was what it meant for Tony. A house with the absence of noise and the noise of absence would be the rule and he and she would adapt to it, if they were lucky, and grow accustomed to that stillness filling out their house and terrace like hot air.

"And you and Mum must look after each other while we are away," Julia said with a sidelong look at her brother.

The platform clock reminded him, second by second, that there was so little time left to discuss issues of great moment, so little time for the hand on arm or elbow, on the shoulder or back and no time for it to linger, forgotten in love, and so little time left while waiting at the station for the train to take his children to London but, Tony reminded himself, there was also pride because Mario was starting at London University and Julia was going to sixth-form college in nearby Hampton Court.

"We've been doing that for 20 years," Tony said. "We won't stop now."

There was so much more to say but Tony could not put more thoughts into words because his voice would be husky with emotion and it was the same voice that had soothed and calmed over the years at those moments of fever and coughing, the homework, the teachers' meetings, the homework not done, and everything was now about to change and they would be lost to him in a landscape of strange places and strangers with their strange ideas, their strange food and their strange habits and endless possibilities, some of them taken, some of them ignored but each decision giving them confidence to make their own way and show them the secrets of their own hearts.

"No more arguing," said Mario.

"Peace and love," said Julia.

And there was more small talk about things that had been said so many times, things concerning the terrace plants, the garden and between topics they were breathing in the silence, thinking of something to say, anything to fill the silence of things never said and Tony experiencing the tension between feeling like a child but being an adult, his children hating to leave but looking forward to being somewhere else.

"London is quite safe, Dad," Julia said. "And anyway, I'll be in the suburbs."

"Leave the big city to adults like me," said Mario.

And everybody laughed.

And Tony was experiencing the contradiction of hating to see them go but hating the moments of parting, and hoping the train would appear soon, and it brought to mind contradictory feelings from years before when he felt pride on introducing Lucy to his family and a little shame at her behaviour towards his parents. Anyway, where was she now? What could be more important than this moment, the once-in-a-lifetime-leaving-of-home, the starting pistol for the rest of their children's lives?

"Take a photo, Dad," said Mario.

"No, let's ask somebody to take one of the three of us," Julia said.

And there was talk and laughter as they sidled up to one another for that photo that might capture this moment. But Tony guessed that nothing, and certainly not words, could capture the complex feelings provoked by this parting. Anyway, thoughts and feelings changed with the passing of time and memory was fickle and Tony knew this journey was being taken by children, his children, but not really *his* children, and they would not be the same youngsters when they came back. The route to London, to further education and the people they would meet, would influence them and overshadow the parents and that meant that those about to board the train, those in the photo would never be seen again.

Tony looked up and along the railway track. He had to change the subject before he burst into tears.

"I envy you this trip," he said. "So much better than flying."

"It's certainly longer," Julia said.

"Yes, but that is the point," Tony said. "Longer, but without being confined to a seat on a bus or a plane."

"You've lost me, Dad."

"Well, on a train, all passengers are disconnected from the familiar. They are an accidental collection of others and, together, they can forge shared experiences, form fleeting friendships they may never forget."

"Sounds like life, Dad," said Julia.

The sun had dropped through a layer of cloud, and its light created a shadow show of the waiting travellers on the wall behind the rails.

"Look at the shadows," he said. "Many of them will be on your train. And you'll forge a shared experience with them so that the shadows become real people and…"

"Dad, Dad…"

It was Julia and she was tugging at the sleeve of his jacket. He looked down expecting to see the top of her head beside his knee.

"Dad, ever the idealist. But things have changed since your day. I suppose when you travelled by train, clattering through the darkness there was always the possibility of adventure or even danger and it could happen at any time, always out of sight and round the next unseen-but-felt curve."

Tony smiled at her words because they were his words and they were words he had used when describing his own adventures to his daughter several times. And she might have added that even if nothing happened, the possibility that something might happen was always there waiting in the next tunnel or at the next station, something life-changing like love or murder, perhaps, or both, at the same time.

Mario opened his mouth to speak but was interrupted by the announcements. For Tony, the only important information was where the arriving train was going and whether they were on the right platform.

"Front of train," Mario said, picking up his cases and rushing along the platform.

And for Tony, it was not adolescents he was watching, rushing along the platform edge, it was his life's purpose disappearing in front of his eyes, his 18-year-old son and 16-year-old daughter; it was two broody teenagers walking away; it was two seven-year-olds walking away; it was two toddlers walking away and it was two cuddly babies disappearing in front of his eyes; yes, it was to all of these versions of his children that he was saying goodbye and, although they did not know it, they were almost saying goodbye to their childhoods. Almost.

Was it going to be a clean break? Were they going to be dependent one moment and independent the next? And what right did any parent have to believe that the transition to "adulthood" was a collection of markers: leaving home, going to university, getting a job, getting married, and having kids?

"Well, now is the time," Tony said.

"Promise to come and see us, Dad," she said.

"Just try and stop me," he said as he turned to pick up their luggage, their lives, his history, the focus of his life, and place it on the train.

Why had nobody prepared him for this moment?

His life was being ripped apart, daylight had been removed and there was only the thought of Lucy and his heart began to tremble.

"Good bye, you two, and take care."

"We love you, Dad."

He felt tears welling. He could not speak.

"Look after Mum."

He smiled and nodded at their backs.

Please turn around, please turn just one more time. Please…

The guard looked at his watch. Whistles were blown, doors slammed, flags were waved and the train hissed. The heart of his life had disappeared. The train moved forward, accelerated, pulled away. Tony wanted the train to stop, but it wouldn't. He had something to say to his children, but he could not recall what that something was. He wanted to swivel round and leave, but he couldn't. He wanted time itself to stop, but it didn't. They had almost gone, but they hadn't. He would see them for dinner this evening, but he wouldn't.

He watched the last carriage disappearing into a curve, and it accelerated away. He watched it until it was a blip on the horizon and he waved one last time and Tony felt himself disappear into a crowd he had not noticed until now. He had had both of them, then most of them and now neither of them.

They had gone.

Gone.

He had never felt so lonely, and his bottom lip quivered.

Tony remained still. He would not exchange places with anybody. Nobody else was the father of those children. Nobody who had ever lived was the father of those children.

The sun set.

The crowd dispersed.

The quiver spread to his top lip, his nose, his forehead, and his face melted.

And he started to cry.

14

September 2005

Yesterday and today

Yesterday was that day, the day he had always been afraid of, the day he watched his children disappearing down the train tracks to England. The day before they left, they had been his life's rhythm. The day before they left, they had been his life's purpose. The day before they left, his life's purpose had been to experience them, their moods, and desires, and feed their developing personalities. Now was their moment, their chance to make mistakes, to learn what independence was.

Yesterday, he learned the meaning of real love, that real love meant giving them space. Real love meant letting go. Yesterday, he learned that real love was not dependent on anything. Yesterday, he discovered that he had choices concerning how to react. Yesterday, he learned he had the power to decide. Was this an exciting moment or a sad moment? Should he have been grief-stricken or proud? Was it the end or the beginning of something? Today, he decided that the leaving of his children was an exciting moment. Today, he was proud. Today was the beginning of something. Today marked a new start in his relationship with his children.

Yesterday, he learned that he was able to acknowledge the sadness and accept it. He learned that leaving home was not only a beginning for the children, it was also a new beginning for parents, a time of renewed growth, a time that belonged to them so that they could develop aspects of themselves that might have been put to one side. Today, he hoped that he and Lucy would find the time to work on their relationship. Today, he knew that the time had come to think about what made them happy. Today, he had no idea how they might achieve that. Today, he was unable to recall when he and Lucy had last talked about "them."

Yesterday, he was proud. Yesterday, he was proud of his children. He was proud to have been at the station to see them on their way to a new stage in their lives. Yesterday, he saw that this was the opportunity he and Lucy needed to reinvent themselves and start afresh. Yesterday, he saw that leaving home meant liberty for his children, but it also meant liberty for him and liberty for Lucy.

Yesterday afternoon, he picked up the phone and rang the Verona school, but the secretary told him Lucy was unavailable. She would ask Lucy to ring him back.

Yesterday afternoon, she did not ring back.
Yesterday evening, she did not ring back.
This morning, she did not ring back.
This afternoon, she did not ring back.
The fact is, she never rang back at all.

15

2006

Blue

There was even a moment when Tony thought he might throw up. His heart was pounding, and beads of sweat were breaking out on his hairline and starting a slow roll down his forehead. He considered going outside, to get some air, to calm himself and his brother, but the mere thought of a still-in-fighting-mode Ricky turning his anger on him did not help at all. Would Ricky listen? Would he react to words of reason? Tony closed his eyes, took a couple of deep breaths. He had never seen his brother lose control of himself, never seen him behave so viciously. Even the "terrible twos," with their desire for independence and the tantrums at not getting it, had passed Ricky by. But Ricky was now in his forties, and a demon had slipped inside his skin and goaded him into committing a savage and violent act.

Ricky was now pacing up and down the car park beside the restaurant-bar. His facial and body movements were abrupt, exaggerated and tense, and Tony had the odd sensation that this was a circus act, a story without words and narrated by a madman. And the sensation persisted despite the fact that there was no audience except him. All the other actors in this drama, with the exception of the barman, had vanished. Tony watched his brother turn his face skywards and place his arms akimbo. Ricky closed his eyes and inhaled before blowing out through his lips. Leaning forward, he put his hands on his knees and closed his eyes for a while before raising himself to his full height and looking over the tree-covered hills in the valley, their variety of shades of green apparently calming him, perhaps with associations of refreshment and peace. Occasionally, he rubbed the knuckled fist of one hand and then, as if washing his hands, rubbed the knuckled fist of the other hand before opening both, letting the fingers hang loose and free while he stood as still as a statue.

Wiping beads of sweat from his forehead, Tony made the decision to stay inside and allow his brother to come to him when he was ready. The violence had emptied this establishment of guests, and the only other person to look at was the proprietor. The man had already brought a bucket to the splashes and spots of blood on the floorboards and wiped them off with a large blue-and-white chequered cloth before turning his attention to the upturned chairs and table, assessing the damage, and muttering about things he had never before seen and that he thought the war was over. Well, his thoughts were correct. The war was over. But Tony already knew that for one individual, and there were many other individuals who felt the same way, the war was still very much alive, and the events of 7 April 1944 lived on in Treviso's collective memory, in the same way that the Battle of Britain lived on, the bombing of Coventry lived on, the battle of Trafalgar lived on.

Tony was not overly surprised by this. It was true that his father had said little about his role in the war, merely commenting that too many good people died, that he and others like him got on with the job at hand, that they were not heroes, that they did what was expected of them in a time of crisis. Nonetheless, with the benefit of hindsight, Tony saw that his father's feelings, attitudes, and actions had been shaped, in part, by the war. Captain Meldrum did not often express these attitudes, but he always tensed on hearing tourists speaking German. Nonetheless, whatever his thoughts concerning his one-time enemies, Tony's father had done his bit to frustrate the development of another conflict by establishing the language school in Treviso. His aim was simply to help spread the international language of English and, consequently, the international communication and collaboration that was needed to prevent another world war. Every time he walked through the doors of the school, Tony was reminded of his father and that his school was his response to all that hate, all those deaths, all that destruction and all that violence.

Tony still felt his heart thumping, and he shook his head at the memory of this most recent act of violence: that growl of defiance, the smacking of Ricky's fist on the big man's face, the streaming blood, the big man lunging forward, Ricky's upper cut smacking into the big man's chin and sending him hard against the wall, smashing his head on the doorframe and landing on the floor like a sack of potatoes.

Tony looked through the window and eyed his brother. Ricky's face still shocked him. Taut and drained of blood, its skin showed he was still in fight mode and, if this meant that he was not ready to calm down just yet, so Tony was still coming to terms with what Ricky had done. It seemed totally out of character. If Tony had not rushed to hold him back there was no telling what might have happened. Ever since he could remember, Ricky had been the caring one, the kind one, the one who might become a social worker. He had never associated his brother with violence, had never seen his brother consumed with such rage, never imagined it was there under his skin and waiting for the right stimulus to emerge and reveal itself. Nor had he ever imagined that it would happen here and on what had become an annual pilgrimage to Cima Palon in order to celebrate the lives of their parents. It was supposed to be a reflective time. It was supposed to be a gentle time. It was supposed to be an appreciative time and a ritualistic time. In fact, the stop-for a-quicky at the Cartina brewery had become a ritual in itself.

The brewery bar also marked and celebrated entry into the mountain land proper as opposed to the pre-Alps around Monte Grappa and the flatter lands around Treviso. Tony and Ricky often expressed their liking for the plain that stretched to Venice and the sea. Nonetheless, one or the other of them might, just occasionally, mention that winter was uneasy or wishy-washy on the plain. Both might comment that the stars stretching above them on mountain tops were more comforting than the uniformity of the stars seen from the plain and that the problem with flatness was that it had no visible end and was always disappearing or threatening to disappear in a haze. But the brothers really came alive when describing their trips through the valleys and into the Dolomites. Mountains not only energised them, mountains put them in contact with history, with movements of peoples and their languages spreading up the valleys. Mountains put them in contact with places on the hilltops where life stagnated and the German language remained dominant. Mountains were obstacles that inspired them both to wonder what may be on the other side. Mountains were a challenge. Mountains were majestic. Mountains were powerful. Mountains dared them to do things in ways that the plain never did.

They had been driving for a couple of hours when they pulled up outside the bar-restaurant at the Cartina brewery. They parked under the large window through which, along with their own reflections and those of the trees, they were not surprised to see a group of men standing at the bar. The car's arrival had provoked a staring interest from this group and while Tony locked the car, he was not disturbed by bursts of laughter fading to chuckles and chuckles fading to sniggers, but when he pushed at the entrance door, it opened to a smouldering silence and expressionless eyes.

Tony ignored the big man standing head and shoulders above the others and when he and Ricky resumed a quiet conversation in Italian, Tony told himself that there was nothing unusual in men drinking in the morning, nothing noteworthy in their low voices or the absence of laughter. If there was anything a touch unusual at all, it was that they had switched to German soon after he and his brother came in. There was nothing excluding about their choice of language, nothing threatening about them stretched out along the bar, a mere coincidence that there was no space for other customers. The men seemed to present no threat. Fortunately, the proprietor rounded the bar and stood at their table to take their order. If there was anything threatening at all, it was when Tony opened his mouth and ordered a half-litre of red wine.

"Un mezzo litro di vino rosso, per favore," he said.

The room fell silent and it was not a deep-rest silence or a time-to-charge-your-batteries silence or a just-live-in-the-present-silence. This silence was accompanied by hands on hips and narrowed eyes staring at Tony and his brother while the barman brought the red wine and placed it on their table.

The big man raised his glass as a signal that he wanted to make a toast.

"Prost," he said with the slightest of smiles and raising his glass higher. Ricky picked up his own glass.

"Salute," he said.

The smile dropped from the big man' face.

Prost," he said again and this time it sounded like an order, an order or something his raised eyebrows suggested the two newcomers should return.

"Prost," Tony said.

But Ricky was having none of it.

"Salute," he said.

The man's eyes narrowed further but he made no attempt to correct him.

"Have you travelled far?" the man asked in Italian.

"Treviso."

"Treviso? Bella, Treviso," he said turning to his friends. "Bella Treviso, eh?" And he smiled, and his friends smiled at some insider-knowledge or at some insider joke designed to exclude.

"Where you go today?" the big man asked in English.

Tony felt like telling him to go to hell. He did not like the big man's leering smile, did not like his attitude but his sheer size suggested caution, discretion.

"To that cross," said Ricky in Italian and with a nod towards the window behind the bar, "on one of those blue mountains there. Cima Palon, to be precise."

The window actually framed a range of blue-tinged mountains. Tony breathed deeply and tried to calm himself by reflecting that there was always blue on horizons and most things far away. Tony and Ricky called it "the blue of distance," of that place seen from this place, of there from here. It was never blue when you arrived on that place. Blue was the colour of a place you could never reach. Blue was the colour of loss and solitude, and of people who could no longer be met because they were no longer there. Blue was for people like his mother and father.

"Cima Palon?" the big man echoed. "*Scheiss Berg*, to be precise."

Ricky tensed. Tony tensed. Not only was Cima Palon the place on which they had scattered their mother's ashes, it was also the place they had associated with their father ever since finding those photos in the garden shed. There were hundreds of personal photos hidden away in the shed, but there were a few that bore witness to the reality of something different, something more outgoing than a place with a closed door and a cobwebbed interior, and this something bore witness to aspects of Captain Meldrum's personality both he and Ricky had been unaware of. These photographs were confirmation that the captain reached the summit of *Cima Palon* towards the end of his period of recovery from the wound received on Monte Cassino. It was a personal achievement of which he was proud. Tony's favourite photo showed a dishevelled Captain Meldrum with hands on hips, one foot in front of the other and an expression of triumph on his face. He was dominant, tough, tired but content and leading his team down a ridge in the early evening. The caption gave no date but written under the photo were the words "*il ritorno.*" A quiet man given the chance to shine in wartime, Captain Meldrum was in his element.

"Why '*scheiss*'?" Ricky said.

"Why Cima Palon?" said the big man.

He sniffed and glared at both Ricky and his brother but without moving his head. A sneer appeared and pulled at the corner of his mouth.

"Why not Cima Palon?" Ricky said.

"*Scheiss Berg*. Shit mountain."

"Try and ignore him," Tony said to Ricky.

The big man said:

"Inglese?"

"Si," Tony said.

"My father and my father's father born in Treviso," the man said.

"And my father was here in the war," Tony said.

"Tedesco?" the big man said,

"No, inglese," Tony replied.

"You are English," the big man said in a surprised tone.

"Si," Tony said.

The big man put his glass down on the counter, spat on the floor, turned to his friends, and muttered something so low that Tony only picked out the words "*Von den Englandern*" and "*Zerstort*."

Tony wondered what, exactly, the big man was referring to. What had been destroyed by the English? The big man certainly had a lot to choose from. In World War 2, the allies had fought a long and bloody battle in Italy. The enemy had been resolute and skilful and the campaign proved to be one of the war's most exhaustive campaigns.

From the corner of his eye, Tony watched Ricky tense. Middle-age vanity suited him. He still displayed the energy of the younger Ricky, and he was proud of his body hair, his physique neat, tidy, and strong and trained in the local gym. But now he was looking towards the floor, rubbing his forehead, and frowning. Tony decided to change the subject.

"You know Cima Palon?" Tony asked. "It was a special place for our father."

"Your father a partisan?"

"No," Tony said. "He was a British army captain."

"Capitano?"

"Si, un capitano inglese."

"Ah, un capitano inglese. An English prick."

"*Mi scusi?*"

"Treviso my city. English bomb my city. English kill

many my family."

"It was an accident," said Ricky under his breath.

"Accident?" the big man said, tilting his head towards his companions. *"L'avete sentito*? Did you hear that? He said it was an accident. *Es war ein Unfall*."

There was a split-second pause between the big man's bellowing laugh and the group taking his cue and laughing with him. Normally, laughter was contagious, a communal activity that bonded, defused conflict and eased stress. But this group laugh was exclusive, a moment of glory expressing their worthiness, a moment expressing something ominous.

Tony stared at the big man, understanding coming in waves of fear. It was difficult to avoid the damage that had been done in Treviso during the war, and now the big man wanted to make something of it. At least one half of Treviso consisted of 1950s blocks and houses and a plaque was due to be unveiled in 2014, 70 years after the event itself. What happened was that this medium-sized town in the Veneto, and in particular, its railway hub, was heavily hit by Allied air attacks during the Second World War. The most intense raid was the operation on 7 April 1944, in which over 2,000 people died and in which whole neighbourhoods were razed to the ground. Since the number of inhabitants was around 60,000, the impact on local society was devastating. A three-storey skeleton of a building without roof or windows, served as a constant reminder of the bombing. Known as "The House of Memory," it hosted annual celebrations in memory of the victims. Just a few years earlier, Fascists had drawn a swastika over the mural that welcomed visitors with the caption: "*Viva i partigiani*."

The big man held up his hand and the laughter lost its momentum and stopped altogether.

"Inglese big shit, no?" he said.

Ricky raised his head, stared into the big man's face,

and muttered under his breath.

The big man let his eyes fall on the two of them while his friends parked their drinks and lined up beside him.

"*Assassini*," the big man said.

"So, that is where we are going," Tony said.

He was paying more attention to his shaking hands than to the big man and wondering how they could leave the bar with dignity. It briefly crossed his mind how easy it was to forget that England had never been occupied. England had never been forced to surrender to German domination. The big man jabbed his finger at Ricky and his brother.

"Your father one big shit," he said. "You stupid people. Father one big fuck. One big asshole."

He turned to his friends but Ricky had jumped to his feet and was striding across the bar towards him. The big man saw the first punch coming and moved his head back and away but he didn't see the follow up that dazed him or the upper cut and the left hook that sent him to reeling backwards and hitting the wall. Ricky moved forwards driving one punch after another into the big man's face. The big man was almost out on his feet but Ricky was fighting like a man possessed. He stepped backwards, swung at the man's face, and hit him square on the jaw. The punch knocked him out cold. The man slid to the floor but Ricky was not finished. He swung his right leg backwards, preparing to smash his foot into the upturned face. But Tony had him by the waist, was pulling him backwards while the big man's friends tried to haul their man to his feet. Ricky froze. His fists were bloodied, his shirt torn and he was pulling air into his lungs. Then, he turned, and walked out into the car park.

16

September 2006

Normal

Tony hesitated, and this hesitation might have drifted into an embarrassing silence had it not been for the normal sounds of the town drifting upward and filling the room and his ears with normal shouts and normal laughter, the sound of normal car engines and normal scooters and all the other normal sounds of Italian life on a normal Monday afternoon, and he realised that normality was good at the moment because normality worked for now and normality was the perfect solution until he decided to act, bring his world back from the brink and to give it some sort of order.

"Let's just go back to normal for the moment," Tony said.

"Good," said Lucy. "Back to normal it is. Let's begin the meeting again, shall we?"

Begin again? It was a great idea. But how could he begin again when, just minutes previously, he suspected he had been a witness to life-changing moments, a turning point in life in general and a hairpin bend in his marriage in particular? And that afternoon had started in the normal way except that he had been hidden, out of sight, on the dormer window seat, pretending to be interested in some incident in the street below. Actually, he had been absorbed in the noises coming from the impressive desk at the heart of Lucy's world: the squeak and scratch of pencil tip on paper, the rattling, the rustling, the deep breaths, the occasional stomach rumble, the unintelligible mutterings.

...like a witch preparing her poisons.

Lucy always made her plans in pencil and took every opportunity to remind others that flexibility was a critical managerial asset so that when plans changed, all she needed was a rubber.

Ah, yes - a rubber, a rubber, our relationship for a rubber or a visit to a lawyer.

Tony let his eyes wander towards the hotel opposite the Verona school. He was, apparently, entranced by its beauty, its gables and turrets and green fish-scale tiles and he might have said so had he been asked, but instead he was picturing Lucy reading the "book of plans," a blue leather-bound oversized notebook she had bought in Venice for a small fortune. In his mind's eye, she was sitting up in bed with the book open in front of her and resting it on a pillow. She was ticking off items accomplished, enjoying a sense of being one step closer to some grandiose life plan with all its side streets, dead ends and marginalised details. And to what extent, Tony mused, did her life plan include her family? Had she come to terms with the failing love at its core? Perhaps, love had no place in her world view. Had she substituted the word "love" with another word, a word like "closeness" or a word like "friendship" or with an expression like "doing well" or an expression like "not doing well"? How was their relationship doing in Lucy's eyes? Were they doing well or were they not doing well or was their relationship collapsing, infirm or dysfunctional? Was it, perhaps, already in the knacker's yard?

Those were some of the questions, but what were the answers, the right expressions to describe what he and Lucy now had? Was it something held together by tradition, by hope, by the absent children? Perhaps neither of them could be bothered to make an appointment to see a lawyer. But for how much longer? Both Julia and Mario now had one foot in England and the other foot in Italy and were in the process of deciding what to do with their lives. Right now, the nest was half empty but in a couple of years they would be gone for good. So, why were he and Lucy still together?

The hairpin-bend moment in their marriage, that life-changing moment had occurred while he was looking at her bowed head and ruminating. Yes, he was living inside her story and she was living inside his and yet, somehow, the plots were different or they were no longer reading from the same script. The life-changing revelation had started with the swivelling of the office doorknob and the rubbing of the door's bottom rail on the carpet. Still hidden away in his position at the dormer window, Tony had said:

"It's your role in the school, isn't it? And you are afraid of losing it."

Lucy looked up from her desk.

"No, it's Ricky," she said.

More rubbing and the clicking of the latch as it found its home in the strike plate and the door thumped shut. Tony noted his brother's revealing, close-fitting suit but it was the eyes that struck him. Their focus was Lucy. In fact, it seemed that there was nothing else and nobody else in the room except Lucy. While he made directly to Lucy, to Lucy's desk, to Lucy's side, and took a seat, not once did his eyes leave Lucy's face.

"*Ciao, amore mio.*"

And the thought drifted through Tony's head that neither he nor Little Red Riding Hood were the only people who noticed that eyes got bigger when faced with somebody they found appealing. Even from his position in the dormer window seat, Tony noted his brother's dilated pupils, the tender stare drinking in her features, memorising her face in a manner which suggested he was afraid he might forget if he looked away too long.

Imagining he felt their synchronised heartbeats, Tony was unable to prevent speculation concerning how Lucy would have reacted to Ricky had her husband not been present. With an embrace and a smile? And what sort of smile, seductive, playful, intimate? But he was present, Lucy knew it, and the words *amore* and *mio* were received with a noisy silence, the eyes of Lucy meeting the eyes of Ricky and her eyes full of warning. Tony saw his brother blink, and he saw Lucy's jaw slacken with the realisation that the words *amore* and *mio* were out of the bag, in the air, ringing in their ears and open to little interpretation.

As always, Lucy was quick to gather her wits.

"Just look at your brother. Doesn't he look great in that suit? The salesman said that men should express their hidden dreams and this is the result."

Tony slid away from the dormer window and got to his feet. He could not say for how long he stared at his brother. He could not say for how long his own jaw was clamped tight. Nor was he ever sure what made him hesitate, while his body swayed forward to grab Ricky by the collar and shake the truth out of him. Was it second thoughts that held him in check? Perhaps, it was the imagined consequences that dragged him back. Perhaps, it was fear of the consequences that enabled him to take a breath, hold it for a few seconds before walking towards Ricky in the manner of a sergeant about to examine one of his new recruits.

"Judging by the suit's shoulder padding," Tony said, "and these logos on the shoes and on the jacket sleeve, these dreams are connected to hunting and conquest. Am I correct?"

The colour had drained from Ricky's face.

"Correct," he said.

"Then, they must've mistaken you for somebody else," Tony said.

"Nonetheless, that's what the man said."

"Did he, now? Just to please your vanity, no doubt."

"That's a bit harsh, bro."

"Harsh? Is it, really? Well, Let me…"

"Nonetheless, you are late," Lucy said. "What time do you call this?"

"Italian time," Ricky said.

"And we're British," Lucy said. "We do things differently."

"We grew up here," Tony said. "We… they… we do things differently here."

"Meaning?"

"Just because attitudes to time are different it doesn't make either one wrong. They're just different."

"He's still late," Lucy said.

Tony was ready to pick up the gauntlet and argue his case but he knew, better than anybody, that the friction between them had nothing to do with time. His life had just taken a crippling blow but he was still standing, still thinking on his feet.

"I'll make it up to you," Ricky said.

"Just get here on time," Lucy said, the sound of her words spiralling upwards with each syllable while her hands fluttered in the air like butterflies. Tony stayed silent and glanced at his brother. He tried to catch his eye but Ricky had got to his feet and ambled away, had his back to him. He now stood at the bookcase behind Lucy's desk.

And here we stand. Two men with doubts about the woman sitting between them.

Tony exhaled and fanned his face with his hand. He felt a second wave of anger rising in his gut. So, here was his wife. She refused to shine a light on her motives. She was vague about her origins. She had no scruples. And Tony suspected she was having a relationship with his brother.

"Let's get down to business," Lucy said.

She settled herself in the high back chair, and opened her notebook.

"So, the agenda…"

Tony moved to the door, half opened it and put his head into the entrance hall.

"Maria Teresa," he said. "Can you fix us some coffee, please."

There was a Mumble from deep inside the school.

"Due espressi e un caffe latte. Si, si, adesso. Grazie."

He swivelled and, smiling into Lucy's eyes, he returned to the executive table, took his seat, leaned forward and clasped his hands on the tabletop.

"So," Lucy said. "Are we here to drink coffee and chat or are we here to work?"

While Ricky strode to the table, Tony was unable to prevent himself from looking at his brother in a new light. And in this light, the tightness of his suit made it easy for Tony's imagination to eliminate clothes altogether and he pictured what these two might do after conspiring over dinner, wondering if or when they had enjoyed their first kiss, their first caress.

"So, what's up for discussion today?" Tony said.

"We do have an agenda," Lucy said.

Tony glanced sideways, at his brother's hairy ankles, the fullness of Ricky's crotch, the hairy forearm wrapped at the wrist by surfing beads.

"Do we?" Tony said. "I didn't know we'd agreed on one."

"It's just provisional," said Ricky taking a chair and isolating his brother by sitting close to Lucy at the side of the table.

"The agenda's been agreed upon by Ricky and I," Lucy said.

Tony shivered. "Ricky and I." The sound of their names together rolled nicely off the tongue. Nice to hear their names together and nice, perhaps, that another man wanted his wife.

"Do involve me next time," Tony said. "That would be nice."

But it was not so nice that another man had actually reached out and touched his wife, and utterly unacceptable that the other man was his brother.

"There's also such a thing as politeness," Tony said. "All it takes is an email."

Lucy made dismissive clicking sound with her tongue and, glancing at Ricky, she almost imperceptibly gave a nod.

"Sorry bro'," Ricky said, leaning forward, allowing his shirt to spread open while he rested his elbows on his knees.

Lucy took a deep breath.

"Point 1 on the agenda," she said.

Do I like the idea that my wife is attractive to other men?

"To reassess the purpose of the school, its products and the way in which we supply them to our clients."

Would I be turned on by the idea of watching her in bed with my brother?

"We propose setting up a marketing department," Ricky said. "Lucy, as a full partner, will be at its head. Let me make my case, in a nutshell, please."

Perhaps, I am the voyeur who never developed.

"Just drop your case for a minute," Tony said. "Dad established the school in order to help create a society that was built on sympathy and understanding, and he believed that sympathy and understanding would grow from better communication and better communication grew from one common language, and that language is English."

Lucy waved an impatient hand, her fingernails slicing through the air to the sound of her jewellery jangling.

"Tony, I've been elected by you and Ricky in your capacity as company members to act as manager and that's precisely what I'm doing. You both have it in your power to convert the school back to a member managed structure, should you wish."

"I don't wish," said Ricky.

"Yes, but Just a minute…," Tony said.

But Lucy was not having "just a minute."

"No, Tony. Like it or not, I have a duty, in my role of manager, to tell you that grandiose ideals are not enough to keep us afloat. Haven't you noticed that the competition's growing? Haven't you noticed that at our numbers have declined? Students have been lured away by the British Council, by the London School, and all the other schools that did not exist 10 years ago. These schools are offering courses that people need in today's world. We're now facing some serious competition."

"So, we need to adapt our offerings," Ricky said. "We…"

"My sources tell me," Lucy said, "that S.E.S. is perceived as being out of date and out of touch and that our products don't meet the needs of corporate clients."

"Sources?" Tony said. "Who exactly are you referring to? And since when have we offered products?"

Lucy lowered her hand to the table. She held it in the position of a karate chop with the thumb bent backwards.

"Tony, don't you see?"

See what? My wife having an affair with my brother?

He saw her hand chopping at the table to the beat of her words.

"How do you think potential clients see us?" Lucy said.

Keeping her wrist firmly on the table, Lucy raised her karate-chop hand. The gesture looked like permission, permission to go, to speak until the hand was lowered.

"Have you any idea?" she said.

Perhaps I might watch them together? My wife as a slut enjoying sex with another man.

And down went the hand and her arm straightened.

"The truth is that we're seen as old-fashioned," Lucy said. "We're out of touch, expensive and inflexible and very hard to do business with. Have you seen our website? It's a disaster."

"Where did you get this information?"

"We had a survey done. We hired an external company to do it for us."

"Without telling me?"

"We are not obliged to tell you."

Tony tried to catch Ricky's eye but Ricky kept his eyes turned down to the floor.

"We need to start from the basics," Lucy said, "and transform our offerings to something more appropriate, price them accordingly and change the way we advertise."

"Sounds good to me," Ricky said.

"English literature with Mrs Harrison, for example. The course doesn't even pay her salary. She'll have to go. And…"

There was a knock, and the door swung open. Lucy remained open-mouthed while her eyes followed Maria Teresa carrying the drinks, sliding the tray on her desk, putting cups on saucers.

"OK, thanks. Maria Teresa. You may go."

"*Prego*," said Maria Teresa.

"Just put the tray on the desk, please Maria Teresa. Thank you so much. Now, where was I?" Lucy said.

"Mrs Harrison," Tony said, "English Literature."

Lucy nodded.

"We had to let her go," she said.

"Let her go? You mean, you threw her out, right? She was one of our first teachers, she…"

"We must adapt and change our image," Lucy said. "Somebody has to take control, make the necessary decisions and act on them."

"So?" said Ricky.

"So, I've brought in corporate clients, and this is increasing revenue. But we need a new post, and that post is Director of marketing, and I propose that, given my success so far, I take over the role. But there are conditions."

"I see," Tony said. "What are these conditions?"

"No teaching hours but a new contract in which I have full power to market the school in consultation with the current owners. I need contract signing powers and a team of marketing professionals responsible for all product offerings. That means, product development, pricing of the product, promotion, recruiting and training where necessary."

"Well said," Ricky said.

Lucy opened her arms as if taking applause.

"Thank you," she said. "Times have changed, and we must, and we need, to move with them."

Lucy said nothing more and from somewhere in the town, the echoing finale of a street singer was drowned in cheers and clapping and Lucy decided on an encore.

"I was elected by the both of you to the position of manager with authority to run the company on a daily basis and that includes hiring. By the terms of the agreement, members are not allowed to interfere with my operations unless you decide to transfer back to a member-managed structure. Do you want to do that?"

"Not me," said Ricky.

Tony hesitated, and this might have drifted into an embarrassing silence had it not been for the normal sounds of the town drifting upward and filling the room and his ears with normal shouts and normal laughter, the sound of normal car engines and normal scooters and all the other normal sounds of Italian life on a normal Monday afternoon.

"Back to normal, then?" Tony said.

Normal? There would be no return to the "normal" he thought he knew. He had seen though her, her normal lies and deception, through the normal confidence and trickery to the normal ugliness of love's death and the grisly truth emerging to the normal jingling and jangling of her jewellery and the rumbling of her stomach. But back to normal would do for now.

"Back to normal, then," said Ricky.

Yes, back to normal would do for now. How often people used these ridiculous words. Life would go "back to normal" after the holiday, after the recession, after the summer. It was nonsense. Life never went anywhere. It certainly never went in reverse. Making plans did not help much either. Destiny could not be controlled by making plans. Most people simply had to put up with the unexpected and accept any degree of uncertainty that life imposed on them. "Back to normal" only happened in films. When strange, out-of-character and hurtful things were done in real life, they could not be undone. People lived in a continuously unfolding present and once something happened, life rolled on to a new place. New meant new. Life did not roll backwards to a place called "normality."

So, what was new? New was Lucy spending most of her working time in Verona. New was the fact that she and Ricky made a great partnership. New was that the

Verona school had outgrown the Treviso school. This was the new normal.

And all of this was mostly true, but only mostly. New was the suspicion no longer nibbling but eating at his soul. "Normal" would be a nice place to stay until he discovered the truth.

I need to know. I need to know what is going on. I will never be able to forgive my wife or my brother if they are betraying me.

"Let's just go back to normal for the moment," Tony said.

"Good," said Lucy. "Back to normal it is. Let's begin the meeting again, shall we?"

17

2007

Perfect

He had expected the mist to be hanging over the rooftops but it was not. It was floating around the piazzas, billowing through alleyways and into the streets and along the length of the river, playing with its ripples, drifting with them under the bridges, and there was no wind to shift it, nudge it away; and in the streets, beams of lamplight dispersed it or cut through it with the muted sounds of car engines and the darker shapes of people, their heels click-clacking beside the cars towards the bar, the restaurant, the *Pasticceria*, the station, the language school. Tony was sitting Buddha-still, sometimes with his eyes open and sometimes with his eyes closed but, open or closed, his inner voices were asking him what he was doing on this swivel chair on the third floor of this perfect hotel offering the perfect stay in the perfect situation.

At least, the word "perfect" was one that the Cortina Hotel used to describe itself in its perfect brochure but

Tony was no longer a believer in perfection and had long since thrown it, and other absolute concepts, out of his life, or so he liked to believe. He believed the process had started with the death of his parents in the last decade of the twentieth century. Their deaths were somehow freeing, for no longer did he have to live up to standards set for him by his mother, his father, or his extended family.

Tony switched off the lights one by one, and his room became a space of dimness, of shapes of diverse depth and size. Leaning forward, he pushed at the floor with his feet, and he and the swivel chair rolled closer to the balcony windows, and he recalled, or he thought he recalled, the day on which he had refused to eat his too-runny porridge, and his mother had said he was a perfectionist and this view had spread like a virus until it was accepted by everybody. Worse still, they extended the range of his apparent perfectionism and applied it to everything, so that, according to them, Tony was only satisfied with, for example, perfect relationships, perfect holidays, perfect evenings out and perfect people.

Tony peered into the gathering mist in the streets below. Up here, he had a fine view of the building on the other side of the street, a three-storey, post-war, angular, and concrete horror that his father had bought for a song in the early 1960s and which now housed the most important of the Veneto schools. Although Treviso officially housed the school's legal headquarters, its size meant it would always play second fiddle to Verona with its businesses, its tourists, and its international connections.

He reflected that the death of his parents had made it easier for him to begin the process of releasing himself from the shackles of "correct" or "perfect" behaviour and its burden of guilt or innocence. In the years that followed their deaths, endless possibilities of being and doing presented themselves and underlined a thought that had been eating away at him for some time. And that thought was that there was no right thing, no right way to be, no right way to live, no right way to die, no right questions to ask, no right friends to have, no right clothes to wear, no right accent to have, no right food to eat, no right reaction to your partner's infidelity and no right way to release sexual urges.

Glancing at the entrance below, he paid no special attention to the neon-lit sign over the doorway; in fact, he scarcely considered it at all. For Tony, the light was simply part of the natural order of things and it acted as a welcome-to-the-school sign by picking out and welcoming all arrivals and departures. What really interested Tony was the building's top floor, a row of blinded or semi-blinded windows offering a view of the interior of his brother's apartment.

With a new pragmatic view of life, Tony's attitude to right and wrong corrected itself and he believed himself free to be the person he wanted to be, and he knew what he wanted to be. He wanted to be the person who did things, and that meant experiencing all that life had to offer from sport to food to friendship to work to sex and so on. And he wanted to do all this with style and swagger. He wanted to do this with no shame. He wanted to do this without the burden of false morality, with no personal censors, and this meant freeing himself from the constraints of his deceased parents and the constraints of their generation and their morality. He wanted to embrace life with all its possibilities and in all its realities. He loved to play with the paradox that if there was no such thing as the right way, what harm would it do to occasionally succumb to the wrong way?

With these new attitudes, it was hardly surprising that Tony was unimpressed by the Cortina Hotel's offer of the perfect stay in the perfect situation. Perfection depended on ones needs, and he had no need for the hotel's charm and elegance, did not give a fig for its close-to-the-river position or the not-so-faraway Roman ruins, and he did not care two hoots about his room's interior with its decoration and classic style. What he needed was the room's position. From the balcony he had a bird's eye view. It was, in a word, perfect. And, with this view, he might find some peace concerning his and her sexual preferences.

And I'm nodding and my heart is racing. I like that. I am ready now, quite ready, to see and face the truth.

He was touched for a second by a feeling of guilt, but he shook his head and allowed the feeling to drift away. Yes, under normal circumstances, he did have scruples and he did respect the privacy of others but these were not normal circumstances and he had obligations to himself, obligations and a right to know the truth and, by extension, a right to do whatever was necessary to discover whether the feelings that troubled him with doubts were true or simply the product of his imagination. But when he was honest with himself, it was not the moral doubts that really concerned him, but the feeling that he had been fooling himself, that commitment was always going to be a slippery slope, that the potential for infidelity was there and sitting between them from day 1 and that even friends sometimes fell out and never really made up again.

So, my love, il mio amore, will you now shine a light on your true nature? Will you reveal your true ambitions to me?

He leaned back in the swivel chair and, without taking his eyes from the school's entrance, he stretched out his hand, allowed his fingers to find the can, slipped a fingernail under the ring tab and pulled. The can opened with a hiss, a sound which suited this apparent change in both his personal morality and his personal development and which marked a point between past and future. Here he was, in this dark present, beer can in hand, and teetering on the edge of the future with its new truth and morality.

Who is to blame here and is "blame" the right word?

Who? Surely, it was the interrogative pronoun "what" and not "who" that was to blame. Surely, it was the concept of love-at-first-sight that was to blame. How can any individual believe that she is in love at the first meeting? How can he convince himself that this individual is the one you are going to share your life with? He told himself that nobody stayed the same, that love should never be accepted so lightly. Nobody remained in that crazy in-love-for-the-first-time state, that first impulse and rush of lust, those I-will-love-you-forever-and-I-will-never-let-you-go moments. And when he had told himself these things, he asked himself when, exactly, the rest of an individual's normal life started. And he convinced himself that for most couples, it was probably true to say that these initial I-will-love-you-forever feelings started on a downward slide over time, a process accelerated by sleepless nights, nappy changing and the demands of being a carer. Yes, Tony accepted this. But nobody, he told himself, should be expected to accept lies and deceit, and the killer blow, for Tony, was her confession that she had lied. She had lied to him and she had lied to his parents about her own mother and father.

He glanced at his watch. It was 21.00 and teaching would soon be at an end. The mist was thickening, probably due to the nearby river, and appeared in the air as wispy and white-feathered blankets floating in the lamplight over the school entrance, and these wispy and white blankets brought silence, and it was a stillness that lured him away to a world of what-might-have-beens, of youthful dreams now clouded with resentment and regret, and he continued to drift until the shattering squeal of an opening door brought him back to the here and now with its laughter and chatter bursting out of the school building and settling in the street below.

"Ciao, ciao."

He scanned the school's clients, as Lucy called them, gathering first in the smaller groups of classroom loyalty.

"*Civediamo, caro.*"

"Ciao."

Soon, these groups dispersed to meet the wider needs of other groups, those of friends, of lovers or of family, and all of them preening, gesticulating, chattering, hugging, and laughing.

"*Ci vedremo, ciao.*"

"*Alla prossima.*"

And one by one, they merged into the night, spinning satellites, fading to occasional echoes, and waving arms in the mist.

"*Civediamo, caro.*"

"Ciao."

"Ciao."

"Ciao, ciao, ciao."

And, for several minutes, there was nothing but the fog floating over the entrance and dripping on the cobbled stones beneath it. The movement, when it came, barely caught Tony's eye so that the word "visible" could not describe it. There was a disturbance, something other than the norm that sharpened his senses, and something vague, a sense of a beginning, and it was coming from the building opposite, the building bought for a song by his father, the building which housed the biggest school in the Veneto, and he watched it all, despite himself, coming to life in front of his eyes: unreal arms reaching, unreal arms cuddling, unreal hands stroking, unreal fingers running on skin, touching, exploring and unreal faces smiling, smile to smile, kiss to kiss, mouths wider and wider and embraces tighter and tighter until, lost in searching, they fell to the sofa. He watched the event unfold through a veil of detachment.

He wondered why he did not care, wondered why his feelings had no place in which to settle, no stomach to churn, no heart to pain, no legs to weaken. He was the shape on the balcony. He was almost invisible, drinking his beer. Lucy was the ghost in the bedroom, a memory of what had been, the barely visible soul now embracing his brother Ricky.

18

November 2007

Imperfect

Tony slipped out of the chair, swung it away from the window and let it crack against the wall. A puff of plaster floated in the brilliance of a passing car's fog lamp but Tony ignored it, grabbed at his overcoat, and pulled at the room door. He had already slipped into the coat and reached the bottom of the first flight of stairs when he heard the door thump shut. Trotting down the final flight of stairs, he prepared that blank give-away-nothing expression he had designed for students but which was also useful for a lobby staff, well trained in observing, seeing truth and lies in the eyes, the face, and its variety of expressions. He could not bear the thought of sharing idle platitudes with these people or answering their questions concerning his general well-being and whether or not he was enjoying his stay. What was he supposed to say? Should he tell them that he had just watched his wife and brother having sex and, by doing so, had confirmed his suspicions that they were having an affair? Perhaps, he should tell them his pet dog had just died or his business was in trouble, but apart from that, he was just fine.

He made no eye contact with the lobby staff, gave them a wide berth, and disappeared through the heated swing doors. He dived into the street and into the warmth and smell of air blowing upwards from the drying-room vents in the hotel basement. He almost kicked what he thought to be a bundle of rags lying by the pavement but, on closer inspection, he saw that the bundle was an individual, face up in the road, his arms outstretched, his eyes closed and his mouth open as if about to utter words of confession or a warning of impending doom. Tony stood before this fallen person wondering if he should get help or ignore him but, realising that the man might be sick or dying, Tony decided to follow the voice of conscience. He hurried back to the main entrance of the Cortina Hotel.

"Could you please call the police," he said. "A man's lying on the pavement and he might be ill."

"Do you mean just round the corner, sir, by the laundry vents?"

"Yes, that's exactly where I mean."

"We'll see what we can do, sir," the concierge said.

"You can't leave him there," Tony said. "He might die."

"We'll see to it, sir. Please, don't trouble yourself."

Tony left the hotel and picked up his stride towards the fog-free town centre. The smell of laundry quickly gave way to the smell of pizza, garlic and cigarette smoke and he was feeling a little better about himself.

Quite right. Celebrate, man. You are nothing short of the good Samaritan.

And he lifted his chin and pulled back his shoulders. He had just witnessed his wife having sex with his brother. How many other people in his situation would stop to consider the well-being of a down-and-out on the pavement at a time like this? But every now and then, he had to rub his eyes, remember to keep his chin up along with his appearance, pull his shoulders back and remind himself that he, at least, and as far as he was aware, was innocent of any crime or wrongdoing.

"Yes, you're a good man," Tony said to himself. "And you don't deserve this. Not from your wife and brother, for God's sake."

And he raised his eyes to the heavens, saw the constellations of stars and tried to give a similar shape and sense to what he had just witnessed. In the manner of a barrister, he asked himself probing questions, questions about how long the affair had been going on, questions about the symptoms he had either ignored or simply not seen, and questions about why he had not seen them or whether he had seen them but had filed them away in some corner of his mind, and questions followed about why he might have filed the evidence away, questions that went right to the heart of the matter. Did he care? Did he really love her or had love long since disappeared from his life? Perhaps, he did care but had persuaded himself that it was just his overactive imagination. Round and round went the questions until Tony found himself walking down a dark and narrow lane along which all the shutters were pulled tight, and the realisation came to him that if he was not careful, he would get lost in a maelstrom of dark and useless speculation. These might include scenarios of the he-would-find-someone-else kind, of the I-will-kill-my-brother kind, of the give-yourself-time-to-heal kind, of the wait-until-I-get-my-revenge kind. But what he found was that at some point, he had unclenched his fists and he needed a pee.

He pulled his coat around him and strode along Via Mazzini until he emerged under the walls of the Roman arena at one end of Piazza Bra. He looked up only once and thought he recognised Lucy amongst the crowds of tourists by the entrance to the arena. When he realised his mistake, he also found he was happy to be walking with the crowd because he could switch off, unwind, drift with the current and allow those questions, questions about divorce, about telling the children, to drift past him and quieten his inner voices. Now that he had come to think about it, what was he going to do next? Should he consider getting a divorce? How were Julia and Mario going to feel and who was going to tell them?

Well, Lucy started it so she should tell them.

The childish nature of this thought both bothered and pleased him at the same time. It bothered him because he had always assumed that becoming an adult would happen at a certain age as naturally as night follows day, that one morning he would wake up and say to himself:

"Today, I cease being a child and I become an adult."

It amused him to see that "adulthood" was a far more elusive concept. His assumption that he would get to a certain age and everything would suddenly make sense brought a smile to his face. He knew now that adulthood came to some but not to others and often depended on the context so that one could behave in an adult fashion one day and in a childish fashion the next. Who was defining the word "adult" anyway and what did the word "adult" actually mean? He always described his father as an adult and, to Tony, that meant someone who was authoritative, decisive, and doubt-free. But there were other understandings of the word, for example: someone who was married, had children, and, if male, was supporting his family, and, if female, caring for her family. Tony was attracted to the definition that described the word "adult" as somebody who was self-sufficient and responsible for his or her own decisions. Much to his surprise, he found himself to be quite comfortable in a world with a variety of meanings to choose from, a world in which the word "adult" meant one thing one day but another thing the next.

He was still questioning, blaming, and ruminating when he found himself opposite the city gate he knew so well, the club he knew so well and he stopped and lifted his head. He had not intended to come to this familiar place but some kind of homing device had brought him here to this place he knew, to these thrills he knew so intimately, and she was waiting, and usually "she" was Karen, but sometimes she was Beatrice and at other times she was Carla and from time to time she was Francesca, and all of them represented a moment of his own brand of infidelity, his lack of conscience, his it's-OK-because-I-am-a-man attitude and any one of his girls might be waiting for him now, sitting astride a massage table with the single bulb over the doorway and framing her face in a deformed halo.

Maybe, I should just leave things as they are.

On these nights, protected by the fog, she might speak indiscriminately from the window to the passers-by, the strollers from the station, the owners of the cars with out-of-town plates, and some of her words caused some of the men to feign shock and horror while other men stole one glance at their own desires and desperate lives before hurrying away, and other men were forced by temptation to look once more with longing eyes and look in vain for their discarded innocence. But others walked forward and while Tony walked with them, he recalled the song, *When I fall in love it will be forever.* For him, forever was future perfect, but forever had been devastated earlier on this November evening in the flicker of an eye. And now, he could act with a clear conscience and, what was more, a most pragmatic thought came to him and it was so pragmatic he could not understand why he had not thought of it before.

Why should he do anything?

Yes, why upset the apple cart. Just leave things as they are. No need to cause unnecessary problems. And we can all be happy.

"Massage inside," the girl insisted.

The students can be happy. Lucy and Ricky can be happy. I can be happy and the children? Why should they know? On the other hand, they are not stupid. They must know already.

Tony was light of foot. He was nodding and smiling to himself, pleased to have made a decision, and surprised, as he always was, at the range of people who walked through the doors of this place. Some were middle-aged couples, perhaps looking to spice up their love life. Others were, apparently, respectable business men, lawyers, doctors, and professionals who were probably overworked without time for dating. But they gave the place a respectability and the feeling that the club was a safe space to be.

When he was honest with himself, which he thought he had been since his parents passed away, he knew he had never been comfortable with sexual and physical intimacy, but here he felt able to let his barriers down and have a perfect connection with a near stranger he might never see again, at least, if he chose not to. He found he was treated with respect and they never shamed or demonised him or judged him but they helped him express his innermost desires and do it at a time when he was vulnerable and expressing his desires had been hidden away for years.

In a nutshell, he felt good about being a client, good about himself and it brought him a degree of happiness. But try as he might, Tony was unable to forget that it was only a degree of happiness. He could no longer dream again the dreams of his youth but he was unable to turn from the shadows of those early days when he had wanted true love and a true woman in two true and loving arms. He had let that time pass away. Too late today to see that his life had never been just a rehearsal for something else.

"It's Karen I'd like to see," he said. "Is she free tonight?"

He made for the bar, ordered a drink, and waited. He always saw young Karen whenever she was available. He had been seeing her since he had begun feeling burdened and trapped by the obligations of family and keeping up that perfect appearance so important to his parents.

She stopped in the doorway, let it frame her like a picture, a portrait, perhaps, of innocence, of sweetness and light.

He held out his hand and said:

"Lovely to see…"

And her lips were silencing him, her tongue flicking in and around his mouth, the sound of their clothes rustling, the feel of her hair falling across his face and tickling his nose.

She was sitting on his knee, stroking his face, loosening his tie.

"I'm glad you came," she said.

As far as Tony was concerned, she could have added the word "uncle." Karen was not so much a typical prostitute as the sweet girl next door. The relationship had started out as a business relationship but he liked to believe he had become her friend and confidant. She was loosening his shirt; her fingers close to his chest. Her eyes closed and the world outside, the sound of scooters, shouting, cars accelerating went silent as she kissed him again. He felt himself sliding away to another world. It was their world, and he experienced emotions he had not felt in years: lust and longing and freedom to do what he wanted, to explore sexual fantasies that were out of bounds with Lucy. He felt so free, unfettered, and joyous and all of this without having to worry about biding by marriage vows or who was collecting whom from school.

"Do you want to talk or shall we…?" she said glancing at the bedroom.

Of course, he knew it was a fantasy. It was a fantasy relationship, a relationship with no responsibility. But he had managed to convince himself that so long as he was aware of the fantasy, that was alright then. And she, as professional as she was, was happy to take his money and play along. She was never demanding. She required nothing from him.

"How was your week?" he muttered.

He vaguely noticed what he always vaguely noticed and refused to acknowledge but tonight he heard that his voice had a ring of familiarity to it, the ring of the returning customer perhaps, but its tone seemed to belong to someone else, someone he had only just met and hardly knew.

19

November 2007

The scarf

They say that fog in the Veneto is usually a product of the sunny but chilly days of autumn. The fog comes down at dusk and drifts with the evening light towards darkness and reduces all things to their essentials shape or sound: the shape of cars, of buildings, and the sounds of trains, of windows shutting, of people whispering or walking home. Fog can make the world a different place.

The fog was particularly thick in the darkness of night when I arrived unannounced and unseen, at the fabulous Hotel Cortina in Verona. However, I was not going to allow the foggy conditions to reduce me to anything, or influence my behaviour. I had a job to do, one step at a time.

One.

A smile for the concierge and several more smiles for the pretty girl sitting next to him. She was about my age and had the look of somebody who liked being looked at.

Two.

A question for both the concierge and the girl.

"Is it true that several famous people have stayed at this hotel?"

I smiled at both employees, enjoyed the soft and warm lights of the entrance hall while the concierge showed off his knowledge. His presentation of the hotel's history was as impressive as it was a little clockwork in style. His list of famous people included: Charles Dickens, D'Annunzio and Hemingway.

"And not to forget Peggy Guggenheim, the art collector," he said. "She'd always stay here on her way to Venice."

The girl said:

"And, apparently, Hemingway wrote a short story in the Hemingway Suite. There are signed books and a typewriter used by the man himself, in our library."

"Wow," I said, genuinely impressed.

"You could also, if you wished, order drinks inspired by the author's tastes."

"That's very kind," I said.

Three.

"I believe my father, Tony Meldrum, is staying at the hotel," I said, "Is he in his room?"

"I'm afraid Mr Meldrum has just gone out, sir," the concierge said. "You've missed him by a few minutes."

That was not a good start. I was looking forward to surprising Mum and Dad on the occasion of Mum's birthday the following day, so I decided to take some time for myself and stroll into my Verona. I had not gone far when I came upon a tramp sleeping in the street. Playing the part of the good citizen, I reported the tramp to hotel staff. They seemed unconcerned. They told me they would take care of the situation, and I made off towards the city walls, the canals, and the less salubrious edge of the town.

The thick fog was even thicker over the water, and the light from the streetlamps winked and blinked through it. It was much colder here, too. Water droplets pricked at my face and hands, while I followed the clouds of my breath into this earthier part of town. I knew the city well. I knew the tourist sites, Juliet's house, the arena, the gardens, and bridges. Yes, there was no doubt that Verona was a city for those who liked to see and appreciate beauty. But for me, Verona's charm and allure lay in its contrast with ugliness, the ugliness of post-war concrete buildings, the ugliness of the circular road, the ugliness of drug dealers, the ugliness of creeping cars with out-of-town plates, the ugliness of dark shapes and shadows behind windscreens, of windows winding down, of girls negotiating, of whispering men, of gloved hands massaging gear sticks, the ugliness of hands offering money, the ugliness of hands taking money.

I was unable to clearly see Porta Nuova station or the church and car park beside it but the sound of whooshing tyres, horns and drifting yellow headlamps indicated the presence of cars, and a muffled whistle, and soft, blurred edges suggested the presence of a train inching away from a station platform and creating images in my head of fiery dragons with terrible, bilious eyes. People with suitcases or backpacks drifted past as wrapped up packages in jacket and scarf. It seemed I was standing in a place populated by ghosts walking noiselessly and wrapped in silence. Fog clung to everything. Somewhere, a drunken cry rose into the sky. Somewhere, steel-capped shoes tapped homeward. Somewhere, there were whispers, and all these sounds were soft, hushed, and illicit.

I was not expecting to see him, so I was merely irritated that somebody could come out of a doorway and into the street without looking. His head was down, his face wrapped in a scarf, his eyes focused on the pavement. He shot out of the doorway and into my chest and knocked the wind out of me. There was no indication that he was aware of this brush with a stranger and there was no apology. But I was not focused on my irritation. Nor was I focused on the mild pain in my shoulder. I thought I had recognised something, a movement of the legs, perhaps, the shape of the head, the scarf around the mouth. Then, I heard more footsteps coming down a flight of stairs and heading for the door.

It was the scarf, the "Made in Italy" scarf that confirmed my suspicions.

The scarf, created from the finest silk cloth, handcrafted, and printed on Lake Garda, made with high-quality wool fabric, this soft-to-the-touch cashmere scarf with its bright colours would always stand out from the rest.

It had stood out from the rest.

It had stood out this evening.

It was the scarf I bought for my dad the previous Christmas.

20

2009

The secrets of silence

The walk from the centre of Asolo to the cemetery was a delight. Without a care in the world, or so it seemed, they strolled along a lane, down the hill from the town and followed a narrow path beside a chapel and up another hill. Most of the way, they were side by side, straw hat to straw hat, and she was drifting in her world and he was drifting in his and, although a random passer-by might not have noticed, the world under Tony's straw hat and the world under Lucy's straw hat were far, far apart.

The visit had started at a time when the sunlight was still brightening and shadows were still shifting in windows and under the porticos, and hunger had connected them, fuelled their search for the open bar with a handful of early-rising British and German tourists and all of this to a background of distant engines buzzing, early morning *ciaos* and *buongiornos* and human shapes flitting about in soon-to-be-opening shops and restaurants.

"Cemeteries are not places I usually come to," Lucy said. "But our stay won't be permanent. This visit's temporary, isn't it, Tony? I certainly hope so."

Tony glanced at her. He wondered if she had attempted a joke, but Lucy did not often make jokes. Her face, half hidden in the shade of her wide-brimmed straw hat, gave very little away, nothing more than a light lifting of the cheeks.

"It might sound strange," Tony said, "but I've always enjoyed being in cemeteries. I find them calming, and they're great places to meditate."

"To be at one with the universe, you mean? They do tend to be filled with positive vibes."

"Perhaps," Tony said, "because visitors are filled with love and positive memories, and they leave these positives behind when they go."

"And flowers," she said.

"Of course," Tony said. "And flowers."

"Well, I look forward to seeing it all."

"It's magnificent," he said. "You'll love it. Just you wait and see."

They had eventually breakfasted in a bar in Piazza Garibaldi. The warmth of the pastries suggested recent arrival, and the coffee machine was humming to the end of its flush-back cleaning cycle. They drank black coffee, ate fresh bread, local salami and Asolo honey with its taste of sun and flowers, perhaps the flowers now dancing in the breeze beside the path at their feet, but neither of them suggested it, in fact neither of them said a word. They had chosen to adopt their own brand of silence and to bring it with them into the stillness and heat that was building in the cemetery. This place of final rest was a serene place, a hilltop place to be exact, and a place that overlooked the farms and vineyards that dotted the valley between Asolo and the green, inviting, and breath-taking Monte Grappa massif now blanketed with orchids, gentians, and edelweiss.

"Why did you bring me here?" Lucy said.

"Because it's a kind of no-mans-land that belongs neither to you nor to me."

"Not yet, at least," Lucy said.

"I used to feel uncomfortable in cemeteries when I was a boy," Tony said. "Their associations with endings and with death were depressing. But I like this one. I thought you might like it, too. It says a lot about the culture and life of the place."

"Don't get too carried away," Lucy said. "We're not here to talk about culture."

"Right," Tony said. "But before we start, I'd like to visit one grave I've never seen."

This never-before-visited grave, the last resting place of Italian actress, Eleonora Duse, was a marble monolith rising from a bed of stones between manicured hedges. A solitary rose had been placed below the engraving of the actress's name. Tony removed his straw hat, held it at his chest while he wiped at his brow with the cuff of his shirt.

"You know," he said, "in Asolo you should slow down and breathe slowly. You should talk to people. You should also be silent and listen to nature. But if you want pleasures of the floral kind, you must remember to bring your own."

"What are you talking about?"

"I forgot to bring flowers," Tony said.

"Then, today's your lucky day," Lucy said. "The grave doesn't need flowers. The beauty of this place lies in its simplicity, and this tells me volumes about who Duse was as a human being."

"They gave her a magnificent spot," Tony said. "Right in front of Monte Grappa, the mountain that she loved."

"The mountain seems to have broken out in colour, doesn't it?"

"Indeed, it does," Tony said. "Just for us."

"Stop it, Tony," Lucy said. "Romance is not one of your core strengths."

Monte Grappa's south-facing lower slopes were blanketed in flowers, and these eventually gave way to pastures, to dots and shapes on the mountainside indicating the presence of huts and farm buildings and, above them, smoke swirled from restaurant chimneys to the blue of the sky, and all of these places, Tony knew, served polenta, cooked cheese, Lamon beans, sausages and mushrooms and other mountain specialities. Tony replaced his hat and, tapping it into place, his eyes and forehead darkened in shadow.

"You know," he said. "This place has a different feel when the seasons change. The cemetery could be visited in an hour but, if you wanted, you could stay here a lifetime and it'd always be something and somewhere different."

"We don't have a lifetime," Lucy said, glancing at the watch glittering on her wrist. "I agreed to give you one morning until 12 o'clock. And here we are. So…?

"Indeed, so…?"

"So, what about us," Lucy said. "Isn't that what we're here for?"

"Yes, it is," said Tony.

He spoke calmly but he had not managed to connect with his feelings that morning and, even if he had connected with them, he would not have been able to express them by putting words to them. There seemed to be a yawning chasm between what he felt and what he was able to articulate. After all, he thought, not every feeling had a word and the words he did know seemed clumsy and inadequate.

"So, let's start, shall we?" Lucy said.

"After you," Tony said.

Lucy snapped her head sideways as if a wasp had passed close to her nose.

"The problem, as I see it, is that there isn't an "us" anymore. And please don't tell me that the kids don't know we are hardly man and wife. Don't you think "us" should be…"

"Confined to the history books? Eliminated? Put out of its misery? Taken to a doctor and put down like sick cats?"

Lucy raised her head and looked her husband in the eye.

"Don't start by putting your solutions into my mouth, Tony. I'm perfectly capable of expressing myself in my own way. I wanted to use a word like *redefined* or *reformulated.*"

Tony took a deep breath and, in the silence, he turned his eyes to the mountain opposite with its restaurants and bars, and pretended to study something. From a distance, Monte Grappa looked like a wonderful place for a picnic, a cooked lunch, a hike, or a bicycle ride. He had been on the mountain many times, and he knew what might be seen by the informed observer with an interest in History. Tony turned his eyes away from Grappa, and tuned in to himself, to his feelings, to his Lucy, to their relationship, and he wondered what he and Lucy looked like to other visitors who might happen to be watching them. Just another couple visiting a cemetery? Just another couple discussing their children, their problems, where to go on holiday?

"Then, perhaps we see things differently," Tony said. "Or, perhaps, we're choosing to ignore the obvious."

He was looking closely at Monte Grappa again and, while he spoke, his eyes were searching for, and finding, all those depressions in the ground, all those odd ditches zig-zagging across the landscape.

"We need to define the problem first," Lucy said. "Only then can we look at solutions."

He turned to find Lucy's eyes with his but found that

the sun, shining through the loose weave of her hat, had covered her face in pinpricks of sunlight and shadow.

"It seems to me," he said, "that we should cover nothing up. We either put it all on the table or we don't mention it and pretend it isn't there?"

"Agreed," Lucy said. "We shouldn't do that."

"I actually want to know what you think," Tony said.

"I think," Lucy said while lowering her head, "that, in one way, we've drifted so far apart that we've got separate lives already. But, in another way, the children and the school bind us together. It's difficult. It's complicated."

He hardly heard her. He had been hoping for something new, but these words he had heard before. He had heard them in his own mouth. He had heard them in her mouth. He had mulled them over before and he was pretending to mull them over now while he looked again at the slopes of Monte Grappa. They looked so peaceful with their restaurants, their bicycle tracks, and their smoking chimneys, but Tony knew what those slopes had once been witness to, and what they had been witness to were still there for eyes to see if they knew where to look. Knowing eyes would recognise the depressions in the ground as shell craters. Knowing eyes would recognise the zig-zagging ditches as trenches. Knowing eyes would recognise the tunnels in the rock as gun emplacements.

"What do you think we should do about it?" Tony said.

The Monte Grappa massif, a place for walks and contemplation of nature's beauty was now blanketed with orchids, gentians, and edelweiss, but it had been a place of unimaginable slaughter, bloodshed and suffering in the Great War. Knowing eyes knew that, had it not been for the battle, Monte Grappa would have become just another mountain where walkers walked, cyclists rode, and picnickers picnicked. Knowing eyes knew that had it not been for all those deaths, Monte Grappa would have become just another mountain in an endless chain of peaks and valleys between Asolo in the south and Germany in the north.

"I think," Lucy said, "we should consider alternative ways of being together."

"Have you found somebody else?" he asked.

He was not interested in hearing the lie he knew was coming. He had heard it all before: she, denying his accusation and she, believing her own denial.

"No," she said.

And there it was again. She was lying in the same way that she had lied to him, to his mum and to his dad and brother so long ago on their terrace in the sun.

"I see," he said.

And what he saw was that, like always, the conversation was going nowhere. Round and round, they would go. Round and round in circles, like teddy bears, one step, two step and they would trade the same words, the same feelings, the same frustration, the same anger and afterwards, the world would continue as it had always continued.

Well, not this time.

"It just occurred to me," he said, scanning the mountains, "that you might be having an affair with my brother."

So, now it was out, his trump card turned over and standing between them. He felt his heart thumping while he waited for her reply and while he waited, he allowed his eyes and thoughts to settle on Monte Grappa again. Vast and bounded by the Piave river on one side, and by the Brenta river on the other. It stood as a mountain truly different from many of its Alpine cousins. Its valleys, rockfaces, cliffs, streams, meadows, and forests were cemeteries and mausoleums, and they remained as eternal memorials to the tens of thousands of young men who had perished on its slopes.

Lucy had still not replied.

"Well," Tony said. "What do you say to that?"

He convinced himself that she had deflated in front of him and that, stripped of her stories, stripped of her fairytale, stripped of her beliefs and all the other pillars of deceit that supported her, victory was his. He assumed she was trembling before him. It never occurred to him that she might be shaking with anger.

"You dare say that," she whispered. "You dare accuse me…"

"I dare because it's true," he said.

"Hypocrite," she said. "Do you think I don't know about your little visits to the girls in town? You're living a lie; you who are so righteous."

For what seemed an eternity, Tony waited. He waited for her anger. He waited for her scorn, her derision, her criticism. She said:

"But we're made from the same cloth you and I, don't you think?"

And that was all she said. Even had he been able to find the words to ask her how she knew about his "little visits," and even had he been able to ask her how she felt about them, she would remain silent. Silence was power and silence was control and she would judge him and punish him in silence, in the same way that his mother had judged him and punished him by dubbing him Mr Perfect and, subsequently, complaining that whatever he did was comparatively imperfect and wanting.

"So, you're saying that what's good for the goose is good for the gander," Tony said.

Well, so be it. He was comfortable with himself. He was comfortable with his sex life. He was not overnostalgic about the past, its expectations, hopes and dreams, but he was optimistic about the future. He had learned that happiness lay inside himself. It did not depend on externals like people or the sunshine or whether or not his wife was being unfaithful. And Lucy said nothing more on the topic. She simply shook her head and remained silent.

Tony Mumbled something, but he was no longer thinking about geese and ganders, he was thinking about what had been in front of his eyes for some time. The nature of all relationships changed over time and his and lucy's relationship was no exception. The once-upon-a-time "them" with their hopes, dreams and expectations had been cremated, but the urn with the ashes was still above the grill on the terrace where it had all started, and they had never discussed what to do with it, at least, until now.

"You know," he said, "I thought we'd come to define our problems and to find solutions, but I think I was wrong."

"Indeed," she said. "We both know what the problems are, but solutions and consequences are still open for debate."

"And just for the record," he said, "I don't have feelings for anybody else."

And so much was true. He did not have feelings for his providers at the massage parlour and they had no feelings for him. But they did, at least, show him some respect but nothing more. Unfortunately, he had discovered that he needed to be a hero. He wanted to be the man who carried the suitcases, the man who washed the car, the man who stood at Lucy's side to protect her from the big, bad world, the man who made the decisions, the man who made the money. But Lucy did not need a hero. She was already heroic.

"So," Lucy said. "The "us" that got married and had children is no longer with us. Life has moved on and, perhaps, we just need to redefine what we want from each other. And please don't tell me that the kids don't know we aren't the traditional man and wife anymore."

"Hardly," he said.

"Mario's 21, and…"

"Yes, I know. Julia's 19."

"They need to hear it from us," Lucy said.

"Hear what from us? We haven't decided anything."

"Why don't you tell them," Lucy said, "that we're redefining what it means, for us, to be married?"

"Which means what exactly?

"It means setting new goals, sharing new hopes and expectations with each other, and learning to enjoy the time we've got together. Tell them this."

"They'll be back in Italy next week," Tony said.

"Why don't you do it, Tony. Soften them up and prepare them. You're so good with words."

"Alright," Tony said, "I'll speak to them."

She nodded.

There was a long pause.

"So," he said, "it was already done and dusted."

"What was done and dusted?" Lucy said.

"Our relationship," Tony said. "We came to discuss our relationship but what we've found is that the answer was already waiting for us. We just hadn't dared to look. We'd already lived through our doubts and our questions and, on this day, this strange day, we've found we already learned to live into the answers. And we didn't even realise it."

Lucy tutted her irritation.

"If I understand you correctly," she said, "you think we have naturally moved on to another place and that this needed clarification, am I right?"

"Exactly," Tony said. "There's not only one set of characteristics that can define a successful marriage. We can decide what our marriage might look like."

"Thank God," Lucy said. "Amen to that."

Tony was quite at home with this. He had changed, moved on, developed his own ideas of what was right and what was wrong, what a good marriage was and what a bad marriage was. He was no longer hanging on to his mother's dream of perfection. Instead, here in Asolo, he listened to the church clock chiming and he waited for the final strike, the final bong, before he shook himself and prepared for a change of perspective.

"However," Lucy said.

"However, what…?"

"There's one problem."

"Probably more than one," Tony said. "Tell me."

"Actually, there are two problems."

"Exactly," Tony said. "So, let's start with the first."

"Ricky's jealous. Did you know?"

"No, I didn't. Jealous of…?"

"He's jealous of you. You're still my husband, you know?"

"So, the second problem?"

"You've seen it already."

"You mean, his temper?"

Lucy nodded and Tony turned his mind back a few years. A bar on the way to the Dolomites. A big man. An explosive reaction from Ricky, a reaction he recalled as terrible and frightening.

"And there's a third problem."

"I thought there might be," Tony said.

"That night on the terrace, the night we met, you remember it?"

Tony nodded.

"It's part of our story," he said.

"Well, it's certainly not part of Ricky's story. He has other memories."

"Really?"

"Yes, really. He says he remembers everything he and I said to each other before you came along and stole me away from under his nose."

"I hardly remember Ricky at all that evening," Tony said.

"Nonetheless, he was there."

"It's 23 years ago," Tony said. "Do you remember this happening? It sounds bizarre to me."

Lucy shook her head.

"It sounds bizarre, I agree, but, apparently, it isn't," Lucy said. "At least, not according to Ricky. It seems that although we might think our memories are like photographs, preserving every moment in detail and exactly as it happened, the fact is that memories are like a collage with the occasional fabrication."

"Fake memory?" Tony said.

"I would guess so," Lucy said. "But perhaps it is our memories that are false. But the fact remains that Ricky believes what his memory tells him. It may not be part of our story, but it's definitely part of his. He swears it's true, says it really happened and, true or not, we are going to have to face it."

21

2010

Almost

"Why's Mummy in Verona, Daddy? And why are you in Treviso?"

"It's really quite simple. I'll tell you."

"Now? Today?"

"Yes, today. Now, in fact."

"Why today? Why now, Daddy?"

"Because you're both here now," he said. "That makes today a special day and now a special now."

A special day, a special morning and a special now, because it was now, this morning and this day on which he had planned to come clean, to tell it from the horse's mouth, as it were, to reveal, if not all of the details to his children, but the simple fact of a marriage in a stage of transition and to reveal it from his point of view. He had planned to do this by suggestion and letting them come to their own conclusions. At least, that is what he had told Lucy, and that was what he had told himself. He would not admit, could not admit that he was afraid of telling them the truth, the whole truth and nothing but the truth. How could he tell his children that their father had found sexual satisfaction with whores in a brothel and that their mother was having an affair with their uncle?

"Are you going to tell us what's going on?" Mario said.

"The truth and nothing but the truth," Julia said.

Of course, he realised that they had guessed something of his and Lucy's situation. But given that both Mario and Julia were still living in the UK, well into their further education and their own lives, it was easier for him to keep the details from them.

"I'll tell you what it's all come to," Tony said.

And what it had all come to was that he and Lucy lived almost separate lives, and they had been living almost separate lives for almost 3 years. This morning of this day and of this week was the morning on which he had decided to make his thin-end-of-the-wedge revelations, and his aim was simple; to help the children begin a process of acceptance and of normalisation, and this process would begin on this sunlit morning on this riverside terrace of their favourite *Pasticceria. Sommariva*, as the *Pasticceria* was known, was now open for breakfast, brunch and lunch, and dinner. Everybody was enjoying the selection of *antipasti*, meat and fish and consuming it to the sound of the river *Sile* rushing from its spring in the Alps, sparkling in the sunlight while running past *Sommariva,* before flowing onwards to the Venetian lagoon

"Sorry, but what was it you wanted to know?" he asked of Julia and, telling himself to keep cheerful and not to put a hard edge to things, he led the way to the terrace. *Pasticceria Sommariva* was bustling. It always bustled, had been bustling since 1920 and, 6 days of the week, was the bustling place to be seen, a place of a lady's grandest entrance, a place of her most fashionable clothes, of a man's loudest laugh, of the most animated of conversations, a place of movement, of shapes, shifting shadows, and a place of pleasure and excitement with a central corridor bathed in light and flanked with eaters.

Julia's cheeks were balloons deflating while she forced the air from between her lips. Eventually, she said:

"It's Mummy I want to talk about, Daddy. You haven't told us why she went to Verona."

"Went? She hasn't gone, dear."

Julia bunched the fingers and thumb of one hand and, with tips touching and pointing upwards, she made pecking movements in unison with her shaking head.

"Has she left you for uncle Ricky, Daddy?"

Tony smiled at the way she combined the English language with Italian hand signals to express frustration and impatience, but he was not going to allow her to pressurise him. He avoided her question in the same way that he usually avoided the sugary delights of this Pasticceria. He knew that Mario and Julia had been looking forward to them, and they had all stopped at the counter and admired the whipped-up egg whites, sweet with honey and mixed with nuts, or bite-sized biscuits flavoured with almonds, tubular shells filled with delight, the flaky, crunchy lobster tails filled with cream.

He inhaled, paused, and said on a breath:

"During the week, she's staying in the place where she's needed."

"And that place is Verona, Daddy?"

"Exactly, dear."

"With uncle Ricky?"

"Where else do you expect her to stay?"

"Why don't you join her?"

"Because I belong here in Treviso. This is my school, my patch, my world."

He took a deep breath and grinned and nodded his head and continued to nod as if he wanted to accompany words he was not saying, while Julia, with questions in her head, stared at him in dismay. She blurted out:

"You mean she left you, Daddy?"

"No, I wouldn't say that, at least not exactly."

Mario's glancing eyes informed his sister, "I told you so," and then he said:

"What would you say, 'exactly,' Dad?"

"I'd say we're all a family," Tony said. "And it should, and will, stay that way."

The children stared at him, stared open-mouthed in the same way that they had stared open-mouthed at the fruit, the chocolate, the hazelnut cream, the super elegant and delicate customised cakes, and the photographs of the rich and famous eating them all.

"But what, exactly, is she doing with uncle Ricky?" Julia said.

"I really wouldn't like to say, not exactly, anyway."

"So, they're having an affair."

"I didn't say that," Tony said.

"No, but you hinted at it."

"Or was it simply your interpretation?"

Mario lifted his arms in the air, leaned back in his chair and took a calming breath.

"What's his relationship with her, Dad?"

"He's a sort of consultant."

Julia's mouth dropped open.

"Consultant? Consultant? Is that what you call it?"

Mario placed his open hand on her forearm.

"In what?" he said.

"Company development," said Tony, "and marketing, and teacher development."

Tony glanced at Julia's wrist. That was something new, that chunky, in-your-face bracelet.

"Is that Mum's thing?" he said.

"Is what Mum's thing, Daddy?"

Tony nodded towards her wrist.

"The bracelet, dear."

Julia made a movement that suggested a wasp had flown too close to her head.

"No... Daddy, you're changing the subject. I, I mean we, want to know what Mum's doing with uncle Ricky. Are you trying to tell us it's just work?"

"They're running the school," Tony said.

"But not at weekends, Dad."

"Right. She'll be back tonight. She knows you are both here. You can ask her yourselves."

Julia looked at Mario and Mario looked at Julia.

"Not quite the answer you wanted?" Tony said.

Indeed, it was not quite the answer they wanted, but then again, today was not "quite" anything they wanted. It was not quite summer, for example but "not quite summer" was, arguably, and according to Tony, the best time of the year. And even if it were not the best time of the year, it was definitely the best side of summer, the part of summer when people had summer's fullness of things in front of them, things to look forward to, things to enjoy, things that emerged with the endless possibilities of imagination. And it was similar to his "not-quite-the-answer-they-wanted" because this answer was on the "almost" side of truth, the side of truth that protected and cared but prepared nonetheless for easier acceptance of the winter cold.

And life went on. It always did in spite of everything. And the conversations went on in spite of everything. From a nearby table a woman's voice said:

"Are you going to the sea or the mountains this year?"

And there was an answer but Tony was conscious only of the babble of talk and not of the meaning of individual words while he mused on life and how it went on despite everything and people remained after wars, earthquakes, disease and illness, love affairs, deceit and treachery. And then, there was Mario and his persistent question.

"Are they having an affair, Dad?"

Tony wagged his head and stuck out his bottom lip and looked around him. *Pasticceria Sommariva* was the place to be seen, the place for morning woman and her style of very short jackets worn with ankle-length trousers and, for evening woman, and her style of shorter skirts of silk or satin and decorated with sequins. The effect was not simply shimmering. The effect was almost shattering.

"Affair?"

"Yes, Dad. Are they a couple, partners, mates? Are they sleeping together?"

"Well, don't ask me. Ask your mother when you see her?"

Mario made a movement of the head that suggested a wasp had flown too close to his nose.

"You know I can't do that, Dad."

"Why not? Because you need more guts? Because it's easier to ask me?"

"That isn't fair, Dad."

"Maybe life isn't fair, Mario."

"I'm asking you because you're here and she isn't here," Mario said.

"It's all very well and understandable that you want to know but while we all retain an interest in the school, we're all together as one family."

"What about you, Dad? Have you found something else?"

"Something? Do you mean somebody, Mario?"

"OK, Dad. Have you found somebody else?"

"Well, let me ask you something, Mario. What do you know, I mean, what do you really know about your parents' relationship? Your tone suggests that you think you know it all but you can't possibly know what's going on between your mum and I."

Silence. Mario looked towards the floor, blinked, and sucked at his bottom lip.

"I saw you, Dad."

Mario swallowed, and a teardrop appeared in the corner of his eye and began a slow and ragged roll down the side of his nose.

"Where did you see me?"

"Coming out of the massage parlour by the station."

The tear had gathered speed, raced past his mouth, and disappeared under his chin.

"I see," Tony said, "Are you sure it was me? I suppose you're sure, otherwise you wouldn't have accused me."

Mario swallowed and raised his head. His expression had tightened and he rubbed at his eyes, looked his father full in the face and sniffed.

"You were wearing the scarf I bought for you, and the way you were walking, it could only have been you. It was you I saw, wasn't it, Dad? And what were you doing in that place, Dad? What were you doing? Having a nice chat with the girls or what?"

Tony looked up at his son, scanned his face for the boy he had been but found only the trace of a tear on the face of the young man he was.

"I see. So, you assumed it was me," Tony said. "But, you know, there may be many reasons why a man visits these places. Maybe the man's just a philanderer. You don't know why. Maybe the man's wife bears some responsibility. But we don't know what that responsibility is, do we? My advice to you is not to act as judge and jury and don't take sides."

"Dad, I'm not a fool. What you are doing is a betrayal…"

"Do not judge, Mario. You love us both.

"Dad, I…"

"No, stop there," Tony said. "You must understand that you'll have a relationship with both your parents for the rest of your life. So, what you do now must respect and preserve that. My advice is to do as little as possible and to not get carried away by anything that *might* be true."

Julia laid her hand on Mario's forearm.

"What does that mean, Daddy?" she said.

"Two things, my dear. First, it means that there's not just one way to be married. Your mother and I are now deciding what marriage means for us. And when we have decided, we'll let you know. Secondly, and importantly, we have to accept that the school binds us together whether we want it to or not."

Mario looked at his sister and she looked at her brother and they both looked at their father but he was away with his thoughts, gone with the breeze, swallowed by the shadows. He shuffled in his chair and leaned towards his children and said:

"It's just lovely to sit here with you both," he said. "Let's not spoil it with talk of…"

And he hesitated, waved his arms, Italian style, and shook his head as though in rejection of some thought or idea that had no place in *Pasticceria Sommariva*.

"Separation, Daddy?"

"Divorce?" said Mario.

"Step mothers and fathers, Daddy?"

Tony nodded.

"Yes," he said. "Those sorts of things. But the possibilities are endless. In time, you'll see this yourselves. I promise you."

"And what does uncle Ricky have to say about all this?" Mario said.

"We've got no idea," Tony said. "But I expect him to tell us when he's ready."

And then, his eyes slanted sideways and he glimpsed the clouds brooding over the familiar outline of Cima Palon, and it occurred to him that there might be some bad weather over the mountains and that it might be heading in their direction.

22

2012

Christmas cheer

There was a gurgling sound, a rumble-of-the-tummy sound that prompted an exchange of embarrassed glances and smiles from those at the round table and "those" included the almost complete family and two potential additions. The almost-complete family consisted of Lucy and Tony sitting opposite each other, Mario and Julia and their friends and, as far as Lucy was concerned, potential family members from England, Diana and Peter. And yet, the party was incomplete. Somebody seemed to be absent, and this absence was indicated by the chair tucked under the table, the carefully laid cutlery suggesting a last-minute cancellation, a late arrival, or a never-more-to-come guest to whose permanent absence they might drink a toast. There was another empty-tummy rumbling sound.

"A hungry ghost?" said Mario.

"More like deep rumbles from the depths of the heating system," Lucy said.

It was, indeed, a time for the word "depth": the depths

of the heating system, the depths of winter, the depth of snow in the mountain, the depths of depression for some at Christmas time and the in-depth questioning of the newcomers now facing a cross-examination by the lady of the house. There was very little light in this building in the hills, and the little light that there was, emanated from the kitchen, the hallway, and the dining-room. A dressed tree, outside the entrance door, might have been visible from a distance as pinpricks of coloured light in the blackness of the hills. If there was any sound to break the silence, it was that of Christmas-evening chit-chat, nervous laughter and the clatter of knife and fork on Lucy's best Wedgwood dinner set.

"Turkey cooked to perfection."

"Did you do all this on your own, Mrs Meldrum?"

Deciding that the question was rhetorical, Lucy smiled her response and glanced through the window at the cold of the night, the cold of the ice on the terrace, the cold of the icy east wind gusting in the leafless trees, over the terrace and into the darkness, up and away and into the night sky.

"Where is Ricky?"

"He's late."

"He's always late," Lucy said.

In the warmth of the house and their casual clothes sat family and friends, although the word "family" might be a misnomer because two of these people were not yet family and, if Lucy had anything to do with it, they would remain "not-yet-and-probably-never" family members and these not-yet-and-probably-never family members were dreading the grilling they knew was about to come and hit them on this brittle evening with its frosty roads and frostier silences. The word "friends" might also be a misnomer. Friends were not usually warned to expect a cross-examination. Nor were friends normally warned that their host was "a terror" and "a bit of a bully" who took no prisoners and had little patience with time-wasters. And, as far as Mrs Meldrum was concerned, any meeting with no agenda was a time-waster, and that included groups of people around the Christmas dinner table. On top of that, she saw food as a distraction in much the same way that social media was a distraction, that planning was a distraction if the time for doing never began.

"Will you be skiing over the new year?"

"Depends on the snow, my dear."

That Christmas Eve, Lucy was being particularly like Lucy, but it was a Lucy reduced to her bare essentials. It was not that she was cold, she was glacial. Distant to the point of invisibility, she revelled in the power of "the mother," that is, the unchallenged power of the hostess to control and to guide and to dominate the kitchen, the dining-room and the long silences that caused the two guests to look around the room with imitation smiles on their faces while they fingered at their cutlery and stared into the darkness, wishing they were outside on the terrace rather than inside in the dining-room and awaiting their turn for a grilling.

"There's a car coming up the hill," Diana almost whispered to the air. "I can see the headlamps."

"The happy Father Christmas?" suggested Julia's friend Peter.

"Yes, that'll be Father Christmas," Lucy said and, with the suggestion of a smile, she added, "eager to be here and to spread his goodwill and cheer with us. But when, oh when, will he learn to be on time? Do you think we should offer him the turkey's cold shoulder?"

Glancing at Lucy, Tony assumed that she had intended to crack a joke, a joke which had, as usual, missed its mark, left its intended audience confused, and which had failed to spark the mirth and merriment that she wanted. Instead, there had been another interpretation of Lucy's comment, an interprctation which caused the newcomers to stop chewing, cutting, or swallowing and look at Lucy and then at each other. Perhaps they had heard disappointment, or perhaps they had heard the familiarity with which she uttered the words; or perhaps they had seen the patronising smile that had given away her true feelings for the world to see. What Tony heard was contempt or low regard, a public announcement that relegated "Father Christmas" to the level of manservant or houseboy.

"In the meantime," Lucy said, "let's eat before dear Santa Claus arrives. He and his beasts might eat it all for us. They must be hungry after all that travelling."

Armed with a knife and fork, Lucy pushed her turkey round her plate before dropping the cutlery and pulling at the meat with her fingers, tearing off a tiny piece, placing it between her teeth, grabbing at it with her lips and sucking it into her mouth. And while she chewed, she allowed her eyes to settle on each of the two new faces at the table. She knew the other eaters had their eyes on her, and the question in these eyes was: who is Lucy going to get her teeth into first?

"Julia tells me you are doing a PhD, Peter," Lucy said.

Peter gulped down his turkey and potato and nodded.

"Yes," he said.

"And in what area will your Doctoral thesis be, Peter?" Lucy said.

"Oh, please call me Pete," said the young man, moving sideways so his shoulder rubbed up against Julia's. "I prefer abbreviated versions of most things."

"Thesis, Peter," Lucy said. "Topic?"

"Memory construction," he said.

"Construction?"

Pete threw a weak smile at Julia before turning his face back towards his plate and stabbing a piece of carrot with his fork and lifting it to his mouth in a fist-like grip.

"The co-construction of memory-making," he said, waving his fork and the piece of carrot in front of his face, "through a shared community identity of Facebook."

"Understood," Lucy said. "Interesting. Please continue."

Peter shoved his fork into his mouth, scraped the piece of carrot off with his teeth and swallowed it.

"For much of history," he said, using his knife like a conductor's baton, "the only way to chronicle life was to write about it."

"Write? Yes, right," Lucy said.

"Right," Peter said. "But we've got more than just a pen and paper to record memories these days. Many of us now take selfies and share them on Facebook, create albums of our lives. And we use these to remember and review the past and memories sometimes change with them."

"In other words," Lucy said. "We can create out very own past. Is that right?"

"Correct. And this often means that there's no way of knowing what part of your memory, if any part of it, is the exact truth, and what part is creation."

"Indeed," said Lucy. "Fascinating."

"Indeed, it is, Mrs Meldrum. "Memory construction's quite usual with memories from long ago. Constructive processing's the retrieval of memory, but memories may be altered by newer information."

"Very interesting," Lucy said. "But, surely, mindlessly scrolling through past albums, depending on photos to recreate our memories, makes memory itself obsolete, Peter, does it not?"

"Pete," said Peter.

But Lucy had broken eye contact with Peter and she was now searching for her next victim.

"And what about you, dear," Lucy said to Diana. "Mario tells me you are in fashion. I don't suppose you take after your father, do you? I mean, fashion being what it is."

"What's fashion being, Mrs Meldrum?"

"A constant and shifting reality which has no end, and which can only be identified in the context of retrospect."

Diana stared at Lucy for some time before saying:

"Wow, I'd never have looked at it like that. And no, my father is..."

"Smile, please."

Mario had jumped up from the table and stood with a wide grin and his phone, positioned over his head, and in camera mode.

"Just creating memories of my own," Mario said.

The phone flashed, once, twice but then there was another flash from the not-so-distant but invisible neighbour property and it drew gasps from Tony, from Lucy, the children, and their partners. Golden streaks and red stars burst in the sky with sounds that made the air tremble. Until then, the world outside, the terrace, the trees and Captain Meldrum's garden shed, had been hidden in blackness, but this had been blown away by the fireworks and each flash revealed winter whiteness gripping the leafless trees, the shed, the bushes and the terrace tiles. There was also Ricky's car but no sign of Ricky.

"Bit late for Guy Fawkes night, isn't it?" Diana said.

"It isn't Guy Fawkes, actually. It's *la Befana*," Mario said. "You'd love her."

Diana was all studs, fishnets, torn stockings, and ripped denim.

"Never heard of her," Diana said.

Lucy turned he attention to Diana, looked her up and down and said:

"She's a witch."

Diana flinched as though a wasp had flown close to her face.

"What?" she said shaking her head.

"*La Befana*," Lucy said. "She's a witch,"

"Oh, I see," Diana said. "But witches don't exist, do they? Well, there are witches, but I mean, not the black-dressed variety with broomsticks and cats."

"Don't you believe in witches, dear?" Lucy said.

Diana shrugged.

"I never met a witch, but one does experience them from time to time."

"So, how would you know if you were experiencing one?"

"I might feel uncomfortable," Diana said.

Tony stirred.

"Ah, Diana," Tony said as if discovering her for the first time, "how long will you be staying in Italy?"

Diana smiled a winning smile at Tony and his wife.

"Until 2 January," she said.

"Just a quick trip then."

Diana grabbed at Mario's arm and glanced into his face.

"Yes, unfortunately," she said.

"Yes, indeed, unfortunately. My wife's right of course," Tony said. "*La Befana*'s a kind of Christmas witch, and she brings stuff for the kids on January 6."

"An Italian father Christmas then," said Diana.

"Almost, but not exactly. Here in the Veneto, we burn the effigy of the witch. Shame you won't be here to see it on the night of January 5. There are bonfires all over this area, and the children get sweets."

"Cool," she said. "And…"

And the dining-room door crashed open and everybody jumped. Nobody had heard the door open or close, but there was Ricky in the doorway with a red face, a red Santa suit, a runny nose, and frozen webs in his hair.

"Ha, ha, ha."

Everybody applauded, except Lucy.

"Don't you mean ho, ho, ho?" she said.

"I stand corrected. Ho, ho, ho."

"Indeed," Lucy said.

Ricky stared at Lucy.

"I see you gobbled up all the turkey, young lady," he said.

He placed his sack on the floor and handed out parcels to all and sundry. He started with Lucy.

"One for our esteemed boss," he said, "a very merry Christmas to you."

And then came a present for Tony.

"To my wonderful brother, Tony, for everything he's ever taken from me; I mean, everything he's ever done for me."

There were smaller packages for the younger and almost-family members.

"One for my nephew and one for my niece and two for your wonderful English friends. A happy Christmas to one and all."

"Happy Christmas, everybody."

"Happy Christmas," went the almost collective response.

"You're late," Lucy said.

And Father Christmas seemed to deflate.

"Ho…ho…ho," he said.

"So, did you get lost, Santa Claus?" Lucy said. "Or did you just lose track of time in the prosecco bar, dear?"

"Ho…ho," Ricky said. "The reindeer needed a drink."

"Or two," said Tony.

"We already started," Lucy said. "We didn't know if you were going to show or not."

She handed the menu across to him. He immediately waved it away.

"I'll have what you're having," he said. "And white wine's fine."

Lucy smiled at him but her eyes were stony. She made

the right moves with her cutlery but she just pushed her food around while the rest of the diners sat in an awkward silence. Ricky's arrival had filled the empty chair but unbalanced the table, killed imagination of the ghost in the room. The ghost had arrived. Ricky went silent and, for about half a minute, there was only the clacking sound of knives and forks on plates. Peter was the first to break the silence.

"Not hungry, Mrs Meldrum?" he said.

"She doesn't know what she's missing," Tony said.

"It's right there on the table in front of her," Peter said. "Of course, she knows."

Lucy allowed her cutlery to drop with a clatter on her plate.

"And now, Peter," Lucy said, "you're allowing your hidden depths to show. So, if you don't mind…"

"Oh, and what did you say you were studying, Diana?" Tony said.

"Fashion," Diana replied.

"The London School of…?" Tony said.

"Indeed."

"Final year?"

"I'm working on my final collection right now."

"Which consists of?"

"I'm not at liberty to say."

"You've got something to hide?" Lucy said.

"We all have something to hide, Mrs Meldrum. Drugs, alcohol, affairs…Tell me about your private life…no I'm only joking."

Tony managed a strained smile, but he wondered if the truth was obvious or that these newcomers had been informed about his marital situation.

"Have you been enjoying your stay in Italy?" Ricky said to Diana

"Yes thanks."

"Been to Venice yet?" Ricky said.

"Yesterday, actually."

"First time?"

"No, I was there with my parents."

"When you were a child?" Ricky said.

"No, just last year. Do you like Christmas, Mr Meldrum?"

"I wonder sometimes. I love the idea of Christmas, its good cheer and love for mankind. But it can be so dull, the dullness of closed shops, empty streets, grey cold and the smell of turkey or goose after eating too much of it."

"Yuk… Sounds grim," Diana said.

There was a flash of the camera again.

"Smile," said Mario, "we can now alter your memories."

Everybody laughed and flash, flash went the camera to capture the smiling moment.

"Did you know," Tony said, "it was in this very room that Lucy and I had our first dance."

"Wasn't it on the terrace?" Lucy said.

"We've heard the story of how you and Lucy came together," Peter said. "It was 1985, wasn't it?"

"Indeed, it was," Tony said.

"Indeed," said Lucy. "The very same room in which, long ago, he and I made such a firm acquaintance, danced the night away before sealing it all with a kiss on the terrace. Nothing much has changed. The walls are the same colour. The same tiles are on the floor."

"Is that how it was," Peter said.

Tony smiled.

"If that's what memory tells you," Ricky said. "But what about the things that've been forgotten or ignored?"

"What things, uncle Ricky," Julia said.

"Things like my brother and I."

"Doing what?" Julia said.

"I suppose you could say that we were casing out the joint."

"Admiring the guests, you mean? Sizing up the possibilities."

"No," Ricky said. "I mean casing out the joint."

"So, checking the place out?" Julia said.

"Scrutinising it? Mario said.

"No, not exactly."

"So," Mario said, "what exactly what were you doing?"

Good question, but Ricky had no answer and nor did Tony. There was no question that the evening still haunted the room, but individual people had been reduced, over time, to ghosts of sweating dancers, ghosts of young women swinging their hips, of touch, of Lucy's neck, her ponytail, those flashing come-hither eyes. Tony tried to recall the music thumping, but he couldn't. He tried recall a kiss, but he couldn't. He tried to recall himself and brother Ricky discussing possibilities on the terrace. But there was no memory. There was just a blank, an empty space.

"I suppose you could say," Tony said, "that we were wondering what our place on the terrace was."

"But you were the hosts," Lucy said.

"Not everybody knew that," said Ricky. "Some of them had never been invited. People like you, Lucy, for example."

Flash, flash went the camera.

"Smile please," said Mario, his camera at the ready.

But Tony was not smiling. He was watching his efforts, the redefinition of his marriage, vanish into the darkness. Redefining "them" presupposed a shared understanding of the past and the future but whatever it was that Tony recalled, it was not shared by Lucy or the man sitting next to her and looking more than a little ridiculous in his Santa outfit.

23

September 2014

Separation

There was nothing special about that particular day. It was just another glorious Sunday of light and lightness, and Tony was on the terrace preparing a light pasta for a light lunch. No, there was nothing special about the day, except that, on this day, Lucy had chosen to tell him that she had been forced, against her will, to make a life-changing decision. Tony had been mixing spaghetti with their favourite sauce, and the terrace breathed the freshness of olives, their aroma suggesting blueness and the deep green of Italian hills basking in sunshine.

"He just made an ultimatum."

Lucy made this remark in a tone which implied that the identity of "he," and the ultimatum he might or might not be making, was common knowledge but Tony, despite the glimmering light, was in the dark. He knew something was amiss because he saw it in the expression on her face, that give-away-nothing expression he had seen in her eyes before. It was the sort of expression that might precede bad news. It was the sort of expression that told people they were, in one way or another, redundant.

"Who did?" he said.

"Ricky did."

"Ricky made an ultimatum?"

"Yes, and…"

"Did he call you?"

"No, it was an email," Lucy said.

"And what does it say?"

"It's either him or you," Lucy said.

"Why now?" Tony said. "What's so special about now?"

While Tony watched the breeze playing with the trees, it occurred to him that his question was rhetorical. There was, in fact, nothing special about now. There was nothing special about this particular time or this particular day. There was nothing special about the Sunday people driving past their house in their Sunday cars to their Sunday hills, nothing special about their car radios playing their Sunday music, and nothing special about this music drifting over their terrace, trees, and plants.

"There's nothing special about now," Lucy said. "Ricky is unpredictable."

A flash of memory, of Ricky's rage, Ricky's fist, the big man's face, the blood.

"Yes, he can be," Tony said. "And this sounds a bit over-dramatic to me."

"Perhaps, he wants to show us who the boss is."

"Doesn't leave us much room to move, does it?" Tony said.

"No, it doesn't."

"In fact, we appear to have very little choice."

"He's not really giving choices," Lucy said.

Tony was still mixing the pasta with their favourite sauce, and the house and terrace breathed the aroma of olives, the world was touched by a warm wind, and Italian hills were basking in the late summer sunlight.

"So, him or me," Tony said.

Tony's comment was not so much interrogative as a statement. Adrift, in the depths of his mind, it had always been there, this doubt about the viability of a three-sided relationship. But now, Lucy had put words to his misgiving and dragged it into the daylight.

"That's the way he put it," Lucy said.

And it had seemed such a good idea on that warm morning in Asolo some five years previously, that quick fix, a papering-over of the cracks but, seen in retrospect, it was clear it was a fantasy, self-deception, or wishful thinking.

"So, he wants you back in Verona and he wants you there now and forever more, is that it?"

"Correct," Lucy said. "He's too traditional. A 'ménage a trois' is not for him."

"So, he sent you an ultimatum."

Tony raised his hand to his sternum as though his heart had missed a beat. He rooted himself to the spot, breathed deeply, widened his eyes, and the pasta pot slipped from his hands and crashed to the floor.

"Don't move," Lucy said, and, to the sound of trees rustling and a love song playing on a car radio nearby, Tony did as he was told. He stayed still while the pasta snaked and writhed around his feet, and Nat King Cole told the world that when he fell in love it would be forever. Tony remained still until the singer insisted that when he gave his heart it would be completely, and Lucy hurried back to the terrace with a liquid-detergent dispenser in one hand and a plastic bucket and sheets of paper in the other.

"An ultimatum?" Lucy said. "More or less, yes. Yes, indeed, that's exactly what he's given us."

"And how long have we got?"

"Does it matter how long?" she said, pushing him back

and away from the floor, the oil and the wriggling pasta. She threw paper over the mess and stood back.

"Yes," he said. "It matters how long."

"Not long," she said

"Tomorrow? Next week?"

Lucy crouched down on her knees, took some more paper from the bucket, wiped up the oil and then squirted some detergent on the floor.

"Soon," Lucy said.

While Lucy wiped, Tony remained still. He was feeling detached, not quite there, as if it was his shadow watching, talking, and listening while the real person stood to one side and looked on.

"How long, Lucy? How long?"

She wiped excess oil from the pot and handed it to Tony.

"Take this," she said.

"Lucy…"

"Just a minute," Lucy said, pushing herself to her feet. "I'll rustle something up."

She turned her back on him, and Tony watched Lucy carrying the bucket into the house. There was a clacking of plates, the electronic hum of an open fridge door, the thump of the door closing, a knife chopping and, some minutes later, Lucy reappeared with a tray of cheese and biscuits and olives. He was still standing where she had left him.

"Your brother," she said, sliding the tray onto the terrace table, "decided he couldn't live with the uncertainty. Didn't he tell you? Didn't you know?"

Tony's detached shadow shook its head and frowned.

"No," he said. "We've never talked about it."

"He was never happy that we two discussed it, and he was excluded from the decision-making process."

"That we presented him with a *fait accompli*?"

"Exactly," said Lucy.

"Why didn't he discuss it with us?"

"Because we didn't discuss it with him," Lucy said.

"My little brother must have a grievance," Tony said. "Something that happened when Dad retired, perhaps? But it's so long ago."

It was, indeed, a long time ago, but Tony believed he could see himself as he had been then, 25 years old and about to celebrate his father's retirement but so distant was that place where memory called that he could never be sure. Who was that person he saw in his mind's eye? Who was the young man, the lord of the terrace, observing the guests? Was it Tony as Tony had been at the time that he saw or was it Tony, the 54-year-old man, the man whose reflection he saw in the mirror every day when he shaved?

"Aren't you looking for something in the past that was never there," Lucy said.

"Don't patronise me," he said.

"No, not patronising you, Tony. I'm simply asking whether you're imagining things."

He recalled, or he thought he recalled, that she was standing alone on the terrace or was she sitting? Was she alone? He had always thought so, but now he was concentrating on it, he found that he was not sure. Perhaps, what he recalled was an idea of her, an idea that later developed into Lucy the loner, Lucy the indifferent rushing out of the past as a smell-induced memory. The terrace had been crowded but she was standing apart from the others, at least that is what memory told him, and memory recalled a warm and sultry evening, and he was searching for reassurance in the faces of fellow teachers, and that one girl, standing alone, just stared at him with her big eyes.

"We can all imagine things," Tony said. "But surely we can distinguish between imagination and truth, can't we?"

He thought he recalled holding her gaze, staring at her probably, but for no more than a few seconds and he thought that he saw something in those eyes that invited him to come over and talk to her, and it excited and teased him. Later, he convinced himself that she was a loner, one of a kind, and thus was she branded, the person he shared with himself and with others.

"Memories can be notoriously fake," she said.

Perhaps his memory was all or partly fake, or perhaps he was replaying choice selections from his memory. And what of those parts that had been omitted or forgotten? Tony did not recall deciding to make a move, but in his memory, he was suddenly in front of her and conversing about this and that and that and this, and then they were dancing in the dance area. And now, here they were, nearly 30 years later, still dancing but waltzing around the possibility of separation or divorce.

"What about the children," Tony said. "What'll we tell them?"

"They're not children."

"Have you told them?" Tony said.

"Do they need telling?"

"Of course, they need telling," Tony said, "before they find out for themselves."

"Don't you think they might've noticed something already? Didn't you know that Mario's now 27 and Julia's 25."

"I did speak to them about us and Ricky several years ago."

"After our trip to Asolo?" Lucy said.

"Yes."

"And what did you tell them?"

"I was evasive" Tony said.

"But you told them something, didn't you?"

"I think I suggested that we were redefining our relationship."

"So, what do you think they'll expect of us?"

"I guess that the children will trust us to make the right decision," Tony said.

"And what is the "right" decision?" Lucy said.

Tony opened his mouth to reply and hesitated before saying:

"Whatever we decide, it must be the right decision. But there are other things to consider."

"Like?"

"Like the school," Tony said.

"What about it?"

"We'll need to work together."

There was a silence and, in that silence, her eyes travelled over his forehead, down to his eyes and nose, his mouth. Eventually, she looked him in the eye with an enigmatic smile.

"Really?"

"Yes, really."

"Suppose we make you an offer you cannot refuse," she said.

Tony shook his head.

"You've lost me," he said.

"We could buy you out."

"Who are 'we'?" Tony said. "You and Ricky?"

Tony blinked when he saw a truth unfolding in front of him. And he blinked again. She of the blue eyes and the come-hither look was holding the right cards, and it had never occurred to him to try and understand the person who had dealt them. She had, possibly, planned this from the beginning, and he had been too blind to see her ambition, but the poison had spread and corrupted until, at last, it had burst out and lay like a pool of vomit on the floor, and he had not seen it until it was too late.

"Yes," she said. "Ricky and I."

He did not need to hear her. He was remembering the evening he had introduced her to his parents, remembering his ability many lovers have of turning a blind eye to any faults. There had been antagonism from the first exchange with his mother. The moment Lucy opened her mouth, uninvited, to speak, she appeared to dare the rest of the world to challenge her, to take her to task for behaving inappropriately, for saying the wrong thing. And he, wrapped up in his love for her, did not see a thing. She was wonderful. She was different. And where now was that fabricated wonder? Where now was that fabricated difference? Tony hardly recognised the person in front of him.

"We could push you out," she said.

"But why, Lucy? Why?"

There was a pause long enough for Tony to consider some answers to his question. She would push him out because she wanted to exercise her power. She would push him out because she wanted to take revenge on his parents. She would push him out because she wanted control. Perhaps, she would push him out because of his own infidelity, his little outings to the massage parlour.

"Why, Lucy? Tell me why."

Tony shook his head at her silence. He dared not ask her when the affair with Ricky had started. He did not want to hear that those wonderful first months and years of his relationship with Lucy, had been an illusion. He wanted to believe that every weekend had been an adventure. He wanted to believe that there had always been some new dream, a new dream town, new dream people, a new dream beach to visit. There was no time for reflection, no time for remorse but he knew now that the dreams they lived consisted of things that happened in the waking world and in the waking world they had come to rest.

"But why, Lucy, why would you push me out?"

Was it because of his visits to the massage parlours? The first time was just before Mario was born. He did not immediately see this as infidelity. Somehow, it was not he, Tony, who was betraying. It was someone he would eventually leave behind, an image of himself. But he had never considered that all his purchased lovers would leave their shadow on him until they at first singed and then branded. At the time, it all seemed so harmless. His lovers came with the present but the future would take them from him.

"Because I can," she said.

And Tony stared at the unfolding truth, the barely acceptable reality. Because-she-could had already led him to the seedier side of town. Because-she-could had already spawned the notion that she was capable of being unfaithful because she was young, because she was pretty and because she was independent. Because-she-could, she held her head so high and seemed to challenge others to touch her. Because-she-could had prompted his own pre-emptive strike. Such a strike meant that their life together had been nothing but a lie from start to finish, more than 20 years wasted on "what ifs," 20 years wasted on because-she-could, 20 years wasted on lies and deception.

It was when the children came that the trouble came to a head. It was not the children themselves but the concept of change that Tony had to come to terms with. Life with children was one of constant newness and there was no time for change in things new. Life with children was a changeless and unchanging world of sleepless nights, nappies, first words, first steps, first days at school, a world of neither shape nor shadow, where the paint had not dried. It was not a world where time stood still because time had simply not yet begun. He would stop his bad sexual habits in the future he had said to himself; but in a changeless and unchanging world, there was no future.

So, there was nothing special about that day, nothing special about Sunday people in their Sunday cars driving to their Sunday hills except that she had chosen that day to tell him that she had been forced to make a decision. Tony had been mixing spaghetti with their favourite sauce and the terrace breathed the freshness of olives, their aroma suggesting blueness and the deep green of Italian hills basking in sunshine.

"Everything has changed," he thought she had said. "He doesn't want to share me."

"How long do we have," he thought he had said.

"It doesn't matter how long," she might have said.

He stared at her, memories of his own infidelity flitting through his head.

"Of course, it matters," he thought he had said.

"He wants me back now."

"Now?"

But she appeared not to have heard his question. She was nodding and smiling to herself as some inner voices were congratulating her on the achievement of a deep and personal need, a need from which Tony was excluded. She turned her head towards him and, almost as an afterthought, she said:

"Not quite now," Lucy said. "Tomorrow. I'll be leaving tomorrow."

24

2015

The will and the way

"For God's sake, bro."

Ricky straightened up, slipped his hands from his pockets, and let them hover at his ears in a gesture of capitulation.

"You dare ask me i
f I'm sure?"

There was a crash, the table bucked once, twice, and the cups and spoons clattered on saucers. Ricky had brought his hands, palms down, hard, onto the tabletop, and he had not finished.

"God damn it," he said, hammering at the table with his open palm. "Of course, I'm sure, really sure."

The vibrating table marked the moment on that winter-cold and foggy morning in Verona when Tony thought his brother might be on the edge of violence, and he on the edge of receiving it. The warning signs had been there in his brother's growing agitation and anxiety, his staring eyes, the clenched jaw, and the furrowed forehead.

"Why, oh why," Ricky said, accompanying his words with more hand-to-table slaps, "would I make up a story like that?"

He took a deep and shaking breath, and leaned across the table to stare into his brother's face.

"She'd been making eyes at me the whole evening," he said.

"Really?" Tony said.

"Yes, really. I'd never seen anybody so beautiful," Ricky said.

"I never knew."

"Until you poked your nose in, she was mine, bro."

"Are you sure?"

The fog was alive. It rose. It fell. It rolled. It thickened and thinned. It swirled up and over, down and round the gas burners, giant mushroom-shaped burners standing sentinel over the table and chairs. The burners popped and flamed orange and blue, and the flame warmed things and people, people like Ricky and Tony sitting at their table in Piazza Bra on a wintry day.

"Am I sure?"

Beyond the fog, out of sight and on the edge of the square, waiters waited and customers shouted orders for coffee, for grappa, for cappuccino and their shouts were dampened and distorted in the fog and, all the while, cups rattled, a coffee machine hissed and spoons tinkled on unseen saucers. Ricky leaned forward, his shoulders rising and falling with deep intakes of breath.

"You really want to know if I'm sure or not?" he said.

"Yes," Tony said. "I really don't remember you being there at all."

He flinched. Ricky's wide-open eyes were unblinking, and the corner of his bottom lip, once gripped by his teeth, was now released.

"Not at all?"

"No, not at all, I'm afraid."

Ricky leaned back in his chair.

"Well, how convenient for you. Poor bro, let down by his memory."

"I didn't see anything," Tony said. "I tell you, Ricky, I didn't know."

"Well, let me tell you what happened, OK?"

"Go ahead," Tony said.

The fog had taken much of the world away. Bits and pieces of shops, bars and restaurants remained visible, but seemed to be floating oddities in the fog. Some of these oddities were of terracotta and yellow walls, some were the peeling remains of murals, others were no more than stretches of brickwork lit up by lamplight, while others were snatches of balcony railings pouring ivy over a wide arch beneath them. Tony's memory told him that the arch marked the entrance to an alleyway full of wine bars, trattorias, and hostels.

"I suppose it was love at first sight," Ricky said. "I didn't see her arrive at the house and nor did I see her come outside. She was just there, suddenly there, alone on the terrace. We were two strangers in the same place and at the same time and when we saw each other across that crowded place, there was an instant attraction, a spark, and I knew I'd found my life's partner. I never looked back."

"That's wonderfully romantic," Tony said.

He wondered if he sounded sincere but one look at his brother suggested that he was not listening. Ricky was utterly still but his face was tilted upwards, and he appeared to be attentive to the world above Tony's head, but there was nothing there but fog and more fog swirling in space.

"And what do you do?" Ricky said. "You swoop down out of nowhere and whisk her away from under my nose as if I'd never been there."

"And you remember being left with…what was her

name? Mary?"

"I think it was Mara," Ricky said.

"No, it wasn't Mara."

They both looked up with expressions that suggested the swirling fog might throw up the name they were searching for.

"Poor Mara," said Tony.

"Or Mary."

"It was Martha," Tony said.

"To hell with her name," Ricky said.

Both boys looked away, perhaps at the dim winter lights draped over doorways and gardens on the edge of the piazza, or perhaps at the seasonal decorations gleaming and winking, the shooting star flying over the side of the Arena, swooping up and down and landing with a splash near the central garden. But the girl's name was not to be found there. Nor did they find it when they looked over to Via Giuseppe Mazzini, Verona's best shopping street, now understated with fairy-lights hanging blurred and barely visible in the air and bathing shadow shoppers in their grubby glow. The past seemed to beckon and it seemed to Tony that it could take you with it and leave you in some unknown or unrecognisable place. But, come what may, neither he nor Ricky were going to remember the other girl's name.

"Her name will come back to us," Tony said.

"Whatever," Ricky said. "But Lucy was mine until you came along. She'd promised me a dance but you got in first."

"And you've never forgotten, is that it?"

"How can you forget a woman when you see her every day?" Ricky said.

"You sound like you really loved her."

"Love or loved? With or without the final letter?"

Tony said nothing. Unwilling to use the "L" word for fear of giving it a reality he was unable to deal with, Tony pretended to listen to the sounds around him. Shouts and whispers, sounds of car horns and bicycle bells were bouncing off the city walls, the city gates, and the arena itself and deceiving the two men with regard to closeness or distance. Figures, either alone or in groups, appeared and disappeared into side streets and alleyways.

"My memory tells me something entirely different," Tony said. "You hardly appear in them at all. I have a vague recollection of you sitting alone and…"

"So, I was the little bit-part brother who didn't exist. Perhaps, Mr perfect lost his perfect memory. How perfectly convenient for you."

Tony felt his face redden and he bit his bottom lip before saying:

"Listen, Ricky. If it was so important to you, why didn't you say something, eh? Why did you just sit there and let me walk all over you? And why are you telling me this now and after all these years?"

He was expecting a reply, a heated reply, but it never came. He expected a slap in the face but it never came.

"You don't get it, do you?"

"Get what?"

"Get what? You were Mr Perfect," Ricky said. "You'd always been Mr bloody Perfect. Mr Perfect, the apple of Mum and Dad's eyes. And who was I? I was just the younger son, the caring one, born and raised to step aside, to play second fiddle to my perfect brother while he took all the perfect prizes. And then, one day, I woke up and thought: *to hell with that.*"

For a moment, Tony was unsure how to react to a comment he had not fully grasped. Was Ricky being sarcastic or candid? Caught between a variety of probabilities he decided to ignore them all and continue with the offensive.

"Then don't talk to me about friendship. You've been deceiving me all these years with your brotherly love or whatever it is you say you feel."

No sooner were these words out and hanging in the air than Tony had doubts about having floated them there. When push came to shove, was it not true that we were all deceivers? Did we not all, each and every one of us, deceive by omitting important information, denying the truth, or exaggerating things, or by agreeing with an individual in order to preserve a relationship? He had even heard it said that the very purpose of language was not to communicate but to deceive.

"As you like," Ricky said. "Have it your own way."

And round and round they went in their circles. Back and forth, they traded the same words, the same insults, the same feelings, the same anger, and the same frustration. At the time, Tony was unable to say why the two of them stayed. Days later, after Tony had ruminated on this exchange, he thought he understood. It was the bond of brothers, once lost, but trying to find itself again against all the odds.

"And so," Tony said. "You set out to claim your rightful place, is that it? Crouching in the shadows until you got your chance to get what you always deserved, eh? Is that how it went?"

"No, that's not it."

"How and when did it happen?"

"I'm not sure how," Ricky said. "Nor can I say when. And I can't say it was something she did or didn't do. And despite what you might think, it was never an attempt to get back at you and pay you back. I was motivated by love."

Tony took a calming breath and nodded. Ricky looked towards the floor.

"It was," he said, "the realisation that this person was the air I breathe. When did it happen? That's not easy to answer. One day, and I can't recall which day, I couldn't stop thinking about her, her voice, her warmth, her eyes.

But I longed for each day to start so that I could be near her. And I had a longing to be near her all of the time and, all the time, I was imagining a future with her, one day, when it seemed that life would be unbearable without her. That's when it happened."

Tony touched his lips with his fingertips, nodded once, twice and several times more as though ticking off Ricky's main points and finding each one to be in order.

"I see," he said.

"How long have you known about Lucy and me?" Ricky said.

"Years."

"She told you?"

"Yes, she did. We told each other of our infidelities."

"I see."

"A few years ago, now, six years to be exact, we confessed to each other"

"But you'd guessed anyway?"

"I'd prefer the word "know," actually."

"How did you know, bro? How did you know that Lucy and I were an item?"

"I just put two and two together. The way you looked at each other, the…"

"When bro? When did you notice?"

Tony was floundering and on the defensive. What should he tell him? That he had spied on them from the hotel opposite? He had seen them in bed together? He tried to recall one other incident, but he was walking through a fog of memories and when he put his hand out to touch one, it dissolved to his touch.

"I can't put a date on it," Tony said.

"Now, I can tell you something else you don't know," Ricky said.

"Don't tell me," Tony said. "She's pregnant."

"Not exactly, dear brother of mine," Ricky said while looking down his nose. "Be realistic please."

"Then what is it?"

There was a long silence as Ricky at first pouted, before glancing at his brother and smiling.

"So," he said, "get your head round this, bro."

Ricky smiled. Tony shook his head.

"Around what?"

"This."

And he remained silent while throwing silent insults at his brother's face, enjoying the power he had over his brother: the power of having knowledge at his disposal, a power that earned respect and control.

"It's my will," Ricky said. "My last will and testament."

"What about it?"

"I going to change it," Ricky said.

"You're going to change your will?"

"That's right. Yes, I am."

Tony shook his head and stared at his brother.

"Why?"

"Because she asked me."

"And?"

There was a long pause.

"In case I should die first, I will leave my share of the school to Lucy."

"And if she dies first?"

"Her share will go to me. Whatever happens, you'll have to share with one of us."

Tony turned his head to stare into the fog hanging over the square. It was blocking the view of the central garden, touching his cheeks, covering his eye lashes, filling his nostrils. There was fog everywhere, even in his bones, and he shivered with cold.

"You know," Ricky said. "There's one advantage of winter that I've never considered."

"What's that?" Tony said.

"Ice-cream," Ricky said.

"You want to tell me about ice-cream?"

"I want to tell you that there's a good reason to eat more ice-cream in winter."

"Really?"

"Yes, really. For one thing, the fat will provide you with extra insulation over the winter months."

"And for another?"

"It melts more slowly than in the summer months. That means you can enjoy it just a little while longer."

"I'll keep that in mind," Tony said.

"You do that, bro," Ricky said. So, if there's nothing else…"

"Just one question," Tony said.

"Which is?"

"Which is this," Tony said. "Can't you see that it's what she always wanted?"

"Who? Lucy?"

"Right first time," Tony said.

"Are you telling me she wanted an ice-cream?"

"Unfortunately, not," Tony said. "Try again."

"The school?"

"Yes, the school," Tony said. "Listen to me, Ricky."

"I am listening, bro."

"When do you intend to…?"

"Oh, later this year, perhaps in the summer."

"So, you haven't seen a lawyer yet?"

"Not yet," Ricky said.

"Can you do me one favour?" Tony said. "The anniversary of Dad's death's coming up." We must do what we always do and celebrate the day."

"So, what do you want from me?"

"Can you at least wait with your will until we've marked the occasion of Dad's passing?"

"I'll do what's right," Ricky said.

"Promise?" Tony said.

Ricky nodded.

"Yes," he said.

25

2016

Stones and roots

Pulling back his arms and bending at the knee, Tony screamed into the wind.

"Rick."

His brother's name bounced once, twice around the mountains. Tony stood still, listening for a response, but he heard nothing but the fading echo and the rattle of stones bouncing into the void. He leaned back again, bent his knees, and threw the name out of his mouth.

"Rick."

Tony knew it was too late. Instinct told him it was too late. The hoarseness of his voice told him it was too late. Ricky was sliding out of control. There was no way he could slide back into control, unless he slammed into something hard and bone-smashing.

"Rick. Rick? Ricky, for God's sake…"

There was a sucking sound, the dead weight of stone drawing close to the mountain edge, a pause, and a drop into endless space. Then, there was a scraping of stone, quieter this time, the last dribs and drabs crackling over the lip of the ledge, down over the crags and into the void.

"Ricky. Please, no…"

Fear gripped him, held his chest in a vice.

"Ricky?"

Tony's mouth opened, his eyes stared, and he held his breath. Fingers were gripping the lip of the ledge. Toe-caps were scraping the rocks. Boot heels were sliding, their tread missing and slipping. Stones were flying to the heart-wrenching tremble of his brother's voice.

"Help me. Help me," Ricky said. "Help me, please."

Tony Froze. Tony heard. Tony saw. Tony stared at the abyss. Tony did nothing.

"Bro. Bro. Help me…"

There was a strangled scream. Muffled, guttural and heart-rending, it hit Tony like a punch to the solar plexus. Sickness was already setting in when Tony's world tilted sideways, and his head started turning. He grabbed at the rocks, felt his heart racing, the sweat dripping down his forehead, his cheeks and down his neck. Into this nightmare came Ricky's voice.

"Bro. For God's sake…"

The quivering began in Tony's jaw, spread to his arms, his legs and he heard it in his breathing.

Tony froze.

Nobody knows. Nobody will ever know.

His stomach turned.

It was an accident.

He was violently sick.

He did nothing. Nothing. Nothing. Nothing. He did nothing…

*

When Tony told me the story of that day on the mountain,

years had passed since the events themselves, and I was struck by his description of the small things, the unremarkable moments that usually elude memory and are lost forever. I recall his detailing of his initial experience of the mountains, their timeless space and stillness and his description of how each minute seemed the same as the one that had gone before. Even at the time, I thought that this picture was too elaborate to be accurate. It probably consisted of wandering memories of other climbs, and he had found a place to put them, compressed into one traumatic experience.

Tony admitted to me that eliminating his brother was a fantasy he had allowed his mind to consider. But on the way up the mountain his mind had been far away from ridding himself of his sibling. He told me he was concentrating on time in general and time in particular. At first, he focused on the repetitions that filled a minute: steps trudging, steps avoiding this and steps avoiding that, steps slipping here and sliding there and, as time went on, each minute was sensed as the backpack pulling and thigh muscles burning. Nothing, he said, was happening until he understood that one-foot-in-front-of-the-other trudging was happening, and once he noticed this, Tony realised that something was always happening. A cloud came. A cloud went. A boot slipped. A bird swooped. Peaks appeared from different angles. Peaks disappeared and peaks reappeared and sometimes they seemed closer and sometimes further away. And there were the minor incidents: arguments over the quickest route, the broken buckle on his ruck-sack, the flashes of irritation at slipping, losing balance or tripping over rubble. Nonetheless, mostly, it was one foot in front of the other towards the sky and further from the green of the trees beneath them and, Tony noted, if these slopes were not blessed with brotherly love, they were, at least, spared hate. Hate had no place in the world of rock, wind, and sky. And yet, in Tony's mind, there was always that thought:

Should I ask him about the will? Has he changed it yet?

This was, at least, what he told me later.

They made tea in the remains of a hut, and they rested there and ate their rolls, and looked down at the route they had taken, and up at the routes they might take to the final ridge now looking desolate in the morning light. They trudged on, and after hours of trudging, tripping, and sliding, they arrived at the top of the world. Waiting for Tony were those words, whispering to him from the edge of consciousness:

Is that all there is to a mountain summit?

So, what was it all about then, that moment, on that day, in that year and on that mountain? Tony told me that just before he and his brother Ricky trudged onto the summit, it had been tempting them onwards and upwards, to enjoy that sense of having earned it. Instead, it was not the summit that captured their attention, it was the world below, so endless, so green, and the world above, so infinite, so blue, so flecked with cloud that attracted their gaze. Maybe next time, Tony thought, the summit itself might take centre stage. It might offer that sense of accomplishment, the revelling in something they had already done many times in order to mark the occasion of their father's birthday.

So, what about the will? Have you changed it or have you had a change of heart?

"Happy birthday, Dad," the two boys said to a lull in the wind. Let me add that although the word "boys" is hardly an appropriate one to describe two men in their fifties, I have adopted it here because it was the children inside these adult bodies who missed their dad, the boys who climbed the mountain every year to remember the man who had encouraged them to "bag" this peak in the first place and who had passed away on this day some 17 years earlier.

"Well done, boys."

"Well done, Tony."

"Well done, Ricky."

Tony later confided to me that, several times that day, he had been obliged to struggle with other memories, memories that had surfaced on the trudge up the scree. He had allowed his mind to empty, and it revealed a dumping ground of things filed away, things he thought to be gone forever but things that revealed their presence to him when they were least expected. These revelations were helped by the fact that there was no need to imagine the summit because they had trodden on it many times before and so his mind was free to drift. As a consequence, when the trail flattened out and he walked up the final metres, Tony was about to raise his arms in a gesture of victory when, instead, there rose up a picture of his wife, Lucy, and his climbing-companion brother having sex in Lucy's flat.

The two boys expressed solidarity with a high five, and they hugged, as they always did on summits, congratulated each other on their achievement until a rush of wind silenced them. According to Tony, they watched the pale horizon and the mists gathering over it and the mist became clouds that rose higher and cast shadows on the hills. The whole valley stretched out beneath their feet. It was a valley of suggestion, a valley of memories from other climbs on this very mountain, and the lives of loved ones, gone but not forgotten. The side they had ascended was steep but it was a gentle slope when compared to what fell from under their boots. They kicked stones over the edge, and they were out of sight in a moment but the boys heard them, at distant intervals, striking the rock until the sound died away in the silence of distance.

Tony felt his brother's hand on his shoulder. He later

said that he almost brought the will-topic up at that point but decided against it because of the wind. Ricky leaned forward and shouted into Tony's ear:

"We'd better be going down."

Tony nodded and patted at his watch face with his index finger.

"And take it…," Ricky began in a moment of calm, but a gust of wind carried his words away and they went unheard.

Tony wiped at his face and he acknowledged that he was tired, his body hot and fatigued from the climb; the stop at the summit not long enough to recover. Picking his way through the debris of this mountain, Tony thought his mind, joints, bones and muscles were stretched in the same way that the hours were stretched because every step and every second required concentration. Sometimes, Tony recognized sections of the path they had climbed earlier, the sphinx-like pile of boulders, for example, or the pile of random rocks that put them one stumble from broken or chipped bones, but most of the time, coming from the reverse direction, the trail was so unrecognizable that, on several occasions, Tony wondered if they had lost the path. And several times, he stopped to rest his knees, to look around, and he felt happy that down there was the world they lived in, but he felt sadness at leaving this place where beauty lived, but he would take the memory home with him, keep it close beside him when he was in front of the computer, with students, parents, angry or demanding teachers and it might remind him of his growing sense of connection to the natural world. But the feelings he had while in the mountains were always difficult to put into words. He tried to explain them to Lucy. To be fair, she stopped writing to listen but she always stopped listening before he had finished.

Despite their fatigue, they started in haste. Ricky went first, stumbling, falling into things, getting scratched but getting moving even though, for both of them, it was clear that they had to take care of each footfall, to be mindful of risk. Eventually, the scree came to an end, the slope they had been part of was gone, and they left the trail, blinked at the sun, and felt both a wash of relief that this scree descent was over and a wash of dread that another would soon present itself.

"We would do well not to forget Dad's comments about ascending and descending," Tony said.

Ricky shook his head.

"Remind me," he said.

"He said something to the effect that on the ascent, the climber's eyes looked up to the sky and made a climber feel small, but…"

Ricky nodded.

"But on the way down," he said, "a mountain always needed concentration and each step needed careful placement and each step brought the mind from the sky to the interior of oneself."

"Exactly," Tony said, "the descent shrinks the world to stones and roots."

"A dangerous place," Ricky said.

And Tony put a hand on his brother's shoulder.

"We should both take care," he said.

"Of what?"

Tony looked at the stones and roots at his feet.

"Of descents," he said, "of being too late and having to make deathbed reconciliations."

Ricky scanned his brother's face and frowned.

"You alright, bro?"

"I'm fine," Tony said. "I just want to say…"

Ricky shook his head and held up his hand.

"Stop," Ricky said. "Keep it until later."

Tony nodded. Ricky was right. The afternoon was the time for the descent and the descent was not the time for discussions of a private nature, discussions about brotherly love, for example, or lack of brotherly love, of late-in-life reconciliations that bore witness to terrible waste. Nor was the afternoon a time for questions about last wills and testaments, especially when the path they were following was getting rougher.

Not only was the path getting rougher, it was skirting deep precipices and chasms until it seemed that there was no path, and they reached an airy rock band, a 10-metre-long mountain pass, so very exposed that it needed concentration both on the way up and on the way down.

The ledge was the last challenge, and Ricky was tackling it first because tradition dictated that Ricky tackled it first, and Tony waited for Ricky's signal that he should take his turn. The usual high 5 and slaps on the back, and Ricky slid sideways for a few metres before dropping to his haunches. He leaned back from the precipice, took his weight on his arms, and stretched out his legs to use his heels as feelers and brakes. It was a manoeuvre that had always worked for both of them. Tony watched every inch of his brother's progress to the ledge, alert to the tumbling stones and rocks, listening for anything extraordinary, a rushing-and-grating stone-fall, for example, or the shrieks and cries of human mishap.

When Ricky disappeared from view, Tony was stricken by a sense of abandonment. Far above the level of human sounds and habitats, open to the elements and dwarfed by the ridges, the peaks and the crags, Tony shrank in his aloneness, his fear, and the insecurity of being in a place of wind and rock with dusk approaching and he, standing on the wrong side of a precipice.

He calmed himself by drifting with his thoughts. This was not the first time he and Ricky had climbed this peak but, no matter how many times they climbed it, Cima Palon would always be different. Tony assumed the difference was down to the fact that it was the internal summit they reached, the summit of emotional and spiritual fulfilment and this, Tony thought, gave them a better knowledge of themselves. He supposed that, in the final analysis, this was what drove them to climb in the first place. Climbing mountains had certainly taught him more than he had anticipated. Climbing mountains had taught him that good boots were vital. Climbing mountains had taught him that cameras were not waterproof and that his problems seemed smaller when he was involved in solving them. Climbing mountains had taught him patience and gratitude. Climbing mountains had taught him to appreciate the simple things in life, like water, a piece of chocolate or an emptying of the bladder or bowels. Climbing mountains had taught him to be mindful, and to be off the hill before the night came. Climbing this mountain made him realise just how much he loved and missed his father. Climbing this mountain made him realise just how much he still needed his father's approval. With tiredness setting in, Tony knew that climbing mountains could be dangerous.

Tony's heart thumped. There were sounds. Experience told him these were something-was-not-as-it-should-be-with-Ricky sounds. Heels were sliding. Rocks were cracking. Stones were cascading over the edge of the mountain and into oblivion. Tony peered into the abyss. Ricky was a shadow, flickering across the rocky buttress, out of control and heading for the mountain edge. Tony's heart thumped again. The shadow torso was now raised, the arms stretched out, and it was heading helter-skelter towards the abyss. Tony cried out in alarm.

"Rick?"

There was no human response. There was the sound of gravel shifting. There was the sucking of his own deep breath. There was the sound of Ricky's heels sliding and accelerating towards a 500-metre drop to almost certain death.

"Rick?"

The desperation in Tony's voice was followed by a rattle of stones bouncing into the void.

No, please, stop, stop, man…

"Help me. Help me," Ricky said. "Help me, please."

Tony's mouth opened, and he held his breath. Fingers were gripping the lip of the ledge. Toe-caps were scraping at the rocks. Boot heels were sliding, the tread slipping and stones flying to the heart-wrenching sound of his brother squealing.

"Help me. Help me," Ricky said. "Help me, please."

Unable to move, Tony looked on and vomited while his brother struggled. But his mouth was still producing extra saliva, his stomach contracted and he heaved again. He felt a bead of sweat rolling down his forehead, his heart thumping against his sternum and both sweat and heart were racing and holding him, preventing him from movement. And then, Tony heard his father's voice. His father's shadow covered him. His father's finger pointed. His father's finger accused, tried, and condemned.

He's your brother. If you don't pull yourself together and help him, you might just as well slaughter him with your hands. Either way, I will hold you responsible for Ricky's death.

Tony closed his eyes, retched once more, and slid down to the ledge where his brother was floundering. The wind had become so violent that fear of vomiting was replaced by fear of death, fear of being thrown off balance and finding himself whirling in space and dropping down to the rocks below. But movement had released him, cut him loose from the fear that had gripped him. Ricky was at a bend in the path, a mere 2 metres away. Tony later said he felt his nerves grow tense with expectation but after that, he must have acted on instinct. He recalled very little except the feeling of his hands around Ricky's wrists and the strain on his muscles when he pulled him up and dragged him to relative safety. He later said he became aware of the familiar feel of his brother's skin and how Ricky found a foothold and slid over the edge, rolled over and lay on his back. Neither man was ever able to say accurately how long they lay on the ledge but Ricky later gave me his version of the conversation with his brother.

"I guess you just saved my life."

"You're my little brother," Tony said.

"And I thought for a moment you were suffering…"

"…from what? Fear? Vertigo?"

"I thought you might want to let me fall…"

"Don't talk. Save your energy."

"I would not blame you, old thing." You know, don't you? I mean…the will. We already changed it. That means that had I died today…"

Tony shook his head.

"I'd be sharing the school with Lucy?" he said.

"Something like that."

"What I know is this," Tony said. "There's still a steep descent. Save your breath. We need to be down before the night comes."

Tony was checking for injuries when he sensed rather than saw Ricky's eyes. They were fixed on his while Tony fretted over his brother's ashen face. He checked Ricky's limbs. He felt Ricky's palms. He looked into Ricky's eyes. He felt the rhythm of his heart.

"You need some sugar," Tony said.

He opened his rucksack and pulled out some chocolate biscuits.

"Eat," Tony said.

Tony's hands were numb, and the air-filled spaces inside his forehead and cheekbones were telling him how cold they were and swelling up and hurting his face. There was wetness on his cheeks and the slow realisation that it was snowing, and Tony wondered what he would do if Ricky was unable to carry on and just as quickly put the idea out of his head.

"Listen to me. Eat the biscuits. Drink some water. We are going to get off this ledge and we'll reach the hut at the bottom of the slope. And we'll do this before night falls. Once we start, you keep your weight forward and you take small steps. Have you got that?"

Ricky nodded.

"So, what did I just say," Tony said.

"Keep my weight forward and take small steps?"

"Right," Tony said,

And Tony leaned forward and Tony put his arms around his brother and pulled him close, held him tight. And tighter and tighter he held him, and he rubbed Ricky's back until he experienced the rightness of holding this person in his arms and feeling at peace with himself and the world. He kissed Ricky's forehead and stroked his hair and only when Tony felt the shaking lessen, did he pull himself away. He then covered Ricky's hands with his and rubbed them warm.

"Now," Tony said, "we're going to get off this mountain. First, we go along this ledge and we do it one step at a time, got that? Just stay close behind me but we must try and keep moving, OK? Always keep moving. There is so little light left."

"Yes," Ricky said.

"And I don't want to hear any nonsense from you, got it?"

"About...?"

"About letting you fall to your death," Tony said. "You're my brother and I love you."

"Got it," Ricky said.

"Got it."

"Are you ready?"

"Ready," Ricky said.

*

I wrote this chapter from memory, not my memory because I was not there, but from Tony's memory. Most people I know always guard their memories carefully and Tony is no exception. Memories tell us the story of our lives and give us a sense of who we are. The problem is that we often think that memories are stored in our brains in the same way that this story of mine is saved on the hard drive of my laptop. The data on my computer can be retrieved next day and the story is still there the following day, word for word, line by line, full stop to full stop.

Unfortunately, memory is different. Remembering is an act of storytelling, and a memory is only ever as reliable as the last time we accessed it. And, because our attention and mental resources are limited, we cannot remember everything. Our memories are, therefore, selective and this is particularly true when we are under stress, like the situation in the mountains, for example. Tony was adamant that he recalled the details I have included in this chapter. For example, I have written:

"Nothing… seemed to happen until he understood that one-foot-in-front-of-the-other trudging was happening, and once he noticed this, Tony realised that something was always happening. A cloud came. A cloud went. A boot slipped on a boulder. A bird swooped. Peaks appeared from different angles. Peaks disappeared and peaks reappeared and sometimes they seemed closer and sometimes further away."

Did Tony really remember this?" Or were these words later additions, assumptions that he believed to be true? Essentially, I am saying that Tony's account of Ricky's fall in the mountains that day is unreliable. Furthermore, when in a state of stress, people tend to focus on the source of the threat rather than their own thoughts. It is, of course, very possible that Tony had some kind of panic attack before helping his brother. We know he had experienced one before and on that very mountain. But, somehow, I doubt it.

26

May 2019

Adam and Eve

Even Julia and I were invited, albeit at the last moment. We accepted at once, and we looked forward to revelling in that warm and comfortable sensation that is born from being with family, the select few who, we are so often told, never turn their backs on you.

Lucy had always been so vague about them. The words "Mum" and "Dad" and "my parents" hardly ever turned up in Lucy's mouth during conversation. Whenever she was asked about her parents, she would either change the topic or claim she did not know where they were or what they were up to. The long and the short of it was that her parents never came to visit and after a while, Julia and I questioned their very existence.

Dad, being the dreadful snob that he is, was not a great help. He seemed uninterested, did not understand why Lucy had agreed to see them at all, and he remained tight-lipped about them. Julia and I, on the other hand, were anxious to hear stories and experiences from their lives.

They were a part of us, and held a key to our own cultural heritage and to a better understanding of who we are and why. So, when Mum phoned and told us that her parents would be visiting, and that they would be staying in Italy for an unspecified length of time, we jumped at the chance to meet them. The word "unspecified" was too vague to play with. Anxious not to lose this opportunity, Julia and I flew to Treviso and we turned up on the terrace to meet our maternal grandparents on a beautiful evening in May.

*

Their visit kicked off around 5.00 o'clock. It started with the car horn tooting, headlamps flashing, engine-revving, car-doors and boot slamming. Soon afterwards, Lucy and Ricky appeared with two elderly people in tow, and they all trudged up the steps, through a gate and into the house. Tony and Mario brought up the rear struggling with enormous strapped-and-buckled leather suitcases.

"Think they have the kitchen sink in this one, Dad"

"Not in that one, Mario. I've got it here."

Finally, by 6.00, everybody was down on the terrace.

Perched on the high stool, one elbow on the bar and his chin resting in the palm of his hand, Tony surveyed the unfolding scene from above. Aloof, he listened, and aloof, he watched, and while his eyes flickered from one speaker to another, he internalised, he examined, and he judged and he remained buddha-still and realised that even after all those years, the arrival of his in-laws was making him curious. He tried very hard not to study their faces for signs of family resemblance, but he could not quite stifle his satisfaction that there was no family resemblance that he had noticed.

Back in the 1980s, he had been young enough to take their absence personally. Later he was resentful because his children had never got to know their maternal grandparents. But hurt and resentment had run their course and had long since fizzled away along with his failing marriage. There was no longer a need to make excuses to himself for feeling indifferent to their arrival, but mild curiosity appeared as nagging short-form questions in his head.

Why now? Had hearts softened with age? Perhaps they were ill. Maybe they were homeless? Why here? Because their daughter was here? Because they wanted to see their grandchildren? Because they were too old to care for themselves? What did they want? A meeting with their wider family? Money? Shelter? To avoid a care home?

Tony decided to stop thinking and to watch, listen and wait. Hearts can change. Hearts can be unpredictable and such moments in life could become milestones. It was, perhaps, ironic that this was the terrace on which he had first met Lucy some 33 years previously. In fact, he mused, it could almost have been the same balmy evening, the same rumblings of distant thunder, the same clicking cicadas, the same scents blowing up from the valley, the same fragrance of flowers and the same stars twinkling in the same positions in the evening sky. But it was not the same evening and Lucy was not the same woman. Age was eating its way through her, thinning her hair, and widening her hips and thighs. But she thought, and often said, that she was still an attractive woman although she hated the word "still" because it was somehow judgmental in tone, and suggested that being attractive had a poor prognosis.

"Everybody, please," Lucy said. "Can I formally introduce you all to my parents?"

She paused, waiting for a silent moment. When she had the attention of the family, she said:

"Please say hello to Adam and Eve."

Silence. Eyes narrowed, foreheads creased and eyebrows rose. It was Julia who prevented the silence from becoming embarrassing by blurting out:

"Lovely to meet you both."

"Likewise," Mario said.

There were murmurs of greeting and welcome from Tony and Ricky. Tony also threw a welcoming but absent-minded smile across the terrace. He had already sent his mind back to another time and another place. It was a time of revelations, of Lucy coming clean and admitting her lies about her parents and where they had come from. It was also a time of heartache, a place in Soho, a place of fine dining in the European tradition, a place of sex and glamour and a place frequented by politicians and sports stars. He also recalled the name of the club. According to Lucy it was called The Adam and Eve club.

"When did you both arrive?" Julia said.

She was sitting on the edge of a wicker chair. Every bit the demure girl, she was leaning forward, legs folded beside her and her hands folded in her lap. A permanent smile, such a sweet smile, had set on her face.

Lucy made a sound, a long sound, and in the manner of a singer searching for the right note. Eventually, she said:

"It's complicated."

Tony rolled his eyes.

"Take your time," he said. "There's no hurry."

They look like they have revelled in life. Am I being charitable? Should I not call a spade a spade? They both seem ragged, used up and at the end of their tether.

Tony was delighted at the expression containing the word "tether." So much better than the word "rope," and he allowed his mind to focus on the word's origins: old English? Germanic? And while Lucy told them all that Adam and Eve had flown in to Venice the previous evening, Tony smiled and nodded and encouraged, and decided the word "tether" was probably Nordic in origin.

"And we decided to spend the night in the airport hotel," Lucy said, "and see a bit of the city before coming here."

"How long are you going to be here?" Mario said. "We'd like to take you back to Venice."

"And drink prosecco on the Lido," said Julia, "on the terrace of the Grand Hotel des Bains."

"Prefer a beer myself," said Adam.

"Whatever takes your fancy," Julia said.

"And there's Asolo," Mario said.

"And Bassano del Grappa," said Julia.

"Not to mention Vicenza, Verona and the Dolomites," Mario said. "Perhaps we should visit Cortina."

Tony glanced at brother Ricky. Hovering at the doorway to the house, between two terra-cotta pots now brimming with white and pink hydrangea, Ricky seemed flustered. Perhaps, he had been expecting to simply drop in, say hello and move on.

"And will we get to see more of you," Julia said, "now you're both here?"

"And who are you, dear?" Eve said.

"I'm Julia, your granddaughter."

Eve nodded but said nothing.

"And I'm Mario."

"Yes, dear."

Tony thought Ricky was looking increasingly unsettled. Perhaps, it was the children's questions and suggestions that were bothering him. The palms of both his hands were pushing at the doorframe, and Tony received a picture of that mythical figure, Samson, betrayed by the woman he loved, blinded by his enemies, and now determined to end his life and the lives of those now gathered in the house and garden by using his immense strength to break supporting pillars and bring the house crashing down on them all.

"They've come a long way," Lucy said, by way of

explanation to a question that had never been asked or answered.

Tony noted that Lucy never mentioned where they had come from. How far was "a long way"? It was all relative.

"Anyway, it's lovely to meet you both," Tony said.

He heard the patronising tone of his voice and recalled the promise he had made to his mother that he would never treat the elderly with disrespect. She had told him that inside an old body there still lived a young person, so he stared into Eve's eyes and searched for the girl who had lived and loved, but he saw only the old woman who was forced to accept that her fate lay in the hands of others. Tony switched his gaze from Eve, to Adam, and back to Eve.

"Lucy's told me a lot about you, both," he said.

"Who did?" Eve said with a smile of her own that touched her lips but which failed to reach the eyes.

"Your daughter."

She shook her head and continued shaking it until Adam leaned over and stage-whispered in Eve's ear:

"He means the girl."

The shaking became a nod and understanding brought life to her eyes.

"Lucy? What was it you said she did?"

"She told me a lot about you," Tony said.

"Did she really?"

"Yes, I hear you used to run a club in Soho," he said.

"Remind me where that was, could you, dear?" Lucy's mother said. "My old grey matter…"

"Not what it used to be?" Tony said.

"Spot on."

"London. The Adam and Eve Club?" Tony said.

There was an intake of breath, an open mouth and flashes of enlightenment in Julia's eyes.

"So," Julia said, "you gave your names to the club or…?"

"Not quite dear," Eve said. "My name is Evangelica."

"What a beautiful name. It's Greek, isn't it?"

"Yes, it…"

"But you did run a club called the Adam and Eve Club," Tony said.

"Dad…"

"Just a minute, dear," Tony said. "The Adam and Eve club?"

"Oh, that one. Yes, we sold up, dear……er…Tony, isn't it?"

"Yes, it is," he said. "And you went to France, didn't you?"

She looked at her husband, who was nodding off.

"At least, that's what Lucy told me," Tony said.

From the corner of his eye, Tony saw Adam raise an affirming finger.

"Yes, that's right, dear. We went to France."

"Sunshine, sports cars and wine, good food and beautiful people," Tony said.

Her chin tilted in Tony's direction but there was nothing in her eyes, no interest, and no emotion. It was unnerving the way those black pupils peered at him.

"Is that so?" she said.

"And not necessarily in that order," Tony said.

"Is that all you can say about France?" Eve said.

"Just a simplification," Tony said. "Didn't you like the food in France?"

"I didn't say that," Eve said.

"No, you didn't," said Tony. "How long will you be in Italy?"

The old lady glanced at him with an irritated expression on her face that suggested Tony was a fool.

"That depends, dear."

Tony leaned back in his wicker chair and rolled his eyes to a wisp of cloud that had temporarily blocked the sunlight.

"I see," he said. "So, we'll have plenty of opportunities to talk. I look forward to them."

"Likewise," said Eve with a smile. She turned her head to Lucy and said, "Can you take me to the toilet, dear?"

Lucy took her by the arm and the two of them disappeared through the door and into the house. Adam appeared to be sleeping. Julia swung round to face her father. Her cheeks were red, her eyebrows lowered and her mouth downturned, and she stared at her father before saying:

"Dad, what do you think you are doing? You just made it clear that you don't want them here."

"They are so drab and colourless," Tony said. "And their clothes are too big for them."

"What's got in to you, Dad? They're old people. What do you expect?"

"They give me the creeps," Tony said. "

"The creeps? Dad..."

Julia was on the point of tears. Mario put a comforting hand on her shoulder.

"Neither absence of colour nor the size of the clothes makes people bad, Dad," Mario said.

"And Mario and me have come a long way to see them," Julia said through her tears. "Please, whatever your feelings towards Mum, give these people a break, will you? Think about us. Just for once, please, think about us."

For several moments, Tony said nothing. There was nothing to say. Julia and Mario were right. He certainly had not warmed to Adam and Eve. But that was no reason to bully them. He consoled himself with the thought that oversized clothes might be reminding him of his own childhood and his mother's tendency to buy his and Ricky's clothes at least one size up. It must have been a hangover from the war years when new clothes had been difficult to come by.

"I am thinking about you, dear," Tony said. "Believe me, I'm thinking of you."

But Julia was going to have the last word.

"You've got a strange way of showing it," she said.

But Tony hardly heard her. It was strange how childhood events could influence your whole life. Even now, Tony found it difficult to put up with trousers that were too long or shirts that were too baggy. When he was a child, he had, at least, grown into them, but Lucy's parents were in their mid-eighties and nobody grew into their clothes in their mid-eighties. These two had already lost so much weight and body tension that they either curled into armchair corners and nodded off or leaned sideways over the armrests, crossing their spindly legs beneath them. But Tony knew that by entertaining this idea, he was refusing to admit the obvious. As it was, he merely smiled his friendly smile and acknowledged that the sight of Lucy's parents sparked off an internal conflict and that this conflict stemmed from competing reactions to these elderly people, one of which was so outrageous, he was unable to immediately express it in words.

"Is anybody hungry?"

It was Lucy. She had now reappeared on the terrace with her mother and a tray of snacks and drinks. She put the tray on a side-table and made a "screwy" movement with her hand from behind her mother's back.

"Has Lucy found us a place to live," said Adam, who had suddenly woken up.

"Apparently, we'll be staying in the hotel, dear; the one next to the school," Eve said. "At least that is what I've been told."

Tony was only half listening. He had believed that if he kept probing, he might hear stories from his parents-in-law, stories about their youth and their years of hope. He had believed that he might, if he was lucky, learn something new about Lucy and her background from her parents' point of view. He somehow guessed that neither on this notable evening nor on other notable evenings would he learn anything new, anything revealing, at least not directly, not from the mouths of these old people.

Tony looked round and found Adam's eyes with his.

"Lucy tells us you have recently come from Thailand," he said.

"Recently?" Adam said. "Was that yesterday or last week? I can't tell you what I had for dinner last night, chum."

There was a fleeting upturn of the corners of the old man's mouth and then his eyes narrowed and he started giggling, a sound which got louder with attempts to suppress it. Tony was about to laugh with him to promote bonding, ease stress and anxiety until he realised that the old man was not laughing along with him, he was laughing at him, and Tony found it unnerving, might even have used words like offensive and threatening had he not remembered the contents of an article he had recently been reading entitled, "Ageing is not for cowards" in which the eminent author, writing in a well-respected journal, had suggested that laughing at inappropriate moments could be an early indication of dementia.

"The man wants to know where we've arrived from, dear," Adam said to Eve. "Thailand? Have we come from Thailand?"

"I think you have," Lucy said.

"So, not Bulgaria?"

"Well, you should know, Mummy," Lucy said. "You were born there."

"Sorry, dear, I almost forgot."

Lucy glanced at Tony.

"And did Mum tell you where she and Dad met?"

"She didn't," Tony said. "So where did they meet?"

"I have already told you," Lucy said. "Don't you remember?"

"The club in Soho? That's what you told me," Tony said.

"Is that where it was? Soho?" Eve said.

"You recall that club in soho don't you?" Tony asked of Eve.

"Course I do, dear. Do you recall that place, dear?" she said to her husband.

But Adam was fast asleep and in his own land of make-believe.

"That's where we decided to take on Lucy," Eve said.

Tony stood up and strolled towards the side table and helped himself to a sandwich and a glass of wine.

"Anybody else hungry?" he said.

He was watching Lucy carefully, enjoying the slackening of her jaw, the curve of the eyebrows. He had seen these signs of embarrassment before, but he had never before seen her mouth actually drop open as it dropped open now, perhaps to the phrasal verb "to take somebody on" with its implications of "somebody" being already there and in existence.

"You mean you decided to start a family?" Tony said.

"Kind of."

"The point is," Lucy said. "They're both broke. Not a penny between them and they need my help."

At this point, Ricky stiffened, lowered his hands from the doorframe and stood motionless as if he had seen a gun pointing at him.

"They're suffering from an early form of dementia," Lucy said, "They've no way of looking after themselves and have nowhere to stay."

Ricky was still motionless except for both arms, which appeared to have a life of their own and which were now fingering at the hydrangea beside him, pulling at their heads and crumpling them in his hand.

"I therefore propose that they come and live with Ricky and me in the school flat until such time as professional help is available. So long as Ricky agrees."

Ricky gave no indication that he had heard anything at all, but stared at the terrace floor in front of him while his fingers squeezed at the flower petals.

"Does Ricky agree?" Tony said.

"Ricky always agrees," said Lucy.

But Ricky neither replied nor shifted, but stared at some point on the floor, looked sideways at Lucy as if he had seen a ghost and turned his head away. As he did so, his eyebrows knitted together and the sides of his mouth rose in an expression of either distaste or disapproval. He stepped away from the door and ambled over to Tony. Stopping at Tony's table, he leaned over and whispered in Tony's ear:

"What on earth is she up to now?"

"I don't know," Tony said but if you need a place to stay there's always a bed for you here."

"You think I'll need it?"

"It's these two old people," Tony said.

"What about them?" Ricky said,

Tony shook his head.

"I don't know," he said. "But change is afoot. Mark my words."

Indeed, Tony did not know, but his gut feelings were remarkably accurate. He had sensed something so out of the ordinary, something so dark that he dared not give it a reality by putting it into words. This extraordinary, unexpected, and dark "something" had arisen when he noticed a reluctance on his part to use the words "parents" to describe these old people. This extraordinary "something" needed to be put in a box with a firm lid. The box needed an attached label and on this label was the word, "unthinkable," and because it was "unthinkable" the thought remained unmentionable. Tony knew that to put words to the unthinkable would be to release them, give them life, the possibility to change lives and this was something that, at the moment, Tony was loathe to do.

In the manner of many late afternoons between March and September, the afternoon breeze was picking up and carrying the same warmth as that of the morning but if Tony was hoping to hear his guests rambling on about this and that or that and this or hear a story or two emerging in a haze of night perfume, he was going to be disappointed. He was not listening. His mind was whirling but he did not blame himself. Collaboration with others was essential for human life and trust meant acceptance of risk regarding the other person. He thought he knew Lucy. He thought he could trust her. He was wrong. He did not even know who she was or where she came from and it was very possible, in fact he was sure, that Lucy didn't know who she was or where she came from either.

27

February 2020

Wonderful

I began this story with the confidence of extreme youth but the more I write, the further this story goes, the older I get, I am really not at all confident in my ability to answer important life questions. For example, are there people in this world best described by the adjective "good" and people best described by the adjective "bad"? And if there are "bad" people, should I avoid them and condemn them because they are bad? Shouldn't I define what I mean by "bad" but, if I did, would that be nothing more than just my opinion? Some people might judge my "bad" people as "good" people. Should I disown my paternal grandmother because she was racist and more than a bit "hoity-toity"? Should I condemn my paternal grandfather for hating Germans and being a snob? As for my maternal grandparents, should I be ashamed of my maternal grandmother because she was, apparently, an immigrant who worked in a dubious London club, and should I condemn my maternal grandfather because he might have been a pimp? But, above all, should I condemn my mother because she told lies about herself, appeared to disown her own parents and kept them from us, their grandchildren?

So, let's look again at both my parents. At the school, they are obliged to categorise people as either good performers or bad performers or, at very best, less good performers. Should I categorise my parents in a similar fashion? After all, I could describe my mother as a bad person, a liar, who has lived a life focused on herself. But I also appreciate that she is more than that. On a personal level, I can understand why she invented her own life history. Not everybody has the perfect childhood we sometimes see in films and TV. Anyway, how many of you, dear readers, can put hand to heart and say that you have never told lies, even little white lies, about yourselves or your parents in order to create a better impression?

As for my father, he is also flawed, trapped in the past and trying to live up to the standards of masculinity, fatherhood, and professionalism he associates with his own father. He is romantic, but a snob. He wondered why his mother was unable or unwilling to see how perfect Lucy was and yet, he treated other women with disdain. He is vacant as a husband and father and deluded into thinking that a business transaction, for example, selling language classes, is like a social service. He despises those people providing other services like drugs and sex even though he indulges in sexual services himself. He clashes with the more pragmatic, progressive Lucy and, in my opinion, he is largely responsible for the family breakup.

What hurts me is that he describes his first memory of my mother as a ponytail. In this respect she was, perhaps, little more than a doll for him to project his ideal wife onto, and when she showed him that she was more than this, he could not handle it. And let's remind ourselves here that people are not perfect, and nor are they solely good or solely bad. As for the bits we don't like? Perhaps, forgiveness is the answer or am I being simplistic? But let us now eavesdrop on Tony and Ricky. They are discussing aspects of some of these questions right now.

*

"This Covid-19 business has slowed the legal process," Ricky said.
"Divorce was never going to be quick," Tony said.
"It never is," Ricky said. "Or so I've been told."
"The stumbling blocks are the financial and business ties," Tony said. "We'll have to split everything."
"And the school?
"And the school," Tony said.
"I'm not comfortable with it," Ricky said.
"With what?"
"All this," Ricky said throwing up his arms
"All this" appeared to be Venice in general and Piazza San Marco in particular. Elaborate, proud and fading, the piazza was, indeed, a wonderful sight that unseasonably warm and sunny February afternoon; a dream of a dream, a mixture of raindrops and sunlight, mist and spray spreading its light into the colours of the rainbow. And all the while, the rain-bringer, that watery and gleaming curtain of cloud, was drifting away and the tables were refilling with customers wishing to have the sun on their cheeks while feeling the presence of historical celebrity and genius in the spaces around them.
"I'm in my late fifties," Ricky said.
"And?"
"She persuaded me to sign over my share of the school to her in the event of my death"
"So?"

"So, if I die, Lucy will have a controlling share of the company."

"Haven't you noticed something?" Tony said.

Ricky shook his head.

"You've lost me," he said. "Noticed what?"

"She controls the schools already and has done for years. The results speak for themselves."

"Yes, but…"

"I'm 60 years old," Tony said. "In 5 years, I'll retire. Somebody needs to take the schools over. Mario and Julia have their own ambitions, their own lives to lead. Lucy's the ideal candidate."

"I can think of better ways of going about it," Ricky said.

A quick intake of breath, a fumble at his throat and Tony tried to hide his excitement at what he was hearing. He watched his wine ripple when he lifted his glass, replaced it on the table before it spilled, and slid both shaking hands under the table. He cleared his throat before saying:

"And I wondered if I was paranoid," Tony said. "I saw it as a conspiracy."

"What do you mean by "it" if I may ask?" Ricky said.

"I thought you both were making moves to force me out," Tony said.

"It's just your imagination," Ricky said. "It's all wonderful."

Tony shook his head in disbelief.

"What? The situation?"

"No," Ricky said. "I mean this place, this café, the weather and the wonderful band and their wonderful music."

"I see."

And, for the most part, both men were focused on the wonderful café, their heads bobbing from side to side, and their fingertips tapping in time to the wonderful music of the wonderful musicians and their repertoire of wonderful perennial favourites and wonderful extracts from wonderful Italian opera and operetta. And even when the musicians paused, both Tony and his brother hummed away, plucked at the crispy-white napkins on the table and tapped their feet in time to the music still ringing in their ears.

"Enjoy it all now," Ricky said. "Who knows what tomorrow will bring."

"More sunshine?" Tony said.

"I'm referring to our freedom," Ricky said.

"I see," Tony said. "The signs are already there."

"What signs?"

"The warning signs," Tony said.

"The warning signs? Ah, you mean impending lockdown?"

"Exactly. Nobody wants to believe it," Tony said.

"People just put their heads in the sand and appear not to see it," Ricky said.

"Appear?" Tony said.

"Yes, appear, because it seems that the virus isn't there for them. All these people apparently refuse to see this reality. They appear to ignore the warning signs."

"Unlike us," Tony said.

"Exactly," Ricky said. "We're not in denial. At least, we don't appear to be."

In that place, appearances of another kind were higher on their list of priorities, and these two ageing Italo-Englishmen, as well-dressed as they were, could compete neither with the dignity nor the elegance of their waiters nor with the youth and vitality of most other guests. As natives of the Veneto, the two men were not exactly tourists, even though both of them recognised that Venice always made feel that way. It was the anticipation of narrow alley-ways and humped-back bridges, the feeling that they were free to go wherever they wanted at a time of their choosing, the thought of canals and the crumbling brick walls that rose from the canals that amazed and excited them and made them feel like sightseers just passing through.

"How do you know," Tony said, "that all these people are in denial?

"Because most people aren't wearing masks," Ricky said.

"Expecting it to just go away?" Tony said. "And ignoring the reality?"

On this unusually warm day, their own expectations had been tarnished on arrival in Piazza San Marco. This was a place holding traces of the past, the affairs of Casanova, the inspiration of Hemingway, the melodies of Vivaldi, but the warmth and its false promise of an early spring had also encouraged the blight of ticket vendors and the crowds and their selfie-sticks. However, from their seats outside this most elegant of cafes, both Tony and his brother enjoyed watching people arriving, sitting, experiencing, embracing, kissing, and laughing, people speaking other languages, people queuing outside the basilica, people apparently ignoring the warnings, the looming lockdown, the dangers of the pandemic.

"Or simply wishful thinking," Ricky said.

And their conversational exchanges continued with comments concerning Covid19, comments with words and expressions like "ignore" and "pass them by," and "creative solutions," "challenge" and "conventional wisdom."

"And it seems there's a plethora of conspiracy theories going around. You heard any?"

"Anxiety," Tony said. "It makes people think like that."

"Or control?"

"Control over…?"

"Conspiracy theories offer some people a sense of comfort," Ricky said.

"How's that?" Tony said.

"They identify the cause of things, the bad guys, if you like."

"Gives the average man or woman a sense of power," Tony said, "a sense of control…"

"Over the uncontrollable?"

"Exactly," Tony said.

"Right. Hmmm…"

The late afternoon sun was shining on the *campanile* and its shadow lay like an omen across the square and darkened the porticos opposite. These were now lit with dull-yellow lights, and waiters skilfully swayed around the tables, the puddles, the people, and the dogs. But on their side of the square, Tony and Ricky were enjoying the premature warmth of the sun, and the waiters were skipping in and out of the shade of umbrellas after a storm that, as if by magic, had revealed, for several minutes, the majesty of snow-covered and distant Monte Grappa before it drifted away, an ice-berg looming in the mist over the Venetian plain.

"So," Tony said, "you're saying that if evil and these evil people did not exist, we'd need to create them, right? Without them, everyday life might appear simply random and out of control."

"Spot on, old chap," Ricky said. "Coronavirus conspiracy theories fit neatly into the idea of controlling the uncontrollable."

"Well, I've read and heard suggestions," Tony said, "by online groups claiming that…"

"The coronavirus doesn't exist? Yes, and I read a theory that the virus was created by greedy executives in pharmaceutical companies to create business for vaccines."

"And there are even suggestions," Tony said, "that 5G networks somehow caused the illness."

"And, apparently, so I've heard," Ricky said, "drinking bleach kills the virus."

"Really? And I thought the virus was created in a lab as a bioweapon."

"And in China, no doubt."

They laughed, and they carried on, and all the while, Tony was wondering why some humans still had a need to believe that there were good people and bad people out there. Wherever "out there" was, the black hats started wars there, provoked economic collapse there and caused pandemics there. The white hats were defenders of the good, the righteous and the status quo and believed that if they got rid of the black hats, everything would be fine.

"People seem to oversimplify," Tony said.

"How's that?" Ricky said.

"It appears they or "we" have a need to create the concept of good people and bad people."

"Saints and sinners?"

Tony nodded.

"Surely the reality's not so black and white."

"Shades of grey?" Ricky said.

"Exactly," Tony said. "Only a fool would say that reality tolerates only good and bad. Yes, we can be destructive…"

"But we can also be constructive," said Ricky.

"So, the truth is in the middle," Tony said. "Side by side with our destructive capacity is our constructive capacity, our capacity to do good and to be good, our impulses to love, to care, to help, to heal."

"Agreed," Ricky said. "I think we should take a more balanced view of both life itself and of the coronavirus in particular."

"Wonderful idea," said Tony, nodding to the tune of his brother's words. And they picked up their wine glasses, held them at eye level for a moment, watched the world distort in the reflections in front of them and toasted their mature cleverness, their mature solution to the world's problems.

"Here's to us," Tony said.

"To us," said Ricky.

If I could just break in again. Of course, on that day in Venice, the boys did not know that the pandemic was about to take everybody by surprise and wash away the old world. But Lucy was always looking forward. While the boys were chatting in Venice, Mum was in Verona and planning for the worst. In this time of increased competition, and of the coronavirus, she ensured the survival of S.E.S. along with the livelihoods of those who worked there. It seems an eternity ago, but Lucy had seen it coming and made sure that students, teachers, student support staff, tech support, and academic managers worked together to practically build something out of nothing. This "something" is what we now call blended learning, a mix of online teaching, telephone teaching and written work and it meant that the school could remain active and that students could continue learning. What Lucy achieved in a short time was miraculous. She thought on her feet, improvised, and came up with something creative, overwhelming, exhausting, supportive and compassionate, something called "emergency remote teaching" as a response to needs that were unforeseen.

"You know," Tony said, "Lucy's always one step ahead of us, and not just regarding work."

He spoke with a mind now absent, a mind uprooted and drifting in the splendour of a previous century, watching people from the twenty-first and either wishing they would go away or wondering what on earth they thought they were doing in history's world. This wonderful café had been the haunt of famous writers and musicians, poets, actors, and politicians and how wonderful it was to sit with their ghosts and feel that they belonged here while the crowds of tourists, with their "wows" and cameras flashing were an unwelcome intrusion into the daydream.

"That's true," Ricky said, "but let's face it, as soon as this thing kicked off, she knew what to do."

A place like Venice inspired talk about art, music, or philosophy and although neither of them had anything against these topics, they were not there to talk about, for example, the similarities between medieval plague and 20th century Covid19. They were there, in their favourite Venetian café, to discuss "this thing" and advances in technology that might allow them to survive during a looming national lockdown.

"Lucy has a knack of seeing the obvious," Tony said.

"And reinventing the schools, adapting them."

"And it looks so easy that you wonder why we didn't see the opportunity, too," Tony said.

"The pandemic has forced her to look at things differently," Ricky said. "Lucy saw the potential immediately."

"And what she found will prove to be revolutionary," Tony said.

"She's very creative," said Ricky. "And that creativity can be both good and not so good."

Tony took a deep breath, and pretended to be interested in a mild disturbance at the base of the campanile. Three policemen were pulling, cajoling, and poking at a body on the steps. Tony could not hear a word, but the man stiffened and then struggled. There was an orange stream of spray, and the man was dragged to his feet, his face creased in pain.

"The threat of lockdown has given her the impetus to show a side of herself that I've never seen," Tony said. "And what she's achieved all over the Veneto, in little to no time, is nothing short of miraculous."

"I've never seen the managers, teachers and tech people work together like that and make something out of nothing."

"And the results have been amazing," Tony said.

"But imperfect."

Tony was waving his hand as though he would conduct the distinctive Lehar sound of the woodwind now taking a prominent role while the brass found expression in soft harmonies.

"Wonderfully imperfect."

"What? The music?"

"No, what she's done," Tony said.

"Wonderful indeed."

"It won't be a return to the way it was," Tony said. "Once she decides on something, there's no stopping her and there's no going back."

"I know she can cause mayhem and so do you, but do you think the school would be still here without her?"

Tony crossed his arms over his chest, lifted his left leg and rested its ankle on his right knee. His nostrils flared as if searching for the scent of jasmine. He looked at his watch.

"So, she wants you out, you say," he said.

"Correct."

"To make room for her parents?"

"That's what she said."

And Ricky looked around him, appeared to watch the customers, some of whom were wearing masks.

"They say it'll soon be mandatory for everybody to wear these masks outdoors," Ricky said.

"Not on my terrace," Tony said, "How long is it since you were there?"

Ricky shook his head.

"Six months? A year?"

"When we met Lucy's parents?"

"Yes, that's it."

"The gardener comes once a week," Tony said. "I just ask him to trim things up a bit."

"So, no major changes?"

"No. Unlike life at your end," Tony said. "There'll always be room for my homeless brother."

Ricky nodded.

"Have they been cleaning up Treviso?" he said. "I mean, have they been disinfecting?"

"Just a bit here and there. It's rather like Venice. Can't you smell it?"

Ricky looked around him as if he were looking at the Piazza San Marco for the first time.

"I can't smell anything," Ricky said.

"Maybe you're getting a cold."

"Yes, it might be catching. Lucy's parents complained about losing a sense of smell and taste when I left this morning."

"It's just their age," Tony said.

He glanced at his watch.

"We can stop in a pharmacy on our way to the station. There's a train to Verona in 45 minutes."

And while they walked across the square, away from the St Mark's basilica and towards the alleyways and the humped bridges, the sound of their wonderful music gave way to other sounds, sounds of people shouting, people laughing, people on phones, people scurrying, people loitering and people informing, and from this crowd of everyman there emerged the sound of something contemporary, something which challenged by its use of chanted and rhythmic speech, its street vernacular, its mix of prose, of poetry and of talking and singing. Tony and his brother glanced at one another other.

"Rap?" Tony said.

Ricky nodded.

"Indeed, it is," he said. "A temporary nuisance, I hope.

Ricky's comment, as dismissive and elitist as it was, could also have been directed at the emerging pandemic. These two boys, if I can still call them boys, were walking away from their old lives but they did not know it. How could they have known it? Nonetheless, retrospect will tell them that in that place and on that afternoon, they had been on the edge of great change. Venice was still wonderful, and would always be wonderful, but the wonderful music, the wonderful musicians in the wonderful piazza were from an old world, and that world was soon to be replaced by something new, something dark, ugly, and destructive, as far from wonderful as it could be and much further away than either of them could ever have imagined.

28

March 2020

Apocalypse

What utter nonsense it all was. They got it all wrong. Neither of us was like that at all...

But Tony had been ordered to Verona immediately and immediately did not mean when he could find the time, it meant now; except "now" was not an ordinary now. "Now" was now with a medical mask, a test certificate and a hand sanitiser because "now" was now in the time of the coronavirus, and nobody knew exactly what the word "now" meant.

The man on the phone had told him in that voice, that crackly voice, that masculine and authoritative airline pilot's voice, what had happened. It seemed unreal, rather like the pandemic itself, with its taped-up-glass doorways, its messages on doors, its empty streets, its shortage of toilet paper and its masks: face masks, dirty masks, germ-infested masks, and dead masks in gutters or torn masks tumbling down pavements in the wind.

Next morning, a trip to Treviso police headquarters, a

signed permission-to-travel document sealed and stamped, a signed permission-to-stay-in-one-of-the-few-hotels-still-open document also sealed and stamped. He was lucky to have found a hotel but a few had been required to stay open, the few that hosted those with a need to travel, the sanitary people and the police and people like him with extraordinary business to attend to. Most hotels were already closed and had become extensions of the hospitals, but their guests were short-stay, just passing through, and on their way to the mortuary.

In the cooler air of evening, Tony was in his car and turning onto *La Serenissima,* the motorway that connected Venice to Verona and Milan. Never had he imagined that this, one of Italy's busiest roads, would be so empty of traffic and he guessed that the other drivers were people like him who had a certified, serious, and justifiable reason for travelling. These restrictions had brought rewards he had not foreseen, and what he saw now was air washed clean, and the first stars were so bright he muttered an edited version of the nursery rhyme his mother had often sung when he was a child.

"Twinkling, twinkling little star, I'm down here and wondering what you are. Why are you shining up there so high, a burning diamond in the sky?"

In fact, the air that evening, so fresh, so breathable, reminded Tony, if he needed reminding, that his life did not always have to stay the way it was, that life in general and his life in particular could change, mature, evolve, develop, regenerate, degenerate and nothing had to remain the same, not even motorway traffic, as long as there was a will to change. Pollution and global warning were avoidable and harmony between humans and the natural world was achievable.

It was approaching 22.30 when Tony left the motorway at Verona Sud and drove into streets quiet and empty and clean, cleaner than clean, as they usually were at this time of evening, but Tony had to remind himself that he was heading into what might be the centre of the worst epidemic Europe had seen since the medieval plague. When he hit the ring road, he wondered if Italians were vulnerable because they were a touchy-feely people with an imbalance, so said the census, of older citizens. Passing the football stadium, he realised he was not affected by numbers or statistics or facts like these. He was unable to see communication style or people getting old, but he could see a lot of emptiness, emptiness in the streets, emptiness in the bars, emptiness in the restaurants, emptiness near the sports stadium, emptiness on the pavements. Emptiness was everything not happening that should have been happening in a city like Verona at this time of night: groups of youths not gathering, ladies of the night not waiting for business, 24-hour supermarkets not open, lovers not walking hand in hand, people not eating pizza, people not drinking wine or *grappa*. Everything that should have been happening was not happening and it was not happening to the sound of sirens, both distant and near, police cars rushing, ambulances racing to save lives, to lose lives, to drop the bodies off at the mortuary.

Tony parked in the hotel's basement parking area, checked in and went directly to his room. In the very early morning, it rained heavily, so heavily that it kept him from sleeping the night through and during the waking time, his thoughts drifted to a place he rarely visited and that night that place was the past. He supposed there was nothing odd about this; with most of his life behind him, the past was the obvious, if not the easiest, place to visit, and Tony had been looking forward to seeing Ricky, the Ricky of old, the caring Ricky, the kind Ricky, the helpful Ricky, the Ricky he had glimpsed again in Venice, in a meeting that had rekindled their relationship, a relationship that had suffered because of a woman. But while he lay in bed listening to the rain, staring at the ceiling, he reflected on what he might have done better had he known what the future held. But as fine as that was in retrospect, real life was lived in real time and nobody knew what the future held, nobody could fully prepare themselves for what was going to happen the next day. Hindsight was a wonderful thing but life was not lived in retrospect. The retrospective was the life as seen on Facebook, those perfect lives with their perfect relationships and their artificial realities that excluded the mundane, the uninteresting, the tragic.

The weather changed again towards dawn. A brisk wind had at first blown the clouds away and by the time he came down to the covid-enforced sparseness of the hotel's breakfast room, the sky was a clear blue without a contrail in sight.

After breakfast, a quick phone call and a visit to the authorities, a chat with the policeman on duty and the information that brother Ricky had recently been staying at the Hotel Arena and that Tony should visit it. The owner was expecting him. He was also told there was a general lockdown and he should make sure to finish his business in the time allotted to him by the permit or he would have to stay, to join others in their frozen lives, their burials, the sound of their hearses passing over the cobbled stones.

Tony found the Hotel Arena wedged between the ancient Roman gateway and the new library. The hotel seemed twisted as if it were in pain. The hotel manager, Signor Caruso, had apparently adapted to his environment in sympathy. He was deformed like Quasimodo and looked as mean as Shylock. Glowering from behind his mask and from behind his desk, he assured Tony that such a terrible thing had never happened in his hotel before. At first, Tony was unsure whether he was referring to the pandemic or to the crime that had occurred in his hotel, but Caruso seemed personally offended by Tony's visit and dropped Ricky's belongings into Tony's hands as if they were covered with dirtiness, but Tony cradled the objects in his arms and he took them jealously with him into the street.

Looking at what remained of his brother, Tony wondered if he had missed something, some hint as to his brother's mental state, at their last meeting in Venice. It was always easy after the event to imagine some clue as to the state of mind of a killer, some small clue offered by an after-the-event recollection. Ricky's effects consisted of a never-sent postcard, a diary, some photographs, and a letter addressed to him.

The postcard had been addressed to Tony and in the top left-hand corner, Ricky had written the place of writing, the date of writing and the opening greeting.

Verona, March 2020. Dear Tony, what a wonderful...

And that was that. So, what was "wonderful"? The weather? An idea? Tony decided that his brother was about to write "wonderful reunion in Venice" and that he would report this to anybody who asked him when he returned to Treviso.

Second, there was the diary kept by Ricky. This was the place in which Ricky recorded a few thoughts on life but his writings were never extensive. Tony turned the pages until he found the last three entries.

> *The dreams I have in an empty room. Wishing to be anybody else but who I have become. Lying breathless in bed with the hum of silence and knowing there is nobody out there to listen now. Knowing I must help myself but dreaming in an empty room.*
>
> *Never satisfied and wanting more. But what more is there? Believing in what she told me, that I was the carer, the compassionate one*

but forced to accept the uncaring, the jealousy and the hate. It was wonderful to see Tony again but Tony the perfectionist will never accept my imperfections. God, I feel so bad. I cannot breathe…

Before covid, it did not matter. There was always hope for change and a better future. Then, today I realised it. I had reached a point in my illness when the future was here and I was staring at it from the shadows, staring and thinking in the darkness; I have lived the lie, and I am no better than Lucy is. I am a thought without a word, a bird without wings. Staring at the future and thinking and dreaming in an empty room. God help me…

And there were photographs, slipped between the pages of the diary. On the back of each photograph, Ricky had written a description of it. The first showed a hand-disinfectant dispenser and a picture reminding people to wear a mask. Both seemed to be on a table at the entrance to a restaurant.

So very simple.

The next photo showed the restaurant terrace and the cubicles separated one from the others by makeshift and wooden partitions.

So practical.

The final photo showed the route marked out with arrows that, essentially, created a one-way system to the toilets and back again.

So human.

Tony told me that he had been half-expecting Ricky to be waiting for him, prepared for Tony's visit in his usual caring and thoughtful way. In a sense, he was there waiting for him because, Tony said, he thought he saw his brother walking in town, but it was just Ricky's resemblance drifting like clouds across the faces of strangers. Tony commented that he felt isolated but untouchable and, although there was no badge of distinction that marked him out from others, he did feel unique and special. But life carried on as normal, death carried on as normal, and the price of coffee or a hotel room did not change because his brother had committed a terrible and unexpected act of violence.

So, Tony had no option but to do it. He had to shadow Ricky's last-known footsteps. He felt he was closing in on the truth and it was a truth that nobody else alive understood, and it had all begun with porridge and an old lady waiting at the kerbside to cross the road.

Tony started at the front door of the hotel. Once so welcoming, the sound of it closing behind his brother must have seemed as final as the day of judgement. There was no going back for Ricky. Tony stuffed the things he had been given into a rucksack and set off with his brother's ghost down Via Mazzini and into Piazza Bra. He felt his ankles rolling to the cobblestones just as his brother would have done and the spring flowers there were a day or two taller than when Ricky had passed that way, and the day was longer, the shadows shorter.

The ancient and narrow streets were almost empty and Tony imagined that they looked very much as they did when the plague visited the region centuries ago. It felt like the plague or, at least, how he had imagined it as a child. Few people had ventured outside. According to the local paper, people went out only for essential supplies. Outside the City *Supermercato*, a family of Veronese were piling bags of toilet paper into the boot of their car. The family, their over-the-shoulder glances, masks pulled up to the eyes, looked panic-stricken. Tony forgave them. He knew that shortages were threatening and he had no difficulty in seeing that panic-buying was a way of managing the stress and anxiety people might feel. In other words, when life was so uncertain or out of control, an effective way of dealing with it was to focus on the actions that were in their control.

Someday, though, Tony knew this would all be a memory, something that happened in the past that most people managed to get through one way or another. There would be many personal memories but there would also be collective memory, in other words, how groups, neighbourhoods, families and streets remembered this peculiar time. Families, for example, might remember some aspects of the pandemic in a collective fashion. But individuals would have their stories to tell, and the stories would be edited and perhaps transformed but however they remembered it, their interpretations would be real and personal.

In the distance, Tony heard microphoned talk and he saw that a service was being held on the grass outside a church near the city wall. Around 50 people, all of them observing the rules of social distancing, dotted the grass at a respectful distance from the church door. The preacher was using a microphone and the singing was loud and hearty. It was the final song and at its end, the congregation offered a loud round of applause. So, what were they applauding? Their survival? The priest who dared to open his church? Or was it a spontaneous outburst of happiness at still being alive?

A familiar face appeared in front of him. He called out to her. It was the school secretary, Maria Teresa. She was walking home. She seemed nervous, tired, and strung out. When he approached her, she told him to step away, to keep a distance but she was prepared to talk.

"Are you scared?"

She shrugged.

"Lockdown is hard," she said. "But most people accept

that it has to happen. Most people observe the rules."

She sounded cheerful and seemed stoic.

"We are not so satisfied with the government's handling of the situation but where else is help coming from?"

On the grass by the church, the congregation had reformed and gathered in groups. They were all wearing masks and waiting outside the church by the city wall. Some of them were now walking behind a hearse and into a garden. Hospital staff in masks, gloves, and protective clothing, were watching on.

"They are allowed to break the curfew to pay their last respects," Maria Teresa said while nodding towards the hearse.

Tony couldn't help but think that these were families and funerals that he knew nothing about but most people, ordinary people, would likely experience something similar and very soon.

"Do you know many people who are sick?" Tony asked.

"Unfortunately, yes," she said. "It is painful you cannot say goodbye. It is painful that they are on their own. I feel very sad. There is sadness everywhere."

She paused, apologising with a quick shake of the head as tears filled her eyes.

"Friends and relatives are slowly dying," she said. "In the streets we see the people who do such important jobs by saving lives, and continue trying to save lives even when it is as clear as day that they cannot be saved anyway. It's heart-breaking."

A look of defiance appeared in her eyes.

"Most of us believe that Covid has given us an opportunity to make changes to social inequalities."

"Do you think the opportunity will be taken?"

She shook her head.

"We can only hope that something good will come out

of this," she said.

Maria Teresa wished him well and she turned and continued her way home and to isolation. He asked himself whether or not she was married. Did she have children? He thought he had known her for years but he knew nothing about her, her circumstances or where she lived, what she felt, whom she loved.

At the edge of the garden, Tony bought a paper. He rarely bought papers but his talk with Maria Teresa had put a thought into his head and he turned to the obituaries. Usually, the obituaries filled barely a page but this day, they filled over 10 pages of single photograph portraits. And that, apparently, was a daily occurrence.

Turning into a garden in the centre of the square Tony stopped to listen. Ricky had loved birds and their song was now deafening as if, muted for the winter, they had found the strength to celebrate spring's renewal, despite the deaths, despite the pain, despite the mourning.

Tony was walking faster now as he tried to follow Ricky's ghost. Faster and faster, he walked until he was skipping along and Tony imagined his brother, muscles taut like violin strings. Ricky would have been carried on by his determination not to change his mind, not to weaken or waver from his task. On the road leading up to the bridge, swaying against the parapet like saplings in the wind, were the heroin addicts. Did the sight of these people hovering on the edges of existence deter Ricky for just one second? Or was he made aware of the fictional character that had been created for him, his own life hovering around lies and dreams, the reality a lie, the dead body of his lover, killed by his own hands and now a bad dream in a hotel room? And how long did the process of strangulation take? Poor Lucy must have been in terrible pain and fear. She must have resisted but she could not resist Ricky's strength. Of course, she would have resisted. She would have tried to claw him off but eventually her strength must have failed her and because of a blocked artery or vein and lack of air, she would have passed out. But how long was eventually? Strangulation could cause coughing, difficulty swallowing, vomiting, urination or defecation, miscarriage, swollen tongue, or lips.

Away in the distance, on the brow of a hill, there was a building with yellow-ochre walls and a red roof. The building was so old it appeared to grow naturally out of the ground like the cypress trees that surrounded it. Ricky must have seen it too. Perhaps it was the last thing he saw as he climbed onto the parapet and threw himself into the void. Whirling through space, was he free from himself, from his lie, from his empty room? Or did the awful thought come to him at the last moment:

"Well, this is it, the final moment. Well, so what?"

Tony took Dick's personal letter from his pocket and unfolded it.

> *Did you know those people were not her real parents? They were foster parents. I liked them, whoever they were, I really did care for them. Mom sat in her easy chair with the TV constantly on. A few days ago, it was game shows. Then it was an American series called Law and Order. She did not speak a word of Italian but she watched the TV till midnight.*
>
> *Dad was a voracious reader. At 89 he went through four or five books a week, just as he has for the past 30 years. I didn't know there were that many detective novels in the world. He used to keep a list of all the books he'd read, so as not to repeat them, but after filling three or four notebooks he gave that up. It took longer to peruse the list than to*

actually re-read the book.

Towards the end, neither of them ate much but I was shocked at the changes in both of them. When covid came, neither of them stood a chance. They were dead within days.

Lucy never knew who her real parents were. So, what do we make of her? What was the truth and what was a lie? Did she really have a master's degree? Did she really come from Lyme? When Adam and Eve died of covid, I recognised the symptoms in myself and decided she would have to come with me. To do nothing was not an option. She had been scheming for years and now she saw her opportunity. On my death she would inherit my half of the school and the divorce would give her half of your share. That means the school would essentially be hers to do with what she wanted. There is little or nothing I can do about my illness but for my sake, your sake and for the sake of our mum and dad, I cannot allow Lucy to inherit anything.

And so, brother Tony, would you make sure that everything I had is left to a charity of your choice. I know I needn't ask, but choose carefully. We all know what a fussy perfectionist you are.

And that was typical of my brother Ricky. Everyone knew it. To Charity indeed! He was so full of compassion, so caring, such a loving fellow.

29

Summer 2021

Into the Night Sky

I have tried. I have really tried to write a story free of bias and prejudice but, while writing this book, a variety of questions and doubts have been my constant companions. For example, can readers can trust me to write an unbiased story? For that matter, can I trust myself to write an unbiased story? How would I know if my stance was objective, partly objective or not at all objective? And what are my credentials? Why am I in a position to know things that others, perhaps, do not? After all, my view of the past is just my view. There are other perspectives, for example: Lucy's perspective or Ricky's perspective.

And what about my sources? Let's face it, memory of first-hand experiences and old photos of the protagonists are hardly reliable. We all know that memory plays tricks on those who remember by editing events in order to fit into that individual's current view of the world. And what about photos? Those records of moments in time, for example: the party on the terrace, or the trip to the mountains, often suffer from the over-imaginative stories that go with them. My point is that while writing the story, I have only memories, both mine and those of others, and photos to help me, and both memory and photos are flawed.

And what about great historical events? How do wars and pandemics, for example, shape our views, our characters and personality? Tony freely admits that he showed scant interest in his parents' stories of World War 2. Community spirit, the white cliffs of Dover, love and loss and later reconstruction did not mean much to him. Essentially, the words "world" and "war" and the number "2" had, indeed, gallantly flown over the white cliffs of Tony's childhood. But the child became adult and 75 years after the war's end, it is as clear as daylight, at least to Tony, that his father was as much a product of the war and things out of his control as they, his children, and their peers, will be products of corona and other things beyond their control even if they are from another generation.

Tony insists that his and Ricky's position regarding the corona pandemic is not dissimilar to their father's position during WW2. They do not know when or how the situation might come to an end. In effect, they, like their father, do not know who will live and who will die. It is highly likely that the after-the-pandemic world will be very different from the before-the-pandemic world but nobody can say how these differences will appear. And Tony told me that in years to come, if he is still alive, and if his grandchildren ask him what he did during the great pandemic, he will tell them those things that his father said to him in the sixties and seventies when he was asked about the war. Tony said he will tell them that a lot of good people died, that he and others like him just got on with the job at hand. He will tell them that they were not heroes. He will tell them that they were just doing what was expected of them in a time of crisis. Readers might think that Tony's comparison is more than a little exaggerated and they may well be right. Nonetheless, at this moment, in the summer of 2021, nobody knows how the emergence of the virus might change things and nor do we know what those changes will look like. That is something that only hindsight will tell us.

When I made notes for this story, it never occurred to me that I might need photographs to help me understand what makes people do what they do or, in my case, what made the characters do what they did, but the truth is that when the book got to that place in time when access to it demanded the memory of others, I soon learned that memory warps, and good material is subjective and unreliable, and reality is (and was) hard to find in the high-running feelings of the remaining bickering protagonists. But I must repeat that caution is needed when analysing photographs both old and new. They say the visual image has power, don't they? But that power depends entirely on the observer and how the observer feels about the picture and what it depicts. A picture has no built-in quality, and a picture has no actual power, does it? That old adage, "a picture is worth 1000 words," bothers me. Why 1000? Why not 10,000, or 5 or 10 or simply none at all? Yes, a visual image may have immediacy and power but add text or speech and you have something that has potential to set the world on fire.

On the other hand, the humble photograph can reveal a great deal if we know where to look for it. Our bodies react spontaneously and honestly even if our words often do not. So, if you study the cues revealed in holiday pictures or everyday selfies, you can learn a lot about the feelings, the reality of lives behind the trite, the dull or obvious, the stale or insipid statements of the actors themselves, statements like my favourite one, one that I often use to describe solid relationships. That statement is, "joined at the hip."

Photos abound in our world today due to the fact that we carry our "cameras" around twenty-four hours a day on our phones, and no time is fuller of pictures than the holidays. But aside from the simple purpose of memory catching, studying photos can tell us a lot about both photographer and subject. Photographs tell the observer what was important in the life of the photographer and they are a part of this person's legacy. Photos reveal what people cared about so much that they wanted to share it.

I never quite understood the relatively small number of photos in the family collection from when I was a child. All of them now represent powerful and emotional links to my past: to my favourite holidays, to my childhood home. Nonetheless, sometimes, when I look at photos of myself as a child, it seems like someone else's memory rather than mine. Sometimes, it doesn't look like a childhood I recall. Sometimes, I wonder if it is actually me.

Ricky's private collection is dominated by photos of himself as a young man. One of these is his profile picture on Facebook. It gives the impression that he is rather tired of adult life with its responsibilities, bank loans, and mortgages. Perhaps behind his masculine, womanising, man-of-action façade is a desire to get back to childhood, a safe world where he cares and where he is taken care of. "Hold me in your arms, stroke my head, and I'll stroke yours," says the profile pic. But, let's face it, this is just my perspective, my opinion, my interpretation.

Finally, I want to say something about happiness. Tony often says that he wants nothing more for us, his children, than to focus on the here and now and be happy. Whenever he thinks about Julia and me, he says, he wants to imagine that we are both dancing, celebrating our lives, unfazed by negatives and focused on the present. There will be more than enough time for us to indulge in nostalgia, he says, and, if we are wise, we will not live our lives in order to make future memories for ourselves. If we do that, he says, we will never appreciate the value of a moment, at least, not until it has become a memory.

If I may add my own point of view, I might add that dad's remarks were a little misguided. Happiness, in my opinion, is something we often (but not always) experience in retrospect. It has often occurred to me that the people we are, and the people we were, differ very little from each other in terms of happiness. Perhaps, we remove the uncomfortable, the boring, the unremarkable and the unpleasant bits from our memories and file them away so that they cease to exist, and what remains are simply the good times. I mean, don't we all look back at a perfect existence, the long summer days of youth, for example, and the endless days of sunshine and laughter? And if we do, it is hardly surprising that the present, with all its dark clouds and rain showers, its worries, and its doubts, is left wanting.

And isn't first love the same? Isn't it true that many of us look back over the years and imagine our first loves were somehow pure, innocent, and perfect? And what is wrong with that? The here and now may be the place to live our lives but those memories of love, however bad they might have been, will always seem perfect. We should nourish these memories, allow them to be picked up by the breeze, to be carried away skywards, to be blown higher and higher until they disappear into the night sky and reappear in the light of the moon and stars.